# The Kvetch Who Stole Hanukkah

# The Kvetch Who Stole Hanukkah

By Bill Berlin and Susan Isakoff Berlin
Illustrated by Peter J. Welling

PELICAN PUBLISHING COMPANY

GRETNA 2010

*To our very own eight miracles—Joshua, Lily, Katelin, Benjamin,*
*Rachel, William, Jake, and Emma—not one of whom is a kvetch!—B. B. & S. I. B.*

*To Darlene, the light of my life*
*To Myra Levine, for explaining the Festival of Lights*
*To Holocaust survivor Phil Gans, who helped enlighten me*
*and calls me friend—P. J. W.*

*The word "Pelican" and the depiction of a pelican*
*are trademarks of Pelican Publishing Company, Inc.,*
*and are registered in the U.S. Patent and Trademark Office.*

**Library of Congress Cataloging-in-Publication Data**

Berlin, Bill.
  The kvetch who stole Hanukkah / Bill Berlin and Susan Isakoff Berlin ;
illustrated by Peter J. Welling.
       p. cm.
  Summary: A kvetch steals all the menorahs on the first night of Hanukkah
in Oyville before he learns an important insight from three children about the
festival of lights.
  ISBN 978-1-58980-798-3 (hardcover : alk. paper)  [1. Stories in rhyme. 2.
Hanukkah—Fiction. 3. Conduct of life—Fiction. 4. Light—Fiction. 5. Jews—
Fiction.]  I. Berlin, Susan Isakoff. II. Welling, Peter J., ill. III. Title.
  PZ8.3.B4564Kv 2010
  [E]—dc22
                                                                    2010009435

Printed in Singapore
Published by Pelican Publishing Company, Inc.
1000 Burmaster Street, Gretna, Louisiana 70053

# The Kvetch Who Stole Hanukkah

In the town of Oyville, in a land far away,
The children prepared for each holiday.
They read about Passover and the Red Sea parting;
They learned of Rosh Hashanah and the New Year starting.

But the holiday that tickled every Vicki, Max, and Monica
Was the Festival of Lights in the season of Hanukkah.
They liked the presents, the food, and the cheer;
They liked the nights when the family drew near.

They pictured Judah Maccabee, his bravery and toil.
They imagined the Temple, its lights needing oil.
When the menorah shone bright, its message was clear:
"A great miracle happened here."

Not everyone in Oyville saw things this way.
There was one person who always said nay.
It was the kvetch who lived high on the hill,
With his grumpy face and his voice high and shrill.

What is a kvetch, you may want to know.
What makes him so gloomy, what makes him say no?
A kvetch is a person who likes to complain.
When others see sun, a kvetch will see rain.

Now, there are times when we all feel quite blue.
We all can be kvetchy, that surely is true.
But to a kvetch the world never seems bright.
To a kvetch most things are never quite right.

It's not like the kvetch had to be that way,
But no one had taught him to let his heart play.
There was some kind of sadness that made him not right,
That made him see dark when others saw light.

So every year on Hanukkah's first day
The people of Oyville would hear the kvetch say,
"The latkes smell bad, the dreidels make me dizzy,
And to hear children laugh puts me in a tizzy."

Every year, it was the same old refrain.
"These Hanukkah songs, they give me a pain.
Hanukkah, shmanukkah—it's all about gifts,"
Shouted the kvetch, and he sounded quite miffed.

But most of all what made him take flight
Was the glow that came from the Hanukkah lights.
When the candles burned down they gave off an aura
That made the kvetch hate every menorah.

His hate seemed to grow with each passing year,
Till the thought of the lights filled him with fear.
He would dream of menorahs with their candles so bright
And awaken in terror, dripping in fright.

"I must gain control, I must find a way
To stop dreidels from spinning and children at play.
There will be no latkes, no more will they fry,
No Hanukkah gelt, no new toys to try."

So the kvetch thought and thought—
 and then thought some more,
Sweating and pacing across his bare floor,
Until finally a smile crept over his face.
"I've got it!" he cried and ran out of that place.

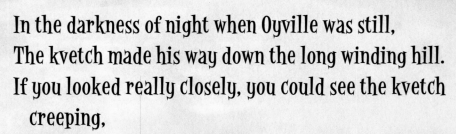

In the darkness of night when Oyville was still,
The kvetch made his way down the long winding hill.
If you looked really closely, you could see the kvetch
  creeping,
But most houses were dark, most people were sleeping.

He sneaked into Oyville on Hanukkah's first night,
Helped through the dark by the menorahs' bright light.
"Aha," said the kvetch, "it's time for my scheme.
No more menorahs! Not another bad dream!"

"No lights and no dreidels, no latkes this year.
No toys and no presents"–his joy was so clear.
He snuffed out the candles and turned off the lights
And carried menorahs through the dark winter night.

When the next day dawned all over town,
The children of Oyville cast their heads down.
The menorahs were gone, the lights were all out.
And no one knew what this was about.

Then they all heard it, a most wretched noise:
The triumphant sound of the kvetch's loud voice.
"Lights out!" he yelled with a jubilant jeer.
"There will be no Hanukkah in Oyville this year."

He took the menorahs to the top of the hill;
He set them all down with unusual skill.
And as he turned to see the new day,
He saw three children a few feet away.

"Mr. Kvetch," the children said, "you've got it all wrong.
The Hanukkah spirit is joyous and strong.
The Maccabees taught us to strive to be free,
To treasure true justice and charity."

"The lights and the gifts show our dedication
To the strength and faith of our ancient nation.
It's a lesson for all that when life seems so dim,
There's reason for hope. You shouldn't give in."

The kvetch stepped back and looked off into space.
A lonely tear rolled down his sad face.
"But . . . but . . . ," he said as he trembled and shook,
"The lights were so bright, I've been too scared to look."

"Perhaps you're afraid to see things so bright
For fear that you'll lose them as day becomes night.
Maybe you'd rather see things as bleak
Because somewhere inside, you feel frightened and weak."

The children stepped forward and took his cold hand,
And the kvetch felt his heart and his spirit expand.
And when he looked out all over the town,
A smile filled his face instead of a frown.

Then the people of Oyville looked up to that hill,
And they took in a scene that made their hearts thrill.
The menorahs shone bright, as bright as the snow.
All the candles were burning, all the lights were aglow.

The kvetch, too, was beaming, his face was so bright,
As the children helped him return all the lights.

And the people of Oyville gave out a great cheer:

# CREATE
# STEREOGRAMS
## ON YOUR PC

## DISCOVER THE WORLD OF 3D ILLUSION

### DAN RICHARDSON

Waite Group Press™
Corte Madera, CA

*Publisher*  **Mitchell Waite**
*Editor-in-Chief*  **Scott Calamar**
*Editorial Director*  **Joel Fugazzotto**
*Managing Editor*  **Joe Ferrie**
*Content Editor*  **Heidi Brumbaugh**
*Technical Reviewer*  **Timothy Wegner**
*Production Director*  **Julianne Ososke**
*Designer/Project Coordinator*  **Sestina Quarequio**
*Production*  **William Salit, Jerald Fox**
*Illustrations*  **Pat Rogondino**
*Cover Design*  **Michael Rogondino**
*Cover Stereogram*  **Dan Richardson**

Printed in the United States of America
94 95 96 97 • 10 9 8 7 6 5 4 3 2 1

Richardson, Dan, 1957–
    Create stereograms on your PC / the Waite Group : Dan Richardson.
        p.   cm.
    Includes bibliographical references and index.
    ISBN: 1-878739-75-1 : $26.95
    1. Computer graphics. I. Waite Group. II. Title.
T385.R497  1994
006.6--dc20

94-5316
CIP

# Dedication

This book is dedicated to Kate, Liam, and George.

# About the Author

Dan Richardson is a digital illustrator specializing in molecular images for scientific and medical publications, an occupation he reached by a fairly circuitous route. His formal education started at Purdue in engineering and ended with a BFA in sculpture from the University of Minnesota. After ten years in Chicago doing sound system design and mixing live bands, he moved to rural Massachusetts.

Dan lives in a cottage in the woods with his family (Kate, Liam, and George), and his computers (Felicity, Nigel, and Bobzilla). Dan is an avid telecommuter, and most of his contact with the outside world happens in the Graphic Developer's Forum on CompuServe. You can reach him on CompuServe at 72537,1341, or from the Internet at 72537.1341@compuserve.com.

Dan's picture credits include numerous textbook and magazine illustrations, as well as a cover for *TIME* magazine.

# Contents

# Table of Contents

## *Chapter 6*  **Random-Text Stereograms** . . . . . . . . . . . . . . . . . . . . . . . . . . . **63**

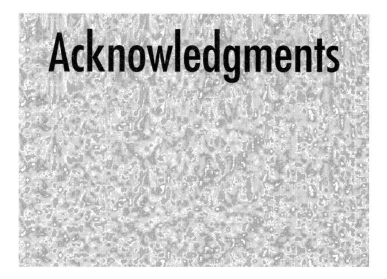

# Acknowledgments

The author wishes first of all to thank his parents, Larry and Katy Richardson, for everything.

Thanks to Tim Wegner for pointing out Mitch Waite, and to Mitch for being there. Joe Ferrie deserves credit for cracking the whip, in a caring sort of a way. I am grateful to Heidi Brumbaugh, Tim Wegner, and Carol Henry for translating my manuscript into English.

Thanks to Johannes Schmid and Florian Kirstein, Frederic N. Feucht, Mike Gardi, Stuart Inglis, Eric Thompson, Rob Scott, Gordon Flanagan, Ed Behl, John Kolesar, David K. Mason, Alexander Enzmann, Alphonso Hermida, John Swenson, The Stone Soup Group, and the POV-Ray team for providing the plethora of freeware and shareware programs used to make the images in this book. Special extra thanks to Johannes, Fred, and Dave for modifying their programs to fit the needs of my readers.

Steve Perrigo, Robert Raymond, and John M. Olsen provided great support and encouragement, as well as contributing their delightful images. Thanks to David Alan Bozak, Lhary Meyer, Greg Gundlach, and Robert Raymond for providing essential research materials. Further thanks to Jim Ver Hoeve for the strabismologist's viewpoint, and many other great words besides. I am indebted to Dr. Christopher Tyler for his patient discussion of the mechanics of depth preception.

And a very special thank you to the entire staff at Waite Group Press for a wonderful job on this and so many other books.

Dear Reader:

What is a book? Is it perpetually fated to be inky words on a paper page? Or can a book simply be something that inspires—feeding your head with ideas and creativity regardless of the medium? The latter, I believe. That's why I'm always pushing our books to a higher plane; using new technology to reinvent the medium.

I wrote my first book in 1973, *Projects in Sights, Sounds, and Sensations*. I like to think of it as our first multimedia book. In the years since then, I've learned that people want to experience information, not just passively absorb it—they want interactive MTV in a book. With this in mind, I started my own publishing company and published *Master C*, a book/disk package that turned the PC into a C language instructor. Then we branched out to computer graphics with *Fractal Creations*, which included a color poster, 3D glasses, and a totally rad fractal generator. Ever since, we've included disks and other goodies with most of our books. *Virtual Reality Creations* is bundled with 3D Fresnel viewing goggles and *Walkthroughs and Flybys CD* comes with a multimedia CD-ROM. We've made complex multimedia accessible for any PC user with *Ray Tracing Creations, Multimedia Creations, Making Movies on Your PC, Image Lab*, and three books on Fractals.

The Waite Group continues to publish innovative multimedia books on cutting-edge topics, and of course the programming books that make up our heritage. Being a programmer myself, I appreciate clear guidance through a tricky OS, so our books come bundled with disks and CDs loaded with code, utilities, and custom controls.

By 1995, The Waite Group will have published over 180 books. Our next step is to develop a new type of book, an interactive, multimedia experience involving the reader on many levels.

With this new book, you'll be trained by a computer-based instructor with infinite patience, run a simulation to visualize the topic, play a game that shows you different aspects of the subject, interact with others on-line, and have instant access to a large database on the subject. For traditionalists, there will be a full-color, paper-based book.

In the meantime, they've wired the White House for hi-tech; the information superhighway has been proposed; and computers, communication, entertainment, and information are becoming inseparable. To travel in this Digital Age you'll need guidebooks. The Waite Group offers such guidance for the most important software—your mind.

We hope you enjoy this book. For a color catalog, just fill out and send in the Reader Report Card at the back of the book.

Sincerely,

*Mitchell Waite*

Mitchell Waite
Publisher

Waite
Group
Press™

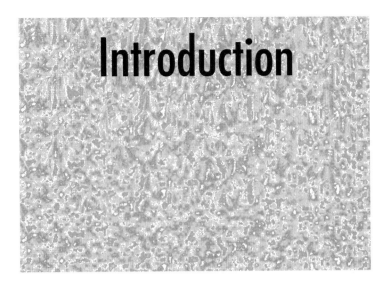

# Introduction

Create stereograms on your PC: If that's what you want to do, this is the book for you. *Stereograms* are flat pictures that reveal 3D depth when viewed in the correct way. Some of them hide a 3D object in another picture, in a wash of random dots that look like TV snow. Some look like ordinary pictures at first, and then various objects in the picture will move nearer or farther away.

This book focuses on the various forms of single-image stereograms, also known as:

- Random-dot stereograms (or RDS)

- Single-image random-dot stereograms (or SIRDS)

- Autostereograms

- Auto random-dot sterograms (or ARDSs)

- Holusions

- Image-mapped stereograms

- Single-image random-text stereograms (or SIRTS)

- Single-image normal-text stereograms (or SINTS)

- Hidden-picture stereograms

- Icon-based stereograms

The disk accompanying this book includes seven programs to help you make your own single-image stereograms on any PC-compatible computer. It also provides instructions and examples showing you how to create stereograms using many other programs with which you may be familiar, such as Fractint, POV-Ray, and Polyray.

When people first encounter stereograms, they usually ask four questions:

⦿ How do I see them?

⦿ How does it work?

⦿ Where did these things come from?

⦿ How can I make them myself?

This book answers all of these questions and many more.

**Chapter 1** introduces you to the various kinds of 3D stereo illusions. It also introduces the tools and programs discussed in the rest of the book.

**Chapter 2** explains the theory behind single-image stereograms. You'll find out why the different viewing techniques produce their own visual effects and read about some visual conditions that may impair a person's ability to see 3D stereo illusions. Chapter 2 also teaches you how to see 3D stereo without the help of viewing hardware. Techniques for learning both cross-eyed and parallel-free viewing are presented.

**Chapter 3** discusses the history of 3D stereo illusions, with particular emphasis on the evolution of single-image stereograms.

**Chapter 4** is a feast for the eyes and mind. The Gallery presents many state-of-the-art single-image stereograms, in full color as well as black and white. Contributing artists include N. E. Thing, John M. Olsen of Infix Technologies, Steve Perrigo, and Robert Raymond of Mirages.

**Chapters 5 and 6** cover text stereograms created with the programs Ued and SIRTSER. Working with text stereograms is a good way to learn how the single-image stereogram principle works.

**Chapter 7** presents an easy, self-contained SIRDS drawing program, RDSdraw. This is a good place to start if you already know how to view SIRDS and you want to jump right in and make some.

**Chapter 8** describes the MindImages highly compact .RLE depthmap format. This format is very useful for transforming stereograms into a data type that is small enough to be shared easily on online services. You will see how to view .RLE SIRDS on your PC screen with MindImages and SHIMMER. Dave's Targa Animator (DTA) is used to convert other images to the .RLE format.

**Chapter 9** demonstrates the program RDSGEN, which creates SIRDS and image-mapped single-image stereograms from depthmaps. (Depthmaps are images you can create using just about any draw, paint, or graphics application.)

**Chapters 10 and 11** show you how to create depthmaps using the freeware and shareware programs Fractint, POV-Ray, and Polyray. These programs are not included here, but the chapters explain how to get them easily, for little or no cost. The depthmaps created in these two chapters can be used in the programs RDSGEN, RDSdraw, MindImages, and SHIMMER.

**Chapter 12** uses the ray tracers POV-Ray and Polyray to create icon-based single-image stereograms, in which you position individual icons in an image to create a 3D illusion. You can apply the methods described in Chapters 11 and 12 to any renderer or ray tracer, such as 3D Studio, RenderMan, or Imagine.

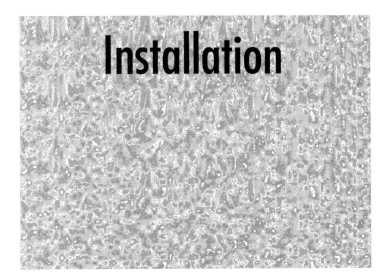

# Installation

The disk included with this book contains software and files needed to work through the examples in the chapters. You must install these programs on your hard disk to use them. The procedure is quite simple.

## Hardware and System Requirements

The installation requires just over 3.2 MB of free hard disk space. To run all of the programs on the disk, you need a PC-compatible computer with a 286 CPU or better, 2 MB RAM (512K of free conventional RAM, 1 MB of extended memory), and a VGA video card. Most of the programs on the disk will run with far less than 2 MB of memory.

## Install the Files

Before installing, please remember to make a backup copy of your installation disk. You will need a blank 3.5-inch high-density floppy disk. Insert the book's program disk into your floppy drive, and enter the MS-DOS command

**DISKCOPY A: A: /V** (ENTER)

or

**DISKCOPY B: B: /V** (ENTER)

depending on whether your 3.5-inch floppy is in your A drive or your B drive. Follow the directions onscreen as DISKCOPY prompts you to insert the source and destination disks.

The installation program, called INSTEREO.EXE, puts 109 files and 7 subdirectories under the master directory \STEREO3D on the hard disk you specify. To run the installation program, follow these steps:

1. Insert the installation disk in your 3.5-inch drive.

2. Change to the drive on which you want to install the files. For example, if you want to install the files on drive C, type the following at the DOS command prompt:

   **C:** (ENTER)
   **CD \\** (ENTER)

3. Type the command

   **B:INSTEREO** (ENTER)

If your installation disk is in a drive other than B, you must substitute that drive letter in the command. When INSTEREO.EXE is done, it reports that it has extracted 118 files. Table I-1 lists the installed directories and describes their contents.

| Directory | Contents |
| --- | --- |
| \STEREO3D | DTA and RDSGEN .EXE files |
| \DTA | DTA documentation and utilities |
| \FRACTINT | Example .PAR and .MAP files |
| \MINDIMAG | MindImages, SHIMMER, and examples |
| \RAYTRACE | POV-Ray and Polyray examples |
| \RDSDRAW | RDSdraw .EXE file and examples |
| \RDSGEN | RDSGEN examples and source code |
| \TEXT3D | Ued and SIRTSER .EXE files and examples |

*Table I-1*  Contents of installed directories and subdirectories

# Change Your Path

In order to run some of the examples as they are described in the book, you need to add the directory \STEREO3D to the PATH statement in your AUTOEXEC.BAT file. You can do this with any text editor, such as MS-DOS EDIT or the program Ued, which you will find installed in the directory \STEREO3D\TEXT3D. Open your AUTOEXEC.BAT file in the text editor and add the STEREO3D drive and directory to the end of the line that begins with PATH. The PATH statement should end up looking similar to this:

```
PATH C:\;C:\DOS;C:\UTILS;C:\FOO;C:\BAR;C:\STEREO3D
```

Save AUTOEXEC.BAT, then reboot your system. The \STEREO3D directory will be added to your path.

# Chapter 1

# A Stereogram Primer

*I*t's a picture on a flat page. It looks like TV snow. Now relax and let your eyes go out of focus. Look *through* the page. Hmmm… Wait a minute. Something's happening. What's this? There's a three-dimensional tunnel, perhaps a foot deep, and it looks  like you can reach right inside it!

Discovering the hidden picture in a stereogram is always a thrill. There's a sense of discovery, of seeking and finding. You're also sharing a secret with other people who know how to see them. Sometimes you find a simple geometric cube, sometimes a wild, organic spiral universe with offshoots and paths that draw your eye here and there around the image. Sometimes a face peers back at you from a swirl of bright colors. There's no telling what awaits inside the repeating patterns. There's something very soothing about viewing stereograms. You relax your eyes, everything else goes out of focus, and a little window opens up into another world.

This chapter provides a general overview of stereograms. The first section introduces basic ideas that will help you understand how stereograms work and how they are constructed. The second section shows how the various types of stereograms are classified, and previews the tools and techniques for creating them that will be discussed in detail in later chapters.

# The Basics

The principles behind these images and the techniques used in producing them are really quite simple, and understanding how stereograms work will add to your pleasure in viewing them.

## Meet Herkimer

Herkimer is a character who lives in your author's computer as a few lines of ray-tracing code. You can see him in Figure 1-1, looking as if he wished he weren't quite so visible.

Herkimer is also in Figure 1-2, hidden in a stereogram. He's not quite as visible here; the computer has hidden him inside the swirling textures. But he's got something else going for him now: When you learn how to view this image, you'll see that he appears in full 3D. Where exactly is he? How did he get in there? How does it work?

## Dot Pairs and Depthmaps

The Herkimer stereogram actually consists of horizontal rows of repeated boxes, placed between 1.1 and 1.3 inches apart. To see Herkimer, you need to learn how to see each corresponding *pair* of boxes as a *single* box, at some distance behind the page. Chapter 2 will teach you this skill, as well as explain why it works. For now, just consider this: Pairs of boxes spaced closer together seem nearer to you, and boxes spaced farther apart seem farther away. Any repeated graphics element can be used instead of boxes. You can make stereograms out of random dots, text characters, icons, or details within larger patterns.

One way to create a stereogram is to make it by hand. You laboriously place each graphic element in an array, and then carefully tweak the distances between the elements until it all looks right. That's the hard way. In practice, it can only be done to create stereograms in which the repeated graphic elements are relatively large in size and few in number. Most stereograms are generated by computers from *depthmaps*. That's the easy way.

Computer pictures are actually a grid of tiny squares called *pixels* (picture elements). Each pixel is one color: the color of that point in the picture. Depthmaps are a special class of computer pictures that contain pixels colored, instead, according to how far they are from the viewer in stereograms created from the depthmap. Thus they serve as a map of the depths in the picture.

Figure 1-3 shows part of Herkimer's depthmap and a stereogram produced from it. The bright areas of this depthmap are the nearest to the viewer, and they map to narrow pairs in the stereogram. Dark areas are far from the viewer, and they map to wider pairs in the stereogram. Each point in the depthmap refers to two points in the stereogram.

## Creating and Transforming Depthmaps

The procedure for producing most stereograms is to create a depthmap and then use software to automatically transform the depthmap into a stereogram. The RDSdraw program, included on this book's disk and described in Chapter 7, integrates the two processes. RDSdraw provides both drawing tools and functions for transforming your drawings directly into stereo 3D illusions.

Because depthmaps are simply ordinary computer pictures colored in a specific way, you can create them with ordinary graphics programs. You can make depthmaps with any draw or paint program, ray tracers, fractal programs, hand scanners, and 3D scanners.

Chapter 9 shows you how to turn depthmaps into stereograms with the freeware program RDSGEN, which comes on this book's disk.

But what if you're not a whiz with a mouse? How can you make interesting, abstract depthmaps without drawing skills? Chapter 10 talks about Fractint, a wonderful freeware program that draws intricate pictures from simple mathematical formulae. Several exercises and a minigallery show you how to use Fractint to create impressive depthmaps.

If you want to make representational or geometric depthmaps, another class of tools is available to help the drawing-impaired. *Ray-tracing programs* create pictures from simple

***Figure 1-1***  Yikes! This is Herkimer

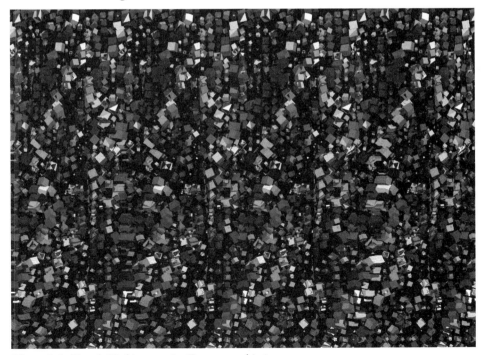

***Figure 1-2***  Here is Herkimer again. Can you see him?

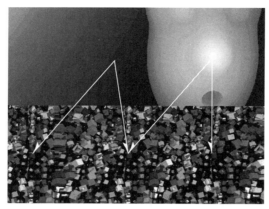

**Figure 1-3** Each point in the depthmap requires two
in the stereogram

text descriptions. An experienced ray-tracing artist can draw a picture of nearly any object
you can think of—without touching a mouse or a pen. Both Herkimer and his image-
mapping screen of boxes were drawn by the freeware ray tracer, POV-Ray. Chapter 11
shows you how to create depthmaps with POV-Ray and Polyray.

# The Variety of Stereograms

The fascination of seeing a full, 3D picture on a 2D page dates back 150 years. Achieving
this effect has traditionally meant taking two photographs and showing one to each eye,
usually with the help of some sort of viewing apparatus. The two pictures are known as a
*stereo pair*. Recent advances in the art have made possible the *single-image stereogram*,
which produces the illusion of 3D from one single image, without any viewing hardware.

All single-image stereograms use the principle of repeated elements that appear at various depths according to their horizontal spacing. The elements may look like rows of small
independent pictures, or a grid of lines. They may be repeated words displayed on a video
screen or typed on a page. You can view a chain-link fence or a wall of bricks as a single-
image stereogram. The types of single-image stereograms are named according to their
repeating element.

## Text Stereograms

View them on any computer, print them on any printer, send them in e-mail—they're
3D pictures made of nothing but ordinary ASCII text. *Text stereograms* come in two flavors, handmade (Figure 1-4) and random computer-generated (Figure 1-5). Chapter 5
discusses the first flavor, and Chapter 6 covers the second flavor, using the programs Ued
and SIRTSER to produce examples.

## Single-Image Random-Dot Stereograms

The *single-image random-dot stereogram* (SIRDS)—a solid field of apparently random dots
containing a hidden picture—was developed as a tool for research into human visual per-

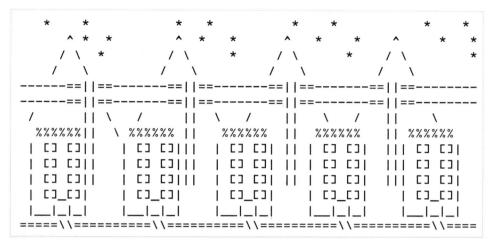

**Figure 1-4** Proper viewing shows this street in 3D

ception. Chapter 7 presents a stand-alone SIRDS drawing program, RDSdraw. With it you can draw a picture and turn it into a SIRDS, right on your computer monitor.

Incidentally, the acronym SIRDS is both plural and singular. One is a SIRDS, and two are SIRDS. Figure 1-6 shows a SIRDS displayed by the program MindImages.

```
0               0               0               0
aztgfwpnhukiomaztgfwpnhukiomaztgfwpnhukiomaztgfwpnhukiomazt
usjrcqgidpxaozusjrcqgidpxaozusjrcqgidpxaozusjrcqgidpxaozusj
deoincklfbagtsdeoncklfbagtsdeoncklfbagtsdeoncklfbagtsdeonuc
xowhrzivbmkytqxowrzivbmkytqxowrzivbmkytqxowrzivbmkytqxowrez
otxmchajzknqygotxchajknqygotxchajknqygotxchajknqygobtxchauj
yboaqxrmctngjhyboqxrmtngjhyboqxrmtngjhyboqxrmtngjhykboqxrfm
jazrwevuhyoiscjazwevuyoisjazwevuyoisjazwevuyodisjazrwevuyno
qlhegswjczrdinqlhgswjzrdiqlhgswjzrdiqlhgswjzrmdiqlhugswjzcr
nhvdxilbwftagrnhvxilbftagnhvxlbftagnhvxklbftaygnhvxpklbftma
ouwgkzbxaypqjvouwkzbxypqjouwkbxypqjouwkibxypqdjouwkhibxypcq
iwulyhnrvkmcqgiwuyhnrkmcqiwuynrkmcqiwuyfnrkmcsqiwuydfnrkmtc
rtzfnmuawdveiyrtznmuadveirtznuadveirtznfuadveqirtznpfuadvse
mkcavisxzhtfyemkcvisxhtfymkcvisxhtfymkcvisxhtufymkcpvisxhet
vjxgpbfwrcodqevjxpbfwcodqvjxpbfwcodqvjxpbfwcoldqvjxspbfwcto
zmaylgnbjhfecuzmalgnbhfecuzmalgnbhfecuzmalgnbhfecuzymalgnrb
scgatlyrxfwndqscgtlyrfwndqscgtlyrfwndqscgtlyrfwndqskcgtlyur
zwghvnidesryabzwgvnidesryabzwgvnidesryabzwgvnidesryabzwgvkn
jdagwypnbzmltujdawypnbzmltujdawypnbzmltujdawypnbzmltujdawoy
vwnelcmidszpoxvwnelcmidszpoxvwnelcmidszpoxvwnelcmidszpoxvwn
vzaomiglwrjyenvzaomiglwrjyenvzaomiglwrjyenvzaomiglwrjyenvza
```

**Figure 1-5** There's a 3D pyramid hiding in these letters

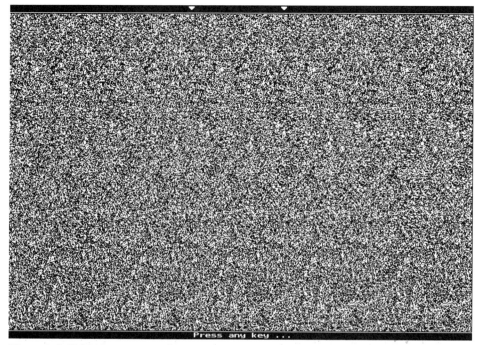

*Figure 1-6* HORN.RLE: A simple SIRDS (© Rob Scott 1992)

## Image-Mapped Stereograms

Computers create SIRDS for you by repeatedly copying a vertical strip of random dots and making small changes in it. If you start with a strip from a picture, instead of random dots, you get an *image-mapped stereogram*. This is the most popular form of single-image stereogram, often seen on posters in bookstores and malls. Figure 1-2 is an image-mapped stereogram, created from Herkimer's depthmap and a computer-generated image of hundreds of little boxes.

## Icon-Based Stereograms

*Icon-based stereograms* usually consist of rows of small pictures, such as Windows icons. These stereograms don't contain hidden pictures. Instead, the elements take on new relationships and a startling 3D reality when viewed in the correct manner. Figure 1-7 shows an icon-based stereogram.

You can create icon-based stereograms with a paint or drawing program. The basic technique involves simply copying a small picture to the Clipboard and pasting it down at regular intervals across the screen. This is a fairly tedious process, even if the program includes tools to help place the objects in your drawing. There's a better way.

Text-based ray-tracing programs excel at the task of positioning objects precisely in a scene. Chapter 12 shows you how to map small pictures onto objects and place them in a stereogram. Since you're doing this in a 3D rendering program, you can also use 3D objects in place of your icons, for a doubly 3D effect.

***Figure 1-7*** An icon-based stereogram

## Alphabet Soup

The variety of stereograms and their acronyms can be somewhat confusing. For your convenience, Table 1-1 lists many kinds of single-image stereograms, their acronyms, the tools you can use to create them, and the chapters of this book that explain how.

| Type of Single-Image Stereogram | Acronym | Repeating Element | Tools | Chapter |
|---|---|---|---|---|
| Single-image normal-text stereogram | SINTS | Text characters | Any text editor | 5 |
| Single-image random-text stereogram | SIRTS | Text characters | SIRTSER | 6 |
| Single-image random-dot stereogram | SIRDS | Dots in a solid field | RDSdraw, | 7 to 11 |
| aka random-dot stereogram | RDS | | MindImages, | |
| aka auto-random-dot stereogram | ARDS | | DTA, and SHIMMER | |
| Image-mapped stereogram | | Details in graphic texture | RDSGEN | 9 to 11 |
| Icon-based stereogram | | Small images | Paint/draw programs and ray tracers | 12 |
| 3D rendered stereogram | | Images of 3D objects | Ray tracers | 12 |

***Table 1-1*** Types of single-image stereograms

# What's Next?

Now that you've been introduced to some of the types of single-image stereograms, it's time to learn how to see these 3D illusions. Then we'll talk about where they come from in Chapter 3, and get a look at the state of the art in the Gallery, Chapter 4. The rest of the book presents all the tools that are on the book's disk and shows you how to use them to create stereograms on your PC.

## Chapter 2

# Seeing in Three Dimensions

**W**hen you reach for your coffee cup, how do you know your hand won't hit the salt shaker behind the cup instead? When someone throws you a basketball, how can you tell when it's going to hit your hands? Somewhere around the age of two months, you began to learn depth perception. By the age of five or six years, most people have it figured out as well as they're going to. This book introduces you to a new twist on this very primary skill.

## Which Thing Is Nearer?

To understand how stereogram viewing works, it helps to think about how your eyes work normally. Since your two eyes aren't in exactly the same place, they don't see quite the same thing. Each eye sees a slightly different view of reality. Figure 2-1 shows a pair of photographs, taken from two cameras placed the same distance apart as a pair of eyes. Look closely to see how the two pictures differ.

What happens if you take two different pictures and show one to each eye? If you can convince your brain that it's really looking at two views of one scene, you'll grasp the illusion of stereo 3D.

*Figure 2-1* How are these two pictures different?

# Perceptual Cues

Depth perception is very complex. Many cues go into the mix. Any or all of these cues can help you decipher the shape of the world around you at any given moment. Table 2-1 lists some of these perceptual cues.

| Perceptual Cue | Meaning |
| --- | --- |
| Accommodation | Eyes and lenses change shape to focus at different distances. |
| Binocular disparity | Two eyes see different views of a single object. |
| Brightness cuing | Brighter objects appear nearer. |
| Convergence | Eyes cross more to look at near objects. |
| Relative motion | Near objects appear to move faster. |
| Occlusion | Near objects can block view of far objects. |
| Perspective | Parallel lines seem to converge as distance increases, distant objects appear smaller. |
| Shadows | Direction of shadows provides information about shape and depth. |

*Table 2-1* Perceptual cues

Your brain integrates a vast amount of information to help you construct a mental model of a 3D world. The perceptual cues contribute to that model, but no single one is absolutely vital. Single-image stereograms bypass most of these cues and trick your brain by exploiting the remaining ones—particularly binocular disparity and convergence—in order to show you something that isn't really there.

# Normal Viewing

When you look at something in the distance, your eyes are nearly parallel and focused at infinity. This also often occurs when you're relaxed and your eyes are unfocused. Figure 2-2 shows two eyes looking at infinity. Your perspective in this figure, as well as in Figure 2-3 through 2-5, is looking downward from the top of someone's head.

When you're looking at something relatively near to you, both eyes cross (*converge*) so they're looking at the same point at the same time, as shown in Figure 2-3. Your eyes and

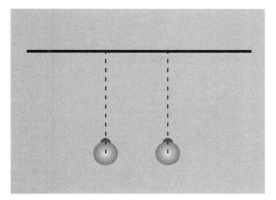

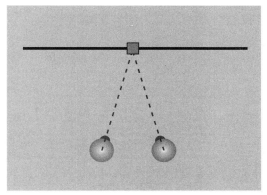

**Figure 2-2** From the top down, two eyes contemplating the void

**Figure 2-3** Convergence and accommodation normally support each other

lenses also change shape (*accommodate*) to bring that point into focus. To see near objects, eyes must cross more and focus closer. To see distant objects, eyes must cross less and focus farther. Normal viewing links convergence with accommodation. Your brain interprets information provided by convergence and accommodation working hand in hand, and normally expects these two pieces of evidence to corroborate each other.

## Parallel and Cross-Eyed Viewing

The two modes of stereogram viewing, *parallel* and *cross-eyed*, both disrupt the normal relationship between convergence and accommodation. Convergence changes while accommodation remains constant.

Cross-eyed viewing uses a convergence that is more *extreme* than normal for a given focal distance. Given a pair of corresponding points, your right eye looks at the left point as your left eye looks at the right point. Your brain interprets them as a single point between you and the picture, as shown in Figure 2-4.

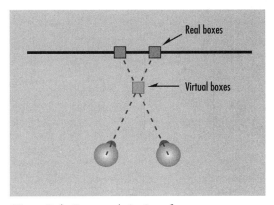

**Figure 2-4** Cross-eyed viewing of stereograms

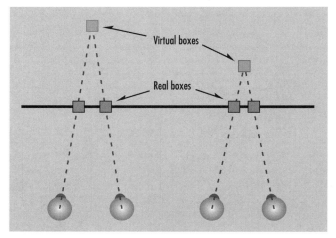

***Figure 2-5*** Parallel viewing of stereograms

Although cross-eyed viewing can be tiring, it's useful because it can handle image pairs that are farther apart than the distance between your eyes. This technique works at all distances, but the distance between corresponding points must increase with the viewing distance. Cross-eyed viewing works for telephone poles in the distance, or two pens in front of your face.

Parallel viewing uses a convergence that is more *relaxed* than normal for a given focal distance. Given a pair of corresponding points, your right eye looks at the right point as your left eye looks at the left point. You brain interprets these as a single point beyond the page or screen, as shown in Figure 2-5.

This technique is often called *wide-eyed viewing*. That name is a misnomer, however, because your eyes never actually diverge, or even reach parallel. A more accurate description of what happens when you view parallel might be wider-than-normal-for-medium-focus-eyed viewing. The technical term for this is *hypoconvergent*.

The parallel viewing technique works up to distances of six or eight feet. The ideal spacing between corresponding points for parallel viewing is solely a function of the distance between your eyes (called the *interocular distance*), independent of the viewing distance.

## Convergence vs. Accommodation

Single-image stereograms generally exploit just two of the many cues that contribute to human depth perception: convergence and binocular disparity. The texture or pattern making up the image provides no information for most of the normal distance cues. There's no perspective, no brightness cues, no motion, no shadows, and usually no occlusion. The 3D illusion produced by stereograms is fundamentally dependent on convergence. The illusion is produced when your eyes converge at one distance while focusing at another. When you're viewing a stereogram, convergence tells you one thing and accommodation tells you something else.

So, in order to view a stereogram, you must learn a new way of perceiving depth, in which you break the normal link between convergence and accommodation.

# Corresponding Points Are the Key

When one eye looks at any particular detail in a single-image stereogram, the other eye looks at the next copy of the same detail. This is known as converging the copies. If the two copies are separated by the right distance and aren't too different, the brain will believe it's looking at two views of a single detail, just like a stereo pair.

Imagine picking two points on this page and converging them. Your brain says "the eyes are somewhere between medium and infinite convergence, and this dot (which is actually two dots) is in focus; therefore, this dot is somewhere between reading distance and infinity." Now imagine converging two points that are spaced closer together. Your brain says "the eyes are more converged and this dot is in focus, so this dot is nearer than the first dot." Figure 2-5 illustrates these two examples.

To approach this concept in another way, look at Figure 2-6, the parallel-view training image. When you parallel-view the top row of this stereogram, your left eye looks at the left-hand planet Earth, and your right eye looks at the right-hand one. Since the two Earth images are identical, you can easily convince yourself they must be the same one. At this point, you ignore the accommodation information and believe the convergence information. Because your eyes are near to their infinite convergence position when viewing the planets, your brain decides the planets must be far away. Convergence takes precedence over accommodation when it's supported by the similarity of two images.

When your eyes travel down the Figure 2-6 stereogram to the question marks, your left eye looks at the left-hand question mark and your right eye looks at the center question mark. Your brain has already given up on the accommodation information, and your eyes are crossed more, because the question marks are closer together than the planets. You interpret the increased convergence to mean the question marks are nearer to you than the planets.

Your eyes are always active—focusing, tracking, converging. If they weren't, the individual rods and cones in your retina would rapidly desensitize, and you would see nothing at all. As you look around a single-image stereogram, your eyes are constantly adjusting convergence in an effort to keep corresponding dots registered. Your brain reads this steady flow of convergence data and interprets it as variations in distance. You may actual-

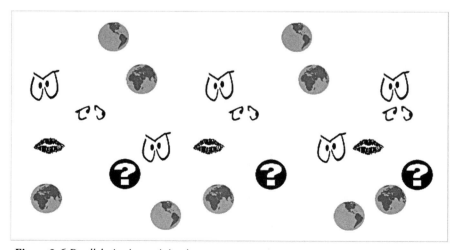

***Figure 2-6*** Parallel-viewing training image

ly be able to feel this adjustment happening as you're viewing images with long, steady level changes.

## Hyperconvergence

The *convergence strip width* of a stereogram is the maximum spacing between repeating elements in the stereogram. If the convergence strip width is too narrow, you can converge too far. Instead of your eyes viewing adjacent corresponding points, they can cross or spread far enough to skip a row or more. Figure 2-7 illustrates this phenomenon, called *hyperconvergence*, which is bad, bad, bad! Well, all right, sometimes it's quite interesting....

Hyperconverging produces unpredictable visual effects. Depths may cancel out, reverse, become stronger, or even oscillate so that viewing is very difficult. Geometric or abstract images may become equally interesting new images. Representational images usually become unrecognizable. One of the images in the Gallery, SISpiral, uses hyperconvergence to create the illusion of additional depth levels. Cross-eyed viewing is more prone to hyperconvergence than parallel viewing.

# Learning Parallel Viewing

With very few exceptions, anyone can learn to parallel-view single-image stereograms. It may take some time, but you can do it. Some people get it almost instantly; some people may take an hour or more. It's important to be relaxed, comfortable, and above all, patient.

This process wants good light, and the page should be as flat as possible. At all times, keep your head level and the page completely flat. Tilting the page to the right or the left defeats the effect. Look again at Figure 2-6, an icon-based stereogram that is designed for teaching parallel viewing. You might want to photocopy the next few paragraphs and have someone read them to you while you look at the figure.

Hold the training picture right up to your nose, so that you can't possibly focus on it. Let your eyes relax, space out, and stare off through the page at nothing in the distance. Ponder the void. Notice the two planets in the top row, without focusing on them. Let them be fuzzy blobs.

With the page actually touching your nose, you should see only one planet, one indistinct gray blob. You should be able to look to the left or the right and still only see one

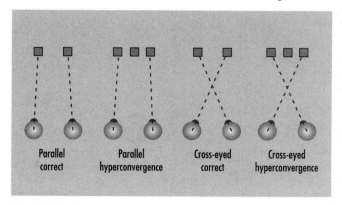

*Figure 2-7* Hyperconvergence

planet in the top row. If you are a young or small person and your eyes aren't that far apart, use two of the three question marks for this exercise.

Pull the page slowly away from your nose to a distance about the width of your hand. Don't try to focus on the page. If your eyes hurt, you're crossing them and working much harder at this than you need to. Relaxation is the key. As the page moves away, another planet will come into your view from each side. Don't focus on them; try to keep looking through the page at nothing. You'll now see three planets where there are actually two on the page. Pull the page very slowly away, and try to keep the three planets from sliding back across the page and becoming two or four.

As you continue to pull the page away very, very slowly, maintaining the three planets, you will notice something peculiar. They're behind the page! Give your brain some time to catch up to this interesting fact. Relax and wait. Let your brain figure out that you want to look at this phenomenon, and your eyes will focus appropriately. Don't force the issue. It's more important to learn to keep the objects from sliding around than it is to focus on them.

As the page swims into clarity, you may want to move it nearer to you or farther away. When it finally locks in, the illusion is quite astonishing. You'll know it when you get it. Some describe it as discovering a new sense, or looking into an alternate universe.

## The Mirror Exercise

This exercise helps you separate convergence and focus. It's good practice for single-image stereogram viewing.

Put your nose right up to your bathroom mirror and look yourself in the eyes. Instead of two eyes, you see one. Each eye is looking straight at itself, and your brain assumes both eyes are looking at the same eye. You can also do this with another person, nose to nose. (Small children find it hysterically funny to see their parents as Cyclopeans.)

Back away from the mirror slowly, without refocusing or crossing your eyes, and try to maintain the illusion. When you are just a few inches away from the mirror, your mystical third eye will be joined by your mystical second nose. Continue backing away without reconverging, until you can focus on your third eye. At this point you have parallel convergence (that's an oxymoron), which is a wider view than you will ever need to see single-image stereograms.

Figure 2-8 shows what the author sees when he looks in the mirror. Parallel-view this figure to see what *you* would see looking at the author.

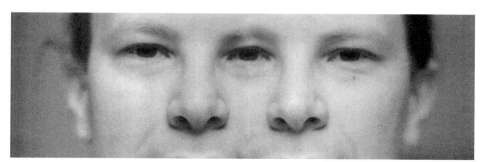

***Figure 2-8*** The author, as he appears to himself in a mirror

## View Your Reflection

This next technique encourages you to focus your eyes at twice the distance to the stereogram. This converges your eyes correctly for viewing the average single-image stereogram.

Display a single-image stereogram on your computer using a program such as MindImages or SHIMMER (see Chapter 8). Turn the brightness knob on the monitor all the way down. Look at your reflection in the monitor, and slowly turn the brightness back up until you can see both your reflection and the stereogram.

While still focusing and converging on your reflection, pay attention to the stereogram and wait for something to happen. If the stereogram has two indexing dots, you want to see them as three. If it doesn't have indexing dots, look for details in the stereogram that repeat across the screen. Try to get two adjacent details to line up on top of each other.

You can aid this effect by setting up a light that shines on your face but doesn't light the monitor screen. This trick works best with older or less-expensive monitors, since better monitors resist screen glare by reducing reflections.

For a variation on the same technique, print out a single-image stereogram and mount it behind a piece of glass. You can tape the print, face, to the inside of a glass cabinet door, or you can put it in a picture frame. Again, look at your reflection in the glass and slowly shift your attention to the stereogram, without reconverging your eyes.

## Look Through the Image

If you have access to a laser or ink-jet printer, you can print a single-image stereogram on transparency film. This makes a great tool for learning parallel viewing. Stand a few feet from a wall, hold the transparency up, and look through it at the wall. Move toward and away from the wall while focusing on it. Notice how the index dots or adjacent repeating features in the stereogram slide left and right. When you have the wall in focus and you can see two features in the stereogram as three, hold still and slowly shift your focus to the stereogram.

Another approach is to print a stereogram on plain paper, and fold the printout so that no paper shows above the stereogram. Hold up the printout and look into the distance, as in the previous example.

You can use this same technique by viewing the wall behind your computer monitor and watching a displayed stereogram with your peripheral vision.

One last tip: Imagine yourself looking through the page or monitor with X-ray eyes. Relax and let it happen.

# Learning Cross-Eyed Viewing

If you learned to cross your eyes when you were a kid, you've got a head start on this technique.

Hold this book in one hand at arm's length, open to Figure 2-6. Hold up a pen vertically about halfway between your eyes and the page, and sight along the tip of the pen at the top row of planets, as shown in Figure 2-9. Look at the pen, keep it in focus, but pay attention to the planets. Move the pen forward and back and watch how the planets appear to slide left and right across the page. When the two planets become three, hold the pen still and shift your attention from the pen to the page. Patience is critical. When the page comes into focus with three planets in the top row, you've got it. Slowly remove

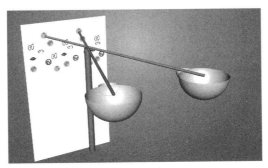

***Figure 2-9*** Learning cross-eyed viewing

the pen and look down the page at the fully 3D illusion. When you've really got it locked in and steady, it's fun to try reaching your hand into the picture.

Notice the reversed depths, as compared with parallel viewing. The image in Figure 2-6 was designed to work equally well with either viewing method. Other images may make sense only when viewed one way or the other.

Cross-eyed viewing has the advantage that you can converge any similar objects if you can get back far enough from them. Try converging the ⓡ and ⓟ keys on your keyboard, or the patterns in your wallpaper. Converge a matching pair of soup cans and then slowly move them apart, for some very strange visual effects. (But please resist the urge to converge the dials on your car's dashboard while you're driving.)

# Which Way Am I Viewing?

Figure 2-10 makes good viewing practice because it's fairly easy to converge, and it tells you whether you're viewing cross-eyed or parallel. The lowercase characters come forward when viewed parallel. Reading downward, they say "wide-near." The uppercase characters come forward when viewed cross-eyed. Reading downward, they say "CROSS|NEAR."

# Can This Hurt My Eyes?

Geologists, archaeologists, chemists, vision researchers, and stereo 3D hobbyists have been free-viewing stereo pairs with these viewing techniques for a hundred years without apparent harm. Viewing SIRDS is a new skill for most people, however, and it uses eye muscles in unfamiliar ways. It's important not to push it too hard. Try for a while. If your eyes hurt, stop and give them a rest.

Exercise common sense. If you go out and run 20 miles after sitting in front of a computer for two years, you're going to hurt afterward. Likewise, if you stare fixedly at your computer monitor in a new way for eight hours, you're going to hurt afterward.

# Does a Vision Impairment Matter?

A small percentage of people are unable to see stereo 3D illusions at all. There are a number of vision conditions that may contribute to this difficulty.

```
    C           C           C           C           C           C
w           w           w           w           w           w
    R           R           R           R           R           R
i           i           i           i           i           i
    O           O           O           O           O           O
d           d           d           d           d           d
    S           S           S           S           S           S
e           e           e           e           e           e
    S           S           S           S           S           S
-           -           -           -           -           -
    |           |           |           |           |           |
n           n           n           n           n           n
    N           N           N           N           N           N
e           e           e           e           e           e
    E           E           E           E           E           E
a           a           a           a           a           a
    A           A           A           A           A           A
r           r           r           r           r           r
    R           R           R           R           R           R
```

**Figure 2-10** CROSWIDE.TXT: This image tells you how you're viewing it

# Astigmatism

Astigmatism is a lens defect that causes blurring or distortion. If you have astigmatism, each eye may see something different even when the objects are the same, and this may hamper your ability to perceive stereograms. SIRDS are particularly difficult for astigmatic eyes, since they eliminate so many helpful auxiliary cues. Some people with astigmatism can see SIRDS animated by SHIMMER (see Chapter 8) even when they can't see them any other way. Some can't see SIRDS at all, and some have no trouble. Presumably, it depends on how horizontal the distortion is, because SIRDS rely on the accurate registration of corresponding points in a horizontal line.

# Monocularism

Newborn infants typically do not have straight, synchronized eyes. Stereo depth perception is a skill learned very early in a child's development, between the ages of two and four months. Apparently, if it doesn't happen then, it can't be learned later. People who are severely cross-eyed (esotropic) in infancy may spend the rest of their lives looking out of one eye at a time. This means they'll have no stereo depth perception, which means they can't see SIRDS or stereo 3D of any kind. People with this condition, called monocularism, learn to judge depth from the other available cues mentioned before, such as accommodation, perspective, and occlusion.

## Other Conditions

Extreme differences in refraction between the eyes, such as one eye with 20/20 vision and the other with 20/70, can also impair one's ability to see stereo 3D. Congenital cataracts, if not treated early, may also cause reduced stereo vision. Acquired esotropia, a condition of crossed eyes that begins between the ages of two and four years, can destroy stereo vision. This condition is correctable, and stereo vision can often be recovered.

# What's Next?

Now that you know what stereograms are, how they work, and how to see them, you're probably wondering where they came from. Chapter 3 presents the family tree of the single-image stereogram.

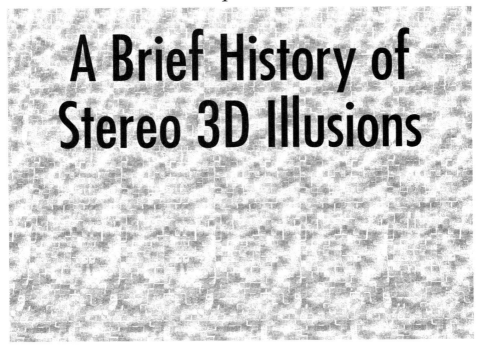

# A Brief History of Stereo 3D Illusions

**W**here did stereograms come from? The single-image stereogram is a visual art form in its infancy. RDS images and SIRDS have a slightly longer history as a research tool. This chapter studies the history of stereo 3D with an emphasis on the developments that led to today's stereograms.

## Assisted Stereo Pairs

The original form of stereo 3D simply imitates the normal function of two eyes. Two separate photographs are taken from two cameras the same distance apart as two human eyes. With the assistance of a little technology, one of these two photos is presented to each eye.

### The Stereoscope

For 2,000 years, people have noticed that each eye sees an object differently. Euclid, da Vinci, Kepler, and many others wrote about this. For just as long, people have been aware that when you close one eye, something changes or seems missing. That missing thing is the perceived depth effect. This is called *relief*, as in bas-relief sculpture. In 1838, Sir Charles Wheatstone made the connection: He realized that the differences in the eyes' views are the source of relief perception. He called this 3D effect *stereopsis*, from the Greek words for "solid" and "vision." This difference in the two eyes' views is known as *binocular disparity*, which literally means "two eyes see differently."

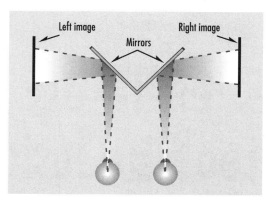

***Figure 3-1*** Wheatstone's stereoscope used mirrors to combine two drawings

Wheatstone discovered that with two drawn pictures he could produce the illusion of depth. He invented a viewer called the *stereoscope* to present one of these two pictures to each eye. The stereoscope used a pair of mirrors at angles in front of the person, with the pictures off to each side. Figure 3-1 illustrates the concept. At about the same time, Daguerre and his contemporaries invented photography. A man named Claudet put daguerreotypes in Wheatstone's stereoscope in 1839, and the revolution was under way.

Wheatstone's stereoscope was cumbersome and difficult to illuminate, but Sir William Brewster solved these problems in 1850. Brewster's *prismatic viewing stereoscope* held the two photos side by side, and used lenses to help the eyes focus while maintaining distant convergence. The introduction of Brewster's invention at the first World's Fair in London is regarded as the dawn of the Golden Age of Stereo.

Oliver Wendell Holmes created the most popular style of stereoscope (Figure 3-2), and it remained in common use until 1930.

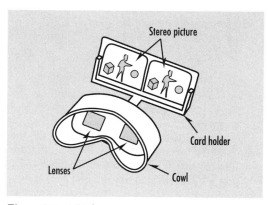

***Figure 3-2*** A Holmes stereoscope

***Figure 3-3*** View-Master stereo viewers

## Popular Gadgetry

In the middle of this century, renewed interest in stereo pairs was prompted by the marketing of a more convenient viewer. The Sawyer View-Master is a compact plastic device that looks like binoculars, as shown in Figure 3-3. It displays stereo pairs mounted on opposite sides of a circular disk, called a reel. Thousands of reels were produced in their heyday during the fifties and sixties and sold in postcard stands and tourist shops worldwide. View-Master is now a Tyco product, still in production.

There are many dedicated hobbyists maintaining and using the stereo-pair cameras produced during this period, including the Stereo Realist, Kodak Stereo, and Stereo Vivid. The members of the National Stereoscopic Association (NSA) and the International Stereoscopic Union (ISU) hold regular conventions and produce publications discussing the topics of 3D photography and stereo viewing. A small number of stereo cameras, such as the Fed and the Sputnik, are now in production in Eastern Europe.

## Virtual Reality

The recent interest in virtual reality has created a third wave of inexpensive, assisted stereo-pair viewers for use with conventional computer monitors. Simsalabim Systems makes the Cyberscope, a plastic hood containing optics and mirrors. It mounts on the face of a monitor and presents a separate image to each eyepiece. Cyberscope-compatible software displays the two halves of a stereo pair on their sides, foot to foot, to preserve a normal screen aspect ratio. This arrangement allows the Cyberscope to work with a variety of monitor sizes, without adjustment.

*Virtual Reality Creations* by David Stampe, Bernie Roehl, and John Eagan (Waite Group Press, 1993) includes a viewer that mounts on the front of a computer monitor. It contains a pair of Fresnel lenses that make it easy for you to focus on a side-by-side stereo pair from a few inches away. The Fresnel viewer works with any software that can display a normal side-by-side stereo pair with the correct size and spacing.

# Superimposed Stereo

Assisted stereo pairs suffer from a number of drawbacks. The primary one is that the image has a definite fixed center. You can't look left or right across that center. The various techniques of *superimposed stereo*—including anaglyphs, Polaroid, lenticular, slit raster, and sequential-field—address these problems by displaying two or more different images in the same place, with technology to present one of them to each eye. Superimposed stereo allows you to look left and right across an image that can be as wide as you desire.

Another drawback is that most stereo pair viewers only work for one person at a time because you need to be positioned directly between the stereo pair. Superimposed stereo, however, can work for large audiences.

# Anaglyphs

In the 1850s, Rollman and D'Almeida independently invented the *anaglyph* projection system. They used two projectors, each containing one image of a stereo pair. Both images were projected onto the same screen, one through a red filter and one through a green filter. The audience wore glasses with one red lens and one green lens, so each eye would only see one of the images. This system can work very well and is still used today. MindImages, one of the programs included with this book, can display images for red/blue or red/green anaglyph viewing (see Chapter 8). Fractint, the freeware fractal-drawing program discussed in Chapter 10, can also produce 3D anaglyphs. VR Basic, available from The Waite Group, lets you create and explore 3D virtual worlds in red/blue anaglyphic stereo.

The main limitation of anaglyphs is that they don't work with full-color images. Also, an accurate color match between the glasses and the viewed image is critical. If the colors don't match well enough, each filter won't totally block the other image, and the images will bleed through to both eyes. Anaglyphs work best with a projected image, because matching the color of a viewing lens filter to that of a projection lens filter is easier than matching to the color of a printed ink or a display.

On the other hand, anaglyphs have the distinct advantages of low cost and ease of use. The audience doesn't need to learn a new viewing technique, and cardboard frames with cellophane lenses work reasonably well for pennies apiece. Audience position is not critical, and the effect works simultaneously for any number of people.

# Polaroid

In the 1940s, a stereo projection system using nearly the same equipment as anaglyph projection solved many of the anaglyph's inherent problems. *Polaroid projection* replaces the red and blue glass in the projectors and glasses with opposing, polarizing filters. A horizontal polarizing filter blocks light that has been projected through a vertical polarizing filter, and vice versa. This works with full-color images, and the lens matching is less of an issue. Disney's movie *Captain EO* uses this system, as do most of Hollywood's 3D movies.

24

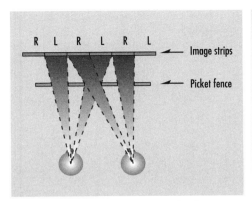

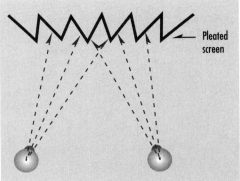

***Figure 3-4***  Different views through a fence  ***Figure 3-5***  Sokolov's accordion projection system

Until very recently, the Polaroid stereo system only worked for projection, since there was no way to put two filters in one place on a printed page or computer monitor. In the early 1990s, advances in microfabrication enabled a company called VRex to produce a sheet of plastic with horizontal stripes the same height as the individual pixels of a computer laptop screen. Alternating stripes are polarized in opposite directions. This sheet, called a µPol (microPol), is laminated to the laptop screen. Software combines a stereo pair, creating a new image that combines (multiplexes) the odd-numbered lines from one image with the even-numbered lines of the other image. Conventional, inexpensive polarizing glasses conduct the odd-numbered lines through to one eye and the even-numbered lines through to the other eye.

This same process works on computer projection panels. It even works on printed images, although each individual print must have a polarizing screen laminated to it with very precise registration. It doesn't work on conventional computer or video monitors, because the location of a particular pixel on the screen is subject to too much variation. On a laptop screen, a pixel is an actual physical object with a known location. It doesn't move around under the influence of temperature, image brightness, or control settings.

## Picket Fence

An interesting and completely separate approach to 3D illusions is the *picket fence* concept. It presents a different picture to each eye without glasses or filters. If you look through a picket fence, each eye gets a slightly different view of what's on the other side. Cut up two billboards into strips, alternate the strips and arrange everything just so behind the picket fence, and each eye will see a completely different picture. Figure 3-4 shows how this works. Several techniques have applied variations on this idea to 3D illusions.

In 1908, a Russian named A. P. Sokolov used two projectors off to each side of the audience, and an accordion-pleated screen to show 3D movies without special glasses. A viewer's right eye saw the pleats facing right, and the left eye saw the pleats facing left. Figure 3-5 illustrates the principle.

First produced in 1928, rows of tiny prisms called *lenticular* lenses were laminated to an image of alternating strips. Each eye looks through an opposite face of each prism at a different strip. The combined image produces crude 3D without viewing hardware. This technique recently resurfaced in the multilensed Nimslo and Nishika cameras.

In the early 1980s, Gregory Gundlach and Grayson Marshall developed the idea of viewing alternating strips through nearly microscopic rows of vertical slits positioned a precise distance in front of a transparency. This technique, called the *slit raster* or *black line process*, can produce astonishingly good full-color 3D without viewing hardware. The technique actually has roots in the work of G. Ives and others dating back to the 1930s and before, but Gundlach and Grayson's independent discovery spawned a wave of interest that continues today.

All of these techniques suffer from high costs and complex production—hardly something for the average person to experiment with at home.

## Sequential Field

In 1981, Lenny Lipton's StereoGraphics Corporation invented the *electro-stereoscopic sequential-field viewer,* which combines electronic shutters with fast video displays. Sequential-field stereo employs glasses with liquid crystal lenses that can turn opaque or transparent in response to an electronic pulse. The controlling software flashes the left image on the monitor and clears the left eyepiece. Then it flashes the right image on the monitor and clears the right eyepiece. It does this 60 times a second, faster than the eye can notice. Each eye sees only one of the two images.

Toshiba produced sequential-field stereo video cameras and viewers in 1988. Sega video games popularized sequential-field stereo 3D. Sega's viewers, though not very high in quality, are much sought after by virtual reality hackers. The StereoGraphics CrystalEyes virtual reality systems represent the state of the art in this technique, providing a flicker-free image without any wires from the computer to the glasses.

The sequential-field concept can produce effective full-color stereo 3D. It's strictly electronic, however, and it requires each viewing person to wear the expensive shutter glasses.

# Free Viewing: No Hardware Required

A conventional, single picture of a mountainside doesn't show you the shape of the mountain, how deep the crevices are, or even necessarily which peaks are near and far. A single picture of a large protein containing thousands of atoms looks like an indecipherable mess without apparent structure. A military tank painted with good camouflage can be completely invisible in a two-dimensional aerial photograph. 3D images have changed all that. Geologists, archaeologists, topographers, chemists, and bomber crews have all used stereo 3D photographs and illustrations to increase their understanding of their subject matter.

The required viewing hardware has always been one of the main drawbacks to stereo 3D viewing. Lenticular and slit raster display techniques eliminate the viewing hardware, but they introduce complexity into the creation of each individual print.

During the course of day-in, day-out viewing, many people dispense with the viewer hardware and train themselves to look at stereo pairs directly. This is called *free viewing*. Though its discoverer remains unknown and uncredited, free viewing may be older even than Wheatstone's stereo pairs.

# Single-Image Stereograms

Sir William Brewster, who invented the prismatic viewing stereoscope, also gets credit for another discovery. Brewster noticed that if he looked at repetitive wallpaper as if he were free-viewing stereo pairs, he got an illusion of depth. This is the first recognized type of single-image stereogram, known as the Victorian wallpaper effect. Figure 3-6 demonstrates this effect, which in principle is an icon-based stereogram. When you view it parallel or cross-eyed, you can see how small variations in the wallpaper printing process give rise to a hidden picture. The wall, once flat, now seems to be broken up into several jagged levels. Modern printing techniques are more precise, so this effect is no longer common.

## The Birth of RDSs

Bela Julesz invented the random-dot stereogram (RDS). Julesz was researching stereopsis and visual perception, with a particular interest in the role binocular disparity plays in depth perception. The title of his book, *Foundations of Cyclopean Perception* (University of Chicago Press, 1971), refers to phenomena that can be seen with two eyes but are invisible to a single eye.

Julesz used computers to create a pattern of random dots, and then to make a copy of the pattern with selected dots shifted various ways. Viewing these cross-eyed presents a different copy of the dot pattern to each eye. When Julesz shifted some of the dots right or left by small amounts, he discovered that the disparity between the two images produced a 3D illusion of an image that could not be seen by itself in either dot pattern. He published a description in the *Bell Systems Technical Journal* in 1960.

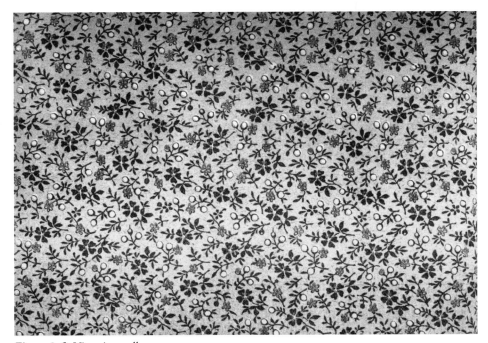

*Figure 3-6*  Victorian wallpaper

Julesz used the RDS to disprove the common belief that depth perception happened in the eye itself. Since neither half of the RDS displays any depth, he could show that depth perception happens in the brain when it combines the two images received by the eyes. The dual-image RDS, sometimes called a Julesz Figure, proved very useful to perception researchers because it isolates two components of human depth perception. Accommodation (focus distance), perspective, occlusion (objects in front of other objects), relative motion, shadows, and brightness cuing (objects are often darker farther away) do not contribute to seeing the 3D image in an RDS. The only things that matter are convergence, (how much your eyes cross so they both see a given point) and the brain's ability to fuse the two different views of one image.

Julesz Figures suffer from the same limitations as any other type of stereo pair. They must be viewed cross-eyed unless they are very small, and cross-eyed viewing can be somewhat strenuous. The image has a fixed center, so you can't look to the left or right. It's not possible to view a large stereo pair without backing up far enough to get the whole thing in view. Stereo pairs can only cover a small part of your field of vision.

One way to address these limitations is using superimposing methods. In fact, Julesz included red/blue glasses and anaglyph RDS images in his book. With superimposing, however, comes the awkwardness and inconvenience of hardware. The solution was eventually found in wallpaper.

Christopher Tyler is credited with taking the next step, after he worked with Julesz at Bell Labs. He remembered Brewster's Victorian wallpaper effect, and realized that he could combine it with the Julesz method of shifting dots to generate a continuous depth image that could be free-viewed. In 1979, at the Smith-Kettlewell Institute in San Francisco, Tyler and programmer Maureen Clarke created SIRDS, which Tyler called autostereograms, on an Apple II computer. He published his work as a chapter in the book *Vergence Eye Movements: Basic and Clinical Aspects* (Butterworths, 1983). He viewed them cross-eyed, just as Julesz viewed his images. Tyler's discovery combined the convenience of free viewing with the wide-image strengths of superimposed stereo, and without the high production requirements of the lenticular or slit raster methods.

## Early Stereogram Artists

The work of Julesz intrigued the artists who discovered it. Alfons Schilling produced hand-drawn stereo pairs using RDS principles in the 1970s. He even painted some single-image stereograms. Masayuki Ito produced a single-image stereogram for *Graphic Design* magazine in 1970. Both Schilling and Ito created single-image stereograms before Tyler.

The Russians beat everyone to the original RDS concept, however. According to Christopher Tyler, Boris Kompaneysky of the Russian Academy of Fine Arts published a hand-painted RDS stereo pair in the Russian journal *Bulletin of Ophthalmology* in 1939!

## Seeing the Light

David Stork and Chris Rocca built directly on the work of Julesz, Tyler, and others. They published an article in *Behavior Research Methods* in 1989, in which they explain the process of creating what they called auto-random-dot stereograms (ARDSs). They also point out that letters or symbols could be used in place of dots. We now call this type of image SIRTS. Stork and Rocca advocated cross-eyed viewing.

Stork, along with D. Brill and D. Falk, created a SIRDS in 1988 that contained the words "SEEING THE LIGHT." This image appeared in the *Behavior Research* article.

They mention that the image can be viewed cross-eyed or parallel (which they call hypoconvergent).

In 1990, Dan Dyckman published a brief article titled "Single Image Random Dot Stereograms" in *Stereo World* (the journal of the NSA). Dyckman wrote that he discovered SIRDS when a friend showed him Falk, Brill, and Stork's Seeing the Light image. Dyckman deduced the principle and produced several images for the article. The title of this article appears to be the first use of the term, but not the common acronym SIRDS.

This article was the first exposure to SIRDS for many of the people now producing them commercially, including Tom Baccei of N. E. Thing. Dyckman advocated parallel (which he called divergent) viewing, and this could be the reason most single-image stereograms are designed today for parallel viewing. One of N. E. Thing's images, Tom's Flower, appears in the Gallery in Chapter 4.

John M. Olsen discovered the single-image stereogram principle independently of Tyler in 1988. Olsen, a student at the University of Utah, and John Halleck, a university employee, were looking at some Julesz-style dual-image RDS images, and thinking about how the first image is used as a random field, with selected dots shifted to produce the second image. He realized that he could use the shifted second image as the random base for a third image. Slide them together, more or less, and you have a SIRDS. Olsen viewed his images parallel.

Olsen continues to be among the many active participants of the Internet alt.3D newsgroup, helping other people improve their understanding of the algorithms and theories behind single-image stereograms. The Gallery in this book includes one of Olsen's Infix Technologies images: Aloft.

# What's Next?

Single-image stereograms are both old and newborn. The popular art form is only a few years old, yet some of the techniques and processes date back over 150 years. Major developments in this art form occur frequently today, as people discover new ways to apply the concepts. Play with the tools in this book, bring your own ideas to your work, and show people what you're doing. You, too, can participate in the continuing evolution of this new medium that is equal parts art technique and computer technology.

The next chapter, "The Gallery of Stereo Illusion," presents the state of the art in stereograms today.

# The Gallery of Stereo Illusion

*I*n this chapter you sample the state of the art in single-image stereograms. Everything you need to produce images of this quality is included in this book, except the talent. You can supply that yourself.

## Contributing Artists

The artists who have contributed images to this gallery range from hobbyists to full-time stereogram professionals.

## John M. Olsen, Infix Technologies

"Aloft" was produced by

Infix Technologies
P.O. Box 381
Orem, UT 84057-0381
(801) 221-9233
jolsen@nyx.cs.du.edu

Infix Technologies has published a number of posters, including a very high resolution bust of Beethoven, image-mapped with musical notes. Infix also does custom stereograms for advertising and promotions.

## Steve Perrigo

Steve Perrigo is a consulting environmental geologist from Kirkland, Washington. His interest in 3D imagery was sparked by viewing single-image stereograms in the malls coupled with a beginner's interest in ray tracing. He frequents the GRAPHDEV forum on CompuServe. His multitude of hobbies and interests are made possible by the patience of his wife, Gail, and his daughters, Allison and Lia.

## Robert Raymond, Mirages

"Dino Skin" was produced by

> Mirages
> P.O. Box 1298
> Moab, UT 84532
> (801) 259-6998
> CompuServe 73063,1024

Mirages is a coalition of artists, programmers, and 3D enthusiasts originally hailing from the red rock country of Moab, Utah. In addition to producing and marketing stereograms highlighting Southwestern themes, Mirages produces custom stereograms on a contract basis.

## Dan Richardson

Dan's interest in 3D computer graphics grew from his work rendering molecular images for scientific and medical publications. His image-mapped and random-dot stereograms in the gallery were all produced with the book version of RDSGEN, as discussed in Chapter 10, with the exception of "Ovals." The commercial programs Draw 3.0 and Picture Publisher 4.0 from Micrografx were used extensively, as was the excellent free Windows paint program Matisse In Gray, courtesy of Fauve Software.

## N. E. Thing

N. E. Thing's image "Tom's Flower" appears courtesy of *MAGIC EYE—A New Way of Looking at the World,* by N. E. Thing Enterprises, Inc., published by Andrews and McMeel.

# The Images

The gallery images are listed in the order in which they appear. The images are meant to be viewed parallel unless otherwise specified.

| Parting | This Fractint depthmap uses an imagemap composed of 10,000 boxes rendered in POV-Ray 2.0. The texture data was generated by OBJREP, John Kolesar's freeware Windows utility for POV-Ray. |
| --- | --- |

| | |
|---|---|
| **Hairwall** | This fractint depthmap reminds the artist of walkways atop castle walls. The imagemap was assembled in Picture Publisher from multiple scans of the artist's hair, taken with a Logitech hand scanner. |
| **World of Words** | The depthmap for this image was hand drawn from several topographical maps. The image-mapped texture was assembled in Picture Publisher from scans of rough draft pages of this book. |
| **Big Hat Rules OK!** | This band logo was created in Draw, and then heavily smoothed and blurred in Picture Publisher. The imagemap was created in POV-Ray using the bozo texture. |
| **Herkimer** | Herkimer's depthmap uses POV-Ray blobs. The imagemap was created in Matisse In Gray. |
| **Eyes** | Depthmap and image-mapped texture taken from the artist's face with a Logitech hand scanner and processed in Picture Publisher. A scan of fake fur added to the texture provides finer visual cues. |
| **See 3D** | This single-image random text stereogram of the words "SEE 3D" was produced using SIRTSER. |
| **Universe Mandelbrodt** | This depthmap comes from a fractal that is a life-sized piece of a Mandelbrodt set roughly the size of the universe, if the universe has a size. Tim Wegner created the fractal with an experimental version of Fractint incorporating arbitrary numerical precision for extremely deep zooms. The image-mapped texture was created in Matisse In Gray. Use parallel or cross-eyed viewing. |
| **Turning** | This Fractint depthmap, reminiscent of a prop wash, was processed in Picture Publisher to reduce the detail. The imagemap was created in Matisse In Gray. Use parallel or cross-eyed viewing. |
| **DNA SIRDS** | A section of a DNA molecule rendered in Polyray. |
| **Dino Skin** | Dr. Ruas Onid, noted paleontologist, made a remarkable discovery under a rock in his backyard: a dinosaur skin specimen totally untouched by the ravages of time! Can you help him identify the species? Find 25 indications of the dinosaur's species. Start with the two fusion "dots" at the top. The 3D image gives another clue. The remaining ones are hidden in the texture of the dinosaur's skin. Also, can you find five instances of the word "dinosaur" in this paragraph?<br><br>The 3D dataset was used by permission of Viewpoint Data-Labs, Orem, Utah. |

**Tom's Rose**

N. E. Thing's lovely flower.

**Arrow Cage**

The arrows in this image are individual bitmaps from clip art and font characters in Draw, exported as .TIF files and converted to .GIF files for image mapping in POV-Ray.

**People**

This icon-based stereogram was created entirely in Draw, using clip art. The image's shimmering colors demonstrate *retinal rivalry*, a condition produced when each eye is looking at an identical but differently colored object.

**Out and In**

This Fractint depthmap uses a POV-Ray imagemap of layers of granite and marble textures, based on Mike Miller's STONES.INC.

**Blue Swirl**

This Fractint depthmap hides in a POV-Ray imagemap using the agate texture. Use parallel or cross-eyed viewing.

**Aloft**

This is John M. Olsen's image of hot air balloons. The depthmap and the stereogram were generated on an HP9000/705 UNIX workstation.

**Planets in Perillel**

This icon-based stereogram was created entirely in POV-Ray. The planetary surfaces are based on images of Venus taken by the Magellan spacecraft, Viking images of Jupiter, and NOAA images of Earth, courtesy of NASA. Use cross-eyed viewing.

**SISpiral**

Depthmap by Fractint, dots by RDSGEN, post-processed with a noise removal filter in Matisse In Gray to create larger-sized random dots. This image is a viewing curiosity.

Begin viewing with the indexing dots in the upper-right corner, and look down to the dropoff halfway down the right side. Now follow the receding spiral back counterclockwise. When you come around to the dropoff again, you'll find that it's down to your new level and you can keep right on descending. With a little patience, you should be able to go smoothly down 2½ cycles or more, depending on the distance between your eyes. Cross-eyed viewing reveals that the slope gets steeper as you go around. Use parallel or cross-eyed viewing.

**Symmetry**

This Fractint depthmap was heavily modified in Picture Publisher. The imagemap was created in POV-Ray with the granite texture. Use parallel or cross-eyed viewing.

**Ovals**

This image was drawn and generated in an early alpha version of Johannes Schmid's vector-based object-oriented single image stereogram drawing program, VECTRDS.

Dive Pit

This depthmap was hand drawn in Picture Publisher. Look for the diving board and the steps up from the bottom. The image-map was created in Polyray using a noise function to create larger scale random dots.

*Parting*

*Hairwall*

*World of Words*

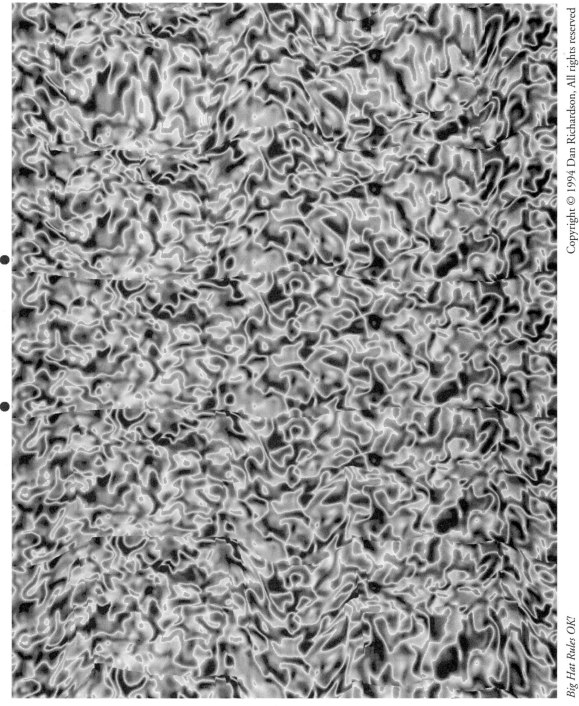

*Big Hat Rules OK!*

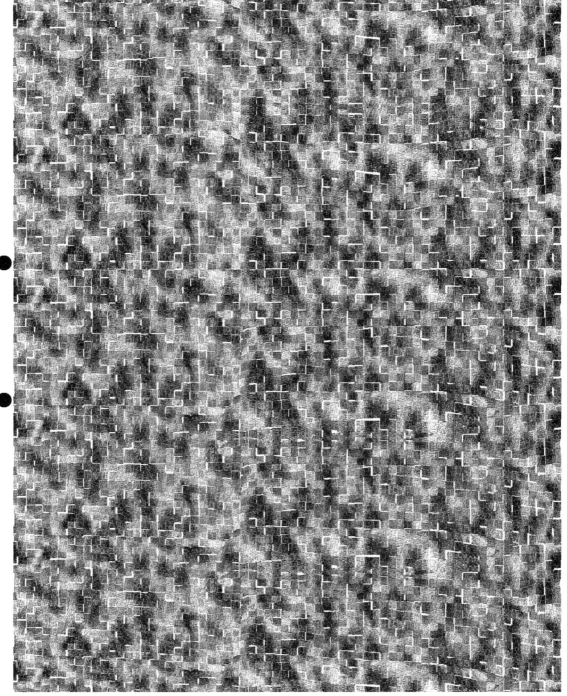

*Herkimer*

40

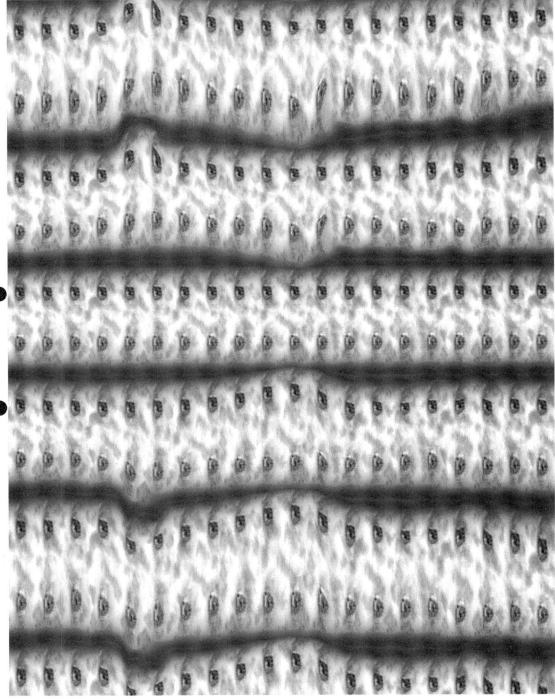

*Eyes*

41

*See 3D*

42

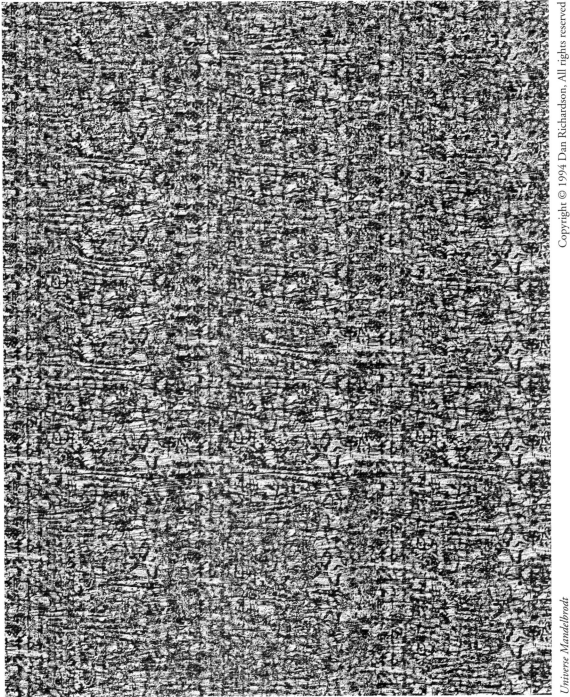

*Universe Mandelbrodt*

43

*Turning*

*DNA SIRDS*

*SISpiral*

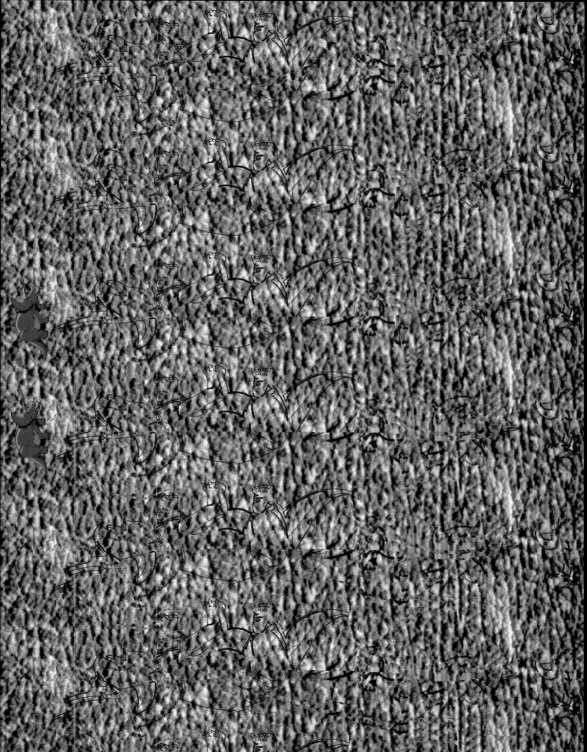

*Dino Skin*

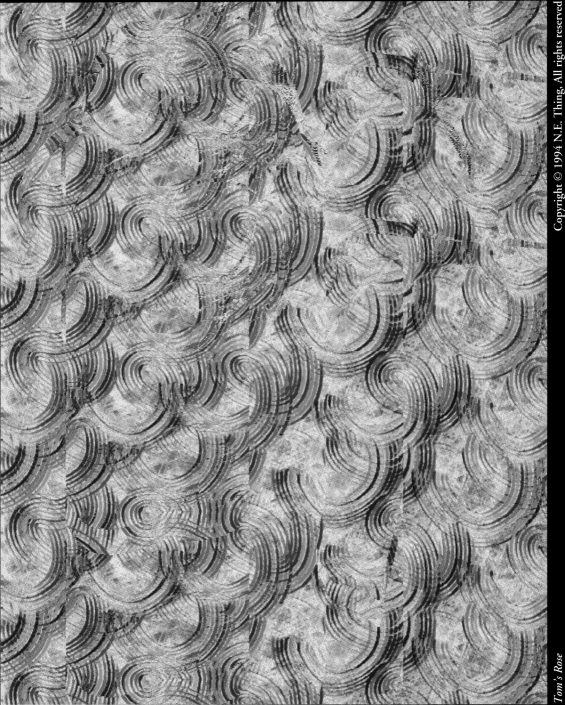

*Tom's Rose*

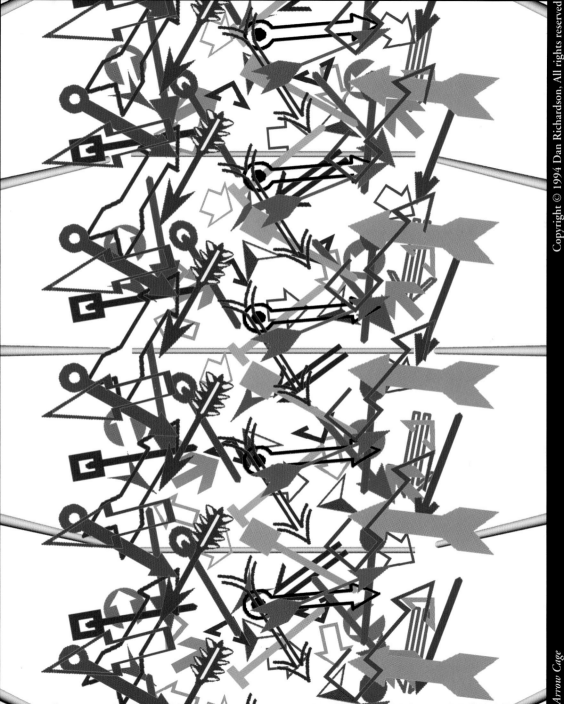

*Arrow Cage*

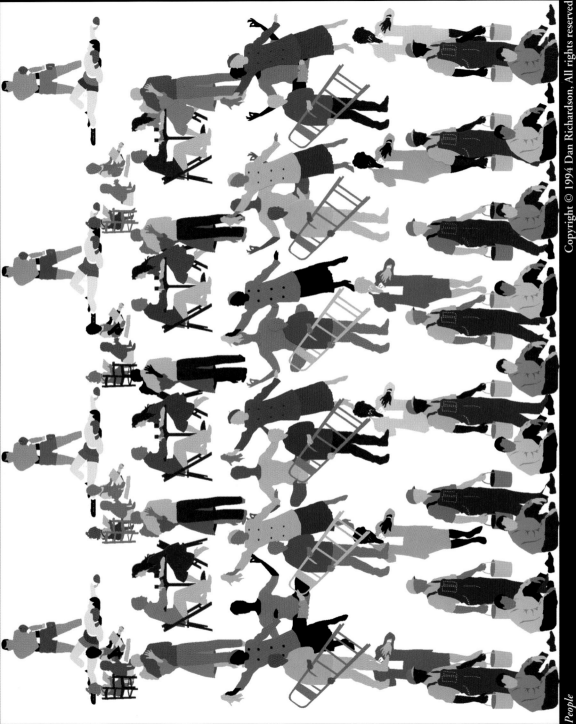

*People*

*Out and In*

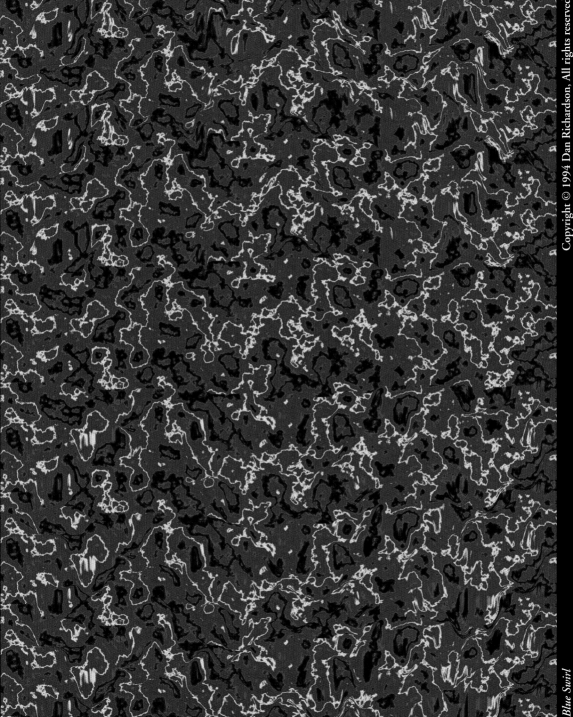

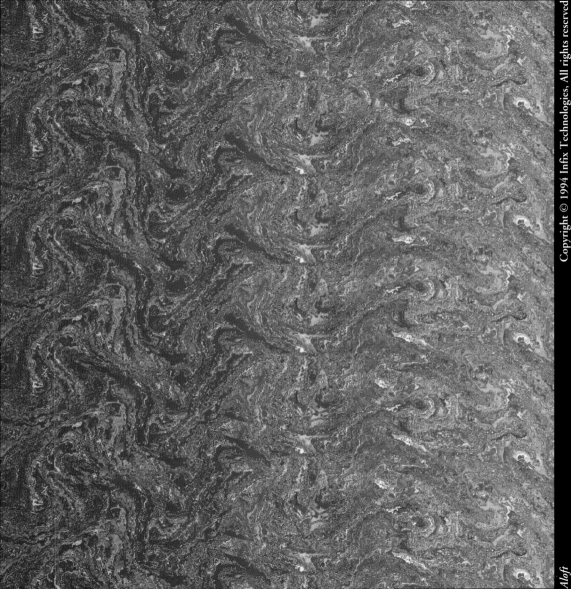

Aloft

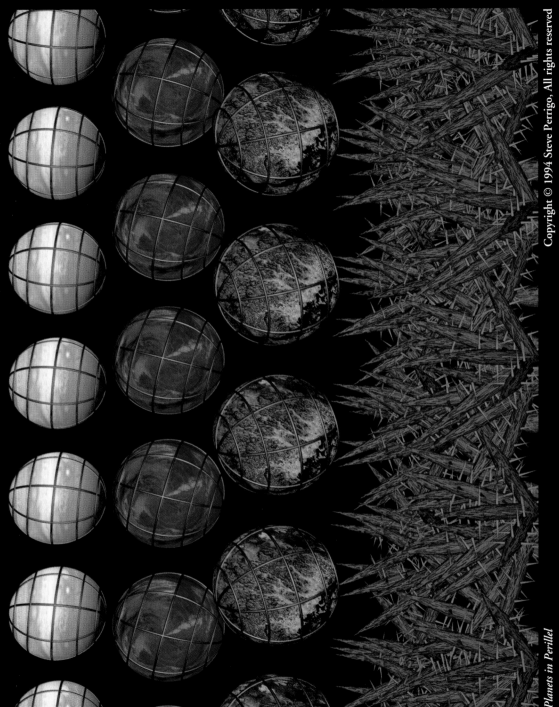

*Planets in Perillel*

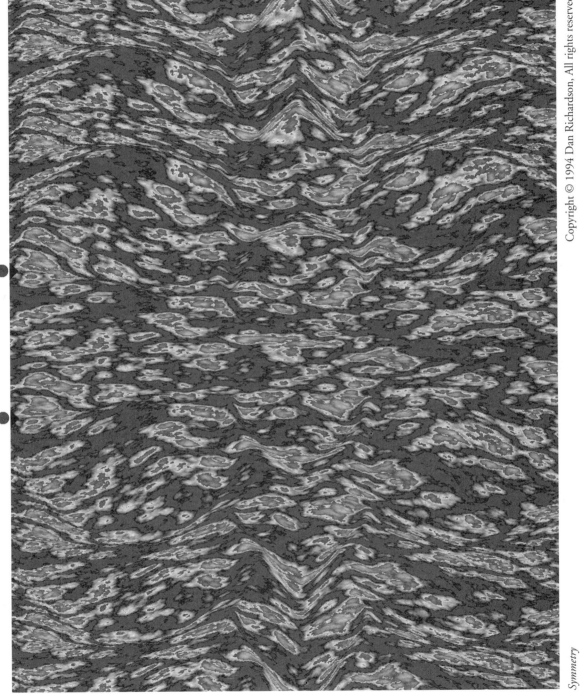

*Symmetry*

*Ovals*

48

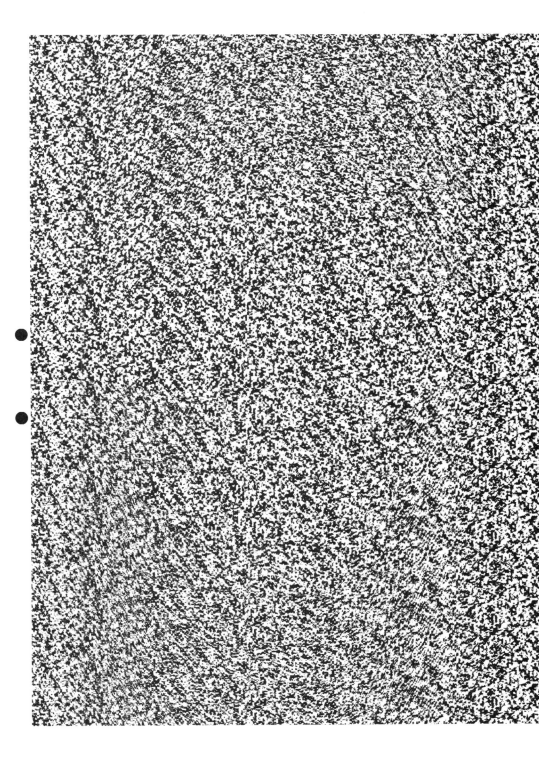

*Dive Pit*

# Normal-Text Stereograms

S ingle-image normal-text stereograms (SINTS) are the simplest and most portable of single-image stereograms. You can create them with any word processor or text editor. You can create them on a typewriter. If you have good handwriting, you can use a pencil and paper. You could even use EDLIN! (I wouldn't, though.) SINTS can be composed entirely of ASCII text, so they are ideal for including in e-mail messages and sending as electronic 3D greeting cards.

When you make a SINTS, you create the 3D illusion by manually adjusting the intervals of space between characters. This experience provides some direct insight into the principles on which single-image stereograms are based. In this chapter we'll reexamine some of those principles in the context of SINTS, guide you through the process of creating your first SINTS, and then discuss a related graphic illusion called DINTS (dual-image normal-text stereograms).

## Intervals and Levels

The basic principle of SINTS is very simple: You can see an illusion of depth in repeated characters. If you view them parallel, characters that repeat at smaller intervals appear to be nearer to you than characters that repeat at larger intervals. If you view them cross-eyed, smaller intervals appear farther away.

Figure 5-1 shows just how far you can push this effect. In this stereogram, each row of numbers uses an interval spacing that is equal to the number printed in that row. For

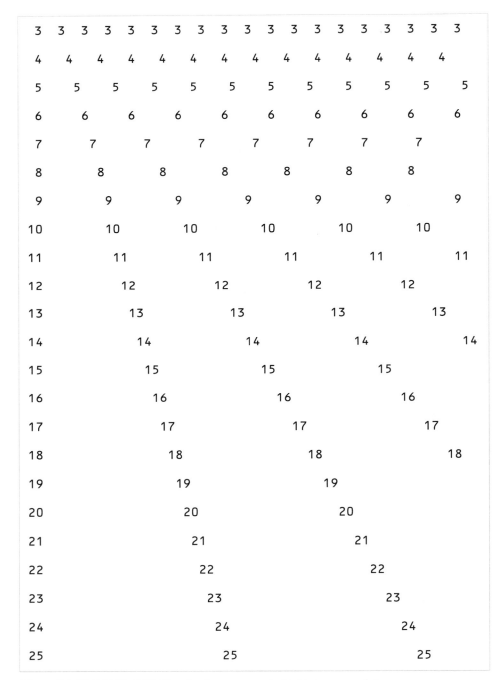

***Figure 5-1*** SPACING.TXT: How far down can you hold this image steady?

example, there are seven spaces between the 8s in the 8 row, so they are at 8-character intervals. Begin viewing somewhere around the 12 row, and look up and down the image.

In this example, parallel viewing shows the rows farther away as you scan down the page. Cross-eyed viewing shows them reaching off the page toward you. How far down the page can you keep the image steady and converged? Hold the page out at arm's length in good lighting, and you may well be able to parallel-view it all the way down to the 25 row. Pay attention to how many rows you can hold together at a time, and the way rows above and below your point of focus fall apart.

Try hyperconverging the top lines. Relax your eyes so the 3s and 4s overlap too far. You may be able to picture them *behind* the 5 row. You may even be able to converge several times too far, especially if you're viewing cross-eyed. If you can, the relative levels will be up for grabs. Your brain will push the numbers forward and back willy-nilly, as it tries to sort out the conflicting information. This illustrates the problems of using too narrow a convergence width.

Notice how you can feel your eye muscles working as you scan up and down the image. This kind of image clearly demonstrates what a physical process single-image stereogram viewing really is. It's not magic after all, is it?

# Creating 3D Text

The best way to learn to do SINTS is just to dive in and start. All this chapter's examples are on the included disk. The book's installation program put them on your hard disk in the directory \STEREO3D\TEXT3D, under the filenames listed in each figure caption. Open them up in your favorite text editor and have a look. If you have MS-DOS 5 or later, you can use Edit. If you don't have a good text editor, skip ahead to Chapter 6 and meet Ued.

This chapter's SINTS were created in 132-character text video mode on a 17-inch monitor. That setup roughly matches the spacing of the 10-point type in which they are all printed. They may look too wide on a normal 80-character monitor. The sequential-spacing image shown in Figure 5-1, SPACING.TXT, can help you determine what spacing is best for your monitor or printer. Once you've figured out what range of spacing works for you, you can get on with building your own SINTS.

Let's look first at three examples showing how to create diagonal text, 3D curves, and a SINTS picture. Try modifying the sample files by substituting characters and adjusting the spacing between characters. Then step back and observe the effects.

## Diagonal Text

Figure 5-2 probably doesn't look like much when you first see it. Viewing it parallel, however, will reveal two levels, with text written diagonally across each level. The two depth levels alternate lines in the file. Adjusting the number of spaces in the row containing the letter *U* doesn't affect the rows containing *E*'s or *A*'s above and below. Keeping the levels separate simplifies the construction, and makes it easier to understand while you're creating it.

Use spaces between the letters, not tabs. You want to be able to adjust the relative positions of the rows by adding and deleting spaces at the beginning of the row. Tabs in a row prevent the characters from moving together, as a unit, making adjustment very difficult.

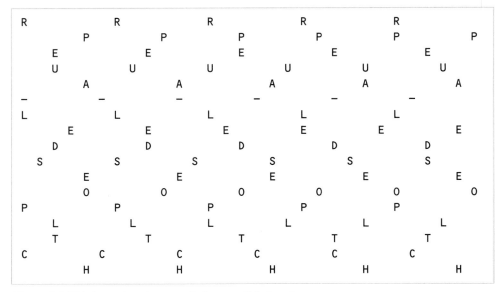

*Figure 5-2* This image is easier to read when parallel-viewed

The image in Figure 5-2 began in Ued as a vertical stripe of letters in the first column. Read every other letter from left to right, and then back.

```
RPEUA-LEDSEOPLTCH
```

Block marking was used on the first row to grab the letter *R* and 11 spaces after it. This block was then pasted in place seven times, creating a row of *R*'s at 12-character intervals. The same procedure was applied to each row, using 12-character intervals in the odd rows and 10-character intervals in the even rows. This made an image with the illusion of two depth levels as shown in Figure 5-3. The words in the two levels are immediately readable without parallel viewing. No mystery.

Spaces were added and subtracted from the beginning of each row until the words lined up on the diagonals. Finally, all the characters after column 60 were deleted to make the figure fit the width of this printed page.

## Curved Text

Figure 5-4 displays a transparent plane across a trough that has curved sides, or tries to, anyway. The low precision available in an ASCII text image makes curves rather difficult. Consider it a challenge.

This image began as a vertical stripe of text that said

```
ROUND CURVE
```

Each row uses a different interval, which meant a lot of tweaking by hand, adding and subtracting spaces while parallel viewing. When the curve looked passable, a blank line was inserted between each row, and

```
flat plane
```

was added on the blank lines at 12-character intervals.

```
R           R           R           R           R
P           P           P           P           P           P
E           E           E           E           E
U           U           U           U           U           U
A           A           A           A           A
-           -           -           -           -           -
L           L           L           L           L
E           E           E           E           E           E
D           D           D           D           D
S           S           S           S           S           S
E           E           E           E           E
O           O           O           O           O           O
P           P           P           P           P
L           L           L           L           L           L
T           T           T           T           T
C           C           C           C           C           C
H           H           H           H           H
```

**Figure 5-3** 2LEVELS.TXT without the leading spaces: Read it up and down

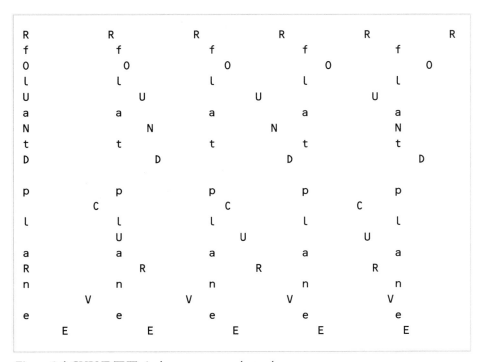

**Figure 5-4** CURVE.TXT: A plane over a curved trough

## A SINTS Picture

Text stereograms can make pictures as well as spell out words. Figure 5-5 depicts a streetscape for parallel viewing. This image is the most complex example in the chapter, since many of the rows contain multiple depth levels. Moving one of the house windows, for instance, will affect the position and apparent depth of the telephone poles. If you put your editor in overwrite mode, you can type in characters anywhere without pushing around the rest of the characters on the line.

In creating this SINTS, the five boxes that make up the buildings came first, and then the mountains and stars, followed by the telephone poles, the windows, the doors, the curbs, and the cars.

## Tips and Pitfalls

The most important tip for SINTS is to avoid making extreme changes in depth between adjacent lines. Single-image stereograms of any type are easiest to view if they don't have large, abrupt level changes. Blank lines between rows of characters may help to ease a rapid transition.

Avoid straight vertical columns that contain characters from different levels. The human brain is wired to combine straight lines into one object, which may fight the illusion you're attempting to create. Insert and delete spaces at the beginning of various lines to see how the image changes as its components move sideways.

The SINTS in Figure 5-6 does several things wrong. Notice how difficult it is to keep the last three lines (8, 12, and 7) registered. It doesn't take much effort to make any of the

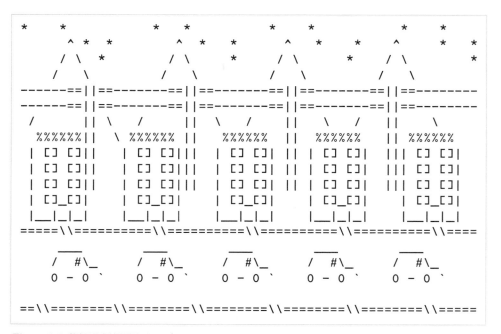

***Figure 5-5*** STREET.TXT: An urban text stereogram

```
4    4    4    4    4    4    4    4    4    4    4    4    4    4
4    4    4    4    4    4    4    4    4    4    4    4    4    4
   7         7         7         7         7         7         7         7
   5    5    5    5    5    5    5    5    5    5    5
   6    6    6    6    6    6    6    6    6
      8         8         8         8         8         8
         7    7    7    7    7    7    7
            9         9         9         9         9         9
               8    8    8    8    8    8
               8    8    8    8    8    8
                  12        12        12        12
                     7    7    7    7    7    7    7
```

*Figure 5-6* BADSINTS.TXT: A stereogram with deep problems

three lines appear in front of the other two. Compare this to the ease of viewing of Figure 5-2. Notice, also, how easy it is to incorrectly hyperconverge the rows containing 4s. This shows up when the 4 rows appear to be the same depth as the 8 rows. You may find the vertical columns distracting, as well.

# DINTS Are Fun, Too

The topic of this book is single-image stereograms, but while you're here in the editor making SINTS, it's a very small step to another kind of ASCII stereogram: dual-image normal-text stereograms. DINTS show up frequently in Internet e-mail signatures, since it only takes a few ASCII characters to make a convincing 3D illusion.

DINTS consist of two separate but similar parts, which combine to form a 3D image when viewed appropriately. The two parts are often spaced too far apart for parallel viewing, so they may require cross-eyed viewing.

## Spacing in Pairs

Figures 5-7 and 5-8 are two examples of DINTS. If you have trouble parallel-viewing them, you might try holding the page out at arm's length. As with any stereogram, you must hold a DINT level relative to your eyes. Tilting a stereogram makes it more difficult to view.

To begin constructing a dual-image stereogram, make a small picture in your text editor. Add a frame, as we did in our examples, to establish a ground plane and help you keep track of where things are. Block-copy the entire picture, and paste a copy right next to the original. View it parallel or cross-eyed. Since each character in the left copy has a twin the same distance away in the right copy, the single image appears flat.

Each character must exist in both copies, since you're trying to convince your brain that each eye is actually looking at the same scene. So have at it with your text editor, moving

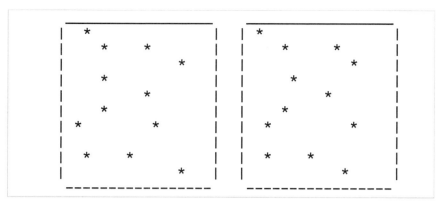

***Figure 5-7*** STARS.TXT: A minor constellation

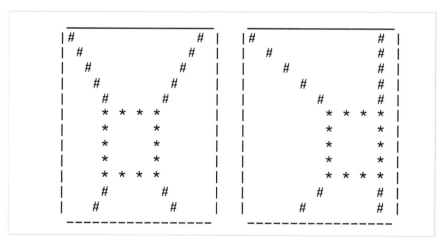

***Figure 5-8*** TUNNEL.TXT: An ASCII passageway

individual characters towards and away from their twins. As you alter the relative distances between matching characters, the characters in the converged image will change levels.

## Blank Lines Can Improve the Illusion

The image of an arrow in Figure 5-9 was difficult to converge until we inserted the blank lines between each row. Try modifying this DINTS in your editor. Delete the blank lines and add extras, then test which changes improve the viewability of the illusion.

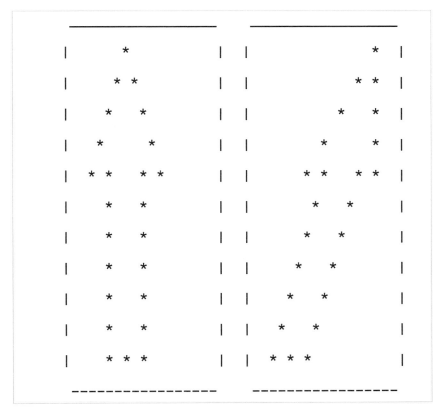

***Figure 5-9*** ARROW.TXT: Blank lines make it easier to converge

## Character Sizes Lend Perspective

The next pair, Figures 5-10 and 5-11, attempt to aid the 3D illusion by using perspective sizing, through carefully chosen different-sized characters. The choice of characters should enhance the apparent depth when viewed in the manner indicated in each image. On the other hand, the sizing of the characters may confuse the illusion if you view an image with the wrong method.

## Combining SINTS and DINTS

The last image, Figure 5-12, uses a combined approach. Each frame relates to the next. Any two of these frames make a stereo pair, since all the frames include the same elements. The series of frames make up one large image, much as the characters in a SINTS contribute to a single 3D image. This gets us back on the single-image track just in time for the next chapter.

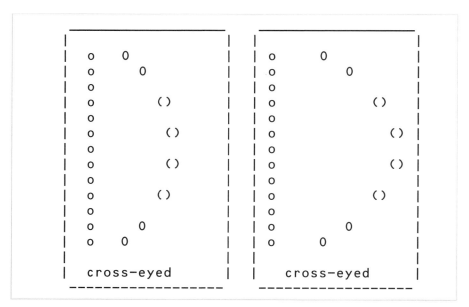

**Figure 5-10** CROSSEYE.TXT: Perspective for cross-eyed viewing

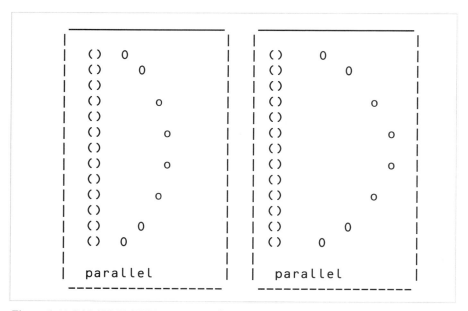

**Figure 5-11** PARALLEL.TXT: Perspective for parallel viewing

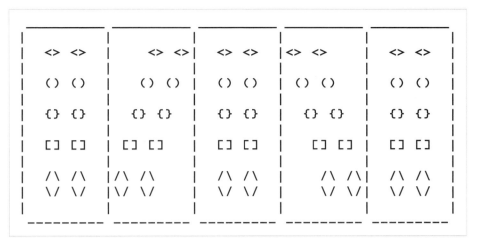

***Figure 5-12*** SINTSROW.TXT: Combining the effects of DINTS and SINTS

Notice that the narrow strip width makes it easy to hyperconverge this image. Doing so completely cancels the 3D effect in two of the middle frames, but makes the central illusion twice as deep.

# What's Next?

In this chapter, you met single-image normal-text stereograms (SINTS). These stereograms enhance a text picture with the illusion of depth, but you can usually tell what the picture is without the special viewing techniques.

Chapter 6 introduces you to SINTS' computer generated cousin, SIRTS, which add the surprise element of hidden pictures to text stereograms.

# Random-Text Stereograms

S ingle-image random-text stereograms (SIRTS) may be the author's favorite form of single-image stereogram. These fully 3D images look like a solid block of random text until viewed either cross-eyed or parallel. You can include them in e-mail messages, print them on any printer, or display them on nearly any computer on the planet. Creating, viewing, and printing SIRTS require no hardware graphics capability.

This chapter shows you how to use two programs included on this book's disk— SIRTSER and Ued—to create, view, and print SIRTS. Ued is an ASCII text editor, and SIRTSER is a utility for converting special source files created in text editors into SIRTS.

## About SIRTSER

SIRTSER is a small DOS command-line utility that generates SIRTS from ASCII source files. You can create the source files with any text editor, such as Ued.

### Licensing Information

SIRTSER is a public domain utility, free for any use. Like all great forces of nature, if you misuse it or it does you harm, it is your own responsibility. The source code (in Turbo C 2.0) is available from the author, Dan Richardson. You can reach him on CompuServe at 72537,1341. From the Internet, his address is 72537.1341@compuserve.com.

## System Requirements

SIRTSER runs on any DOS PC. It uses text display, needs no graphics hardware whatsoever, and is perfectly happy with less than 200K conventional memory. It does not need or use expanded or extended memory. A command-line history TSR, such as MS-DOS's DOSKEY, is quite useful but not required.

## Installation

There is no setup necessary. This book's installation program puts SIRTSER on your hard disk in the directory \STEREO3D\TEXT3D. To see SIRTSER's documentation and information screen, change to this directory and type the command

**SIRTSER** (ENTER)

# About Ued

Ued is an excellent, simple DOS text editor. It is user friendly, can edit up to nine files at once, and has a wide range of cut-and-paste options. This makes it great for editing SIRTSER source files. It's useful for editing other text files, too, such as POV-Ray source files (described in Chapters 11 and 12). It also makes a quick and versatile ASCII file viewer.

## Licensing Information

Ued is shareware. If you like it and decide to continue using it, you are requested to send $20 to

Useful Software
340 Dale Crescent
Waterloo, Ontario
Canada, N2J 3Y3

You can reach the author, Mike Gardi, on CompuServe at 70242,3102. From the Internet, his address is 70242.3102@compuserve.com.

For more information, please see the file UED.DOC in the directory \STEREO3D\TEXT3D.

## System Requirements

Ued runs on any DOS PC with a conventional 80x25-character text display. It can use the 43-line mode of an EGA display, as well as the 28- and 50-line modes of a VGA display. Ued requires only 128K of RAM, plus enough room for the files you want to edit. It will use all available conventional 640K RAM, if needed, but it does not need or use expanded or extended memory.

## Installation

There is no setup required. This book's installation program puts Ued in the directory \STEREO3D\TEXT3D. You can use Ued's configuration program, UEDCFG, to set various options and defaults, but the program should be fine right out of the box. The file UED.DOC contains details about the program, configuration, and registration. This chapter covers all the Ued commands needed in this book.

# Generating a SIRTS Pyramid

Let's start by generating a stereogram from a previously created source file, PYRA-MID.TXT. In this section you'll generate several stereograms from this same file, using different command lines to demonstrate SIRTSER's various options.

## Using the Default Settings

Change to the directory that contains SIRTSER and its support files, by typing

**CD\STEREO3D\TEXT3D** (ENTER)

Then type the command

**SIRTSER PYRAMID.TXT PYRAMID.RTS** (ENTER)

SIRTSER reports its default settings and tells you the filenames it's reading from and writing to, as shown here:

```
SIRTSER rev 1

Reading text file pyramid.txt and writing to pyramid.rts
-c character set is 1, full height optimized
-s strip width is 14
-w total width is 79
-r random number generator seeded from clock, -r0
-h starting with a 2 line header
-m adding a 4 space left margin
-t ending with a 2 line tail
```

SIRTSER then generates a SIRTS and writes it on your hard drive under the filename PYRAMID.RTS.

## Viewing the Source File

To view PYRAMID.TXT, the source file from which PYRAMID.RTS is generated, enter the command

**TYPE PYRAMID.TXT** (ENTER)

You should see four concentric squares of numbers, as shown in Figure 6-1.

Each digit in a SIRTSER source file represents a perceived depth level. A source file of nothing but zeroes produces a flat SIRTS with all the characters repeated at the same interval. This interval, which produces a zero depth level, is the convergence strip width.

Any digit greater than 0 represents the number of levels a particular point is away from the zero depth level. Higher levels appear closer to you when viewed parallel, and farther from you when viewed cross-eyed. This type of file, in which a grid of numbers makes up a map of the depth level at each point, is known as a *numerical depthmap*. SIRTSER uses this depthmap source file to generate a stereogram with up to ten apparent depth levels;

```
111111111111111111111111111111111111111111
111111111111111111111111111111111111111111
111112222222222222222222222222222222211111
111112222222222222222222222222222222211111
111112222233333333333333333333332222211111
111112222233333333333333333333332222211111
111112222233333444444444433333322222211111
111112222233333444444444433333322222211111
111112222233333444444444433333322222211111
111112222233333444444444433333322222211111
111112222233333333333333333333332222211111
111112222233333333333333333333332222211111
111112222222222222222222222222222222211111
111112222222222222222222222222222222211111
111111111111111111111111111111111111111111
111111111111111111111111111111111111111111
```

*Figure 6-1* PYRAMID.TXT: A SIRTSER source file

one for each single-digit number from 0 to 9. Characters at level 1 repeat at an interval one space smaller than the convergence strip width. Characters at level 2 repeat at an interval two spaces smaller, and so on.

Graphical depthmaps, which use colors or brightness to represent depth values, are discussed in Chapters 9, 10, and 11.

## Viewing the Output File

To view the stereogram that SIRSTER generated from the source file in Figure 6-1, enter the command

**TYPE PYRAMID.RTS** (ENTER)

> If you have loaded the handy MS-DOS command-line history TSR, DOSKEY, you can simply press (↑), backspace over the TXT, and type **RTS**. See your MS-DOS manual for details.

You will see five O's at the top of a screenful of characters. This screen is a single-image stereogram, and the O's are the convergence dots. Figure 6-2 shows typical output. Look for the top of a four-step pyramid. Parallel-viewing shows it protruding from the screen, and cross-eyed viewing shows it sunk into the screen.

Your screen will not look exactly like Figure 6-2 for two reasons. First, SIRSTER randomly generates the individual characters each time it's run, unless you tell it not to. Second, you have a computer screen capable of 80 characters on a line, but this page can handle only about 60.

```
           O                O                O                O
&Wf07ZFDL?Q]SB&Wf07ZFDL?Q]SB&Wf07ZFDL?Q]SB&Wf07ZFDL?Q]SB&Wf
V6W[#A2|YdUh0kV6W[#A2|YdUh0kV6W[#A2|YdUh0kV6W[#A2|YdUh0kV6W
YZ54N0?lV|GS#tYZ5N0?lV|GS#tYZ5N0?lV|GS#tYZ5N0?lV|GS#tYZ5N!0
S6{l&70|Y1K[NkS6{&70|Y1K[NkS6{&70|Y1K[NkS6{&70|Y1K[NkS6{&T7
P%ZACY{#G@FS[OP%ZCY{#@FS[OP%ZCY{#@FS[OP%ZCY{#@FS[OPD%ZCY{?#
3PD#R6HEOL8GTh3PDR6HEL8GTh3PDR6HEL8GTh3PDR6HEL8GTh3?PDR6H#E
k98|H]t@2QOCJ{k98H]t@QOCJk98H]t@QOCJk98H]t@QOTCJk98KH]t@QVO
f3[GAHQ95LD?]Bf3GAHQ5LD?Bf3GHQ5LD?Bf3GKHQ5LDP?Bf3G/KHQ5L1D
&U!5[F%Z6Q}S19&U![F%ZQ}S1&U![%ZQ}S1&U![G%ZQ}SF1&U![PG%ZQ}JS
DL#G@[kJ9d4b&2DL#@[kJd4b&DL#@kJd4b&DL#@MkJd4bR&DL#@WMkJd4!b
UR]hCP|#A?YJZMUR]CP|#?YJZUR]C|#?YJZUR]CX|#?YJ6ZUR]CTX|#?YlJ
!VtH802&Zb]TD1!Vt802&b]TD!Vt802&b]TD!Vt802&b]dTD!Vt6802&bR]
8#AC{hVk&J?6dW8#A{hVkJ?6d8#A{hVkJ?6d8#A{hVkJ?26d8#AP{hVkJM?
#USZhR|JC8]90E#UShR|J8]90E#UShR|J8]90E#UShR|J8]90E#MUShR|LJ
}QNKW%1]OL9TtV}QNW%1]L9TtV}QNW%1]L9TtV}QNW%1]L9TtV}7QNW%1&]
29FbkXY3DKO{P#29FkXY3DKO{P#29FkXY3DKO{P#29FkXY3DKO{P#29FkhX
}#AOJKd@679M%[}#AJKd@679M%[}#AJKd@679M%[}#AJKd@679M%[}#AJ|K
{!#}tFb8SVWIYJ{!#}tFb8SVWIYJ{!#}tFb8SVWIYJ{!#}tFb8SVWIYJ{!#
8&49}OFYH%Dh{18&49}OFYH%Dh{18&49}OFYH%Dh{18&49}OFYH%Dh{18&4
```

***Figure 6-2*** The SIRTS pyramid: using SIRTSER's default settings

# Changing the Convergence Strip Width

Recall that convergence strip width is the maximum number of columns between repetitions of a feature in the SIRTS. The maximum convergence strip width you can parallel-view is equal to your interocular (literally, "between the eyes") distance. Comfortable viewing happens when the convergence strip width equals a physical measurement between 1.75 and 2.25 inches. The tricky part is that the physical size of an output file will depend on the width of your monitor or the printed output's type size. SIRTSER spaces the index O's above the image at strip-width intervals. This makes it easy to measure the physical width.

The examples so far have used SIRTSER's default setting of 14 characters as the convergence strip width. This corresponds to roughly 1.75 inches on a 14-inch monitor, or 2 inches on a 17-inch monitor. It's a bit small for a page printed in 10-point type. You can select a different strip width using SIRTSER's –S (Strip width) option and specifying a convergence strip width setting from 3 to 99. The convergence strip width you use depends on the size of the characters in your final displayed or printed output. For example, to set a convergence width of 9, type the following commands:

```
SIRTSER PYRAMID.TXT PYRAMID2.RTS —S9 (ENTER)
TYPE PYRAMID2.RTS (ENTER)
```

This displays a new stereogram similar to the one shown in Figure 6-3. The O's at the top are much closer together. You don't have to cross or relax your eyes nearly as much to

```
         0        0        0        0        0        0
Jk!YlN69QJk!YlN69QJk!YlN69QJk!YlN69QJk!YlN69QJk!Yl
IOB%OlPJ&IOB%OlPJ&IOB%OlPJ&IOB%OlPJ&IOB%OlPJ&IOB%O
5FfPN2d{&5FfN2d{&5FfN2d{&5FfN2d{&5FfN2d{&5FfIN2d{&5
6&KSht|H%6&Kht|H%6&Kht|H%6&Kht|H%6&Kht|H%6&KWht|H%6
JhR&YF5M8JhRYF5MJhRYF5MJhRYF5MJhRYF5MJh2RYF5MHJh2RYF
68ZK@DJ|J68Z@DJ|68Z@DJ|68Z@DJ|68Z@DJ|68Z@DJ|68#Z@DJ|968#Z@D
ClPDXShAYClPXShAClPXhAClPXhAClPXhAClPXhAZClPXh#AZClPHXh#AZC
3FLPSO85T3FLSO853FLS853FLS853FLS853FLS85C3FLS815C3FLJS815C3
I%KLhJO8EI%KhJO8I%Kh08I%h08I%h08I%LhO8I%HLhO8IQ%HLhOS8IQ%HL
3b1LOUP6#3b10UP63b10P63b0P63b0P63bNOP63b%NOP63|b%NOPR63|b%N
ZL{N@54DhZL{@54DZL{@4DZL@4DZL@4DZLk@4DZLQk@4DZXLQk@4MDZXLQk
}34#&hEWt}34&hEW}34&EW}3&EW}3&EW}3@&EW}3V@&EW}H3V@&EdW}H3V@
1NMC{7WRU1NM{7WR1NM{WR1NM{WR1NM{WR1NM{WR21NM{W|R21NMJ{W|R21
NO!3S#fP8NO!S#fPNO!SfPNO!SfPNO!SfPNO!SfP5NO!SfVP5NO!?SfVP5N
?#UR!}I8J?#U!}I8?#U!}I8?#U!}I8?#U!}I8?#BU!}I8E?#BU!}
WZfd7IOlKWZf7IOlWZf7IOlWZf7IOlWZf7IOlWZf7IOlWZHf7IOl|WZHf7I
X63LV29NEX63V29NEX63V29NEX63V29NEX63V29NEX63V29NEX63&V29NEX
#S}V?Hk16#S}?Hk16#S}?Hk16#S}?Hk16#S}?Hk16#S}?Hk16#S}E?Hk16#
!8|JJ}%Wk!8|JJ}%Wk!8|JJ}%Wk!8|JJ}%Wk!8|JJ}%Wk!8|JJ}%Wk!8|JJ
4lLIR!}M@4lLIR!}M@4lLIR!}M@4lLIR!}M@4lLIR!}M@4lLIR!}M@4lLIR
```

**Figure 6-3** SIRTS with a narrow convergence strip width, easily hyperconverged

see the image, as you did for previous examples. The smaller convergence strip width makes all the characters repeat at shorter intervals.

In fact, if you relax your eyes too much, you may see another image altogether. You may see false steps, distortions, and steps that appear to change level as you look at the area around them. This occurs when your eyes skip a repetition or two. Instead of viewing adjacent repeating features, you converge every other repetition or even every third or fourth. This is called *hyperconverging* the image.

Single-image stereogram viewing depends on your eyes tracking the relative distances between adjacent repeating objects. Once you hyperconverge, all bets are off. Hyperconverging an abstract stereogram may produce a new and interesting illusion. Hyperconverging a representational stereogram, or one containing hidden 3D text, usually produces an unrecognizable mess.

# Changing the Output Character Set

PYRAMID.RTS uses SIRTSER's default character set, which consists of uppercase letters, numbers, and full-height characters. SIRTSER's –C (Character) option allows you to select one of several character sets, as shown in Table 6-1.

| Option | Characters Specified |
|--------|---------------------|
| –C1 | Uppercase letters, numbers, and full-height characters (default) |
| –C2 | All ANSI standard, low ASCII characters |
| –C3 | Uppercase letters only |
| –C4 | Lowercase letters only |
| –C5 | Numbers only, requires –S strip width from 3 to 9 |
| –C6 | All standard low ASCII, plus some high ASCII characters |
| –C7 | All standard low ASCII, plus all high ASCII characters |
| –C8 | High ASCII characters only |
| –C9 | High ASCII line-drawing characters only |

**Table 6-1** SIRTSER –C character sets

## An Example of Lowercase Only

To create and view a SIRTS composed of only lowercase letters, enter the following commands:

```
SIRTSER PYRAMID.TXT PYRAMID1.RTS –C4 (ENTER)
TYPE PYRAMID1.RTS (ENTER)
```

SIRTSER generates a stereogram pyramid out of randomly selected lowercase letters, resembling the one shown in Figure 6-4.

You may notice some points out of place. Since there are only 26 lowercase letters, SIRTSER doesn't have as many characters to choose from. With fewer characters available, it's more likely characters will repeat at inappropriate times. The single-image stereogram principle depends on controlled repetition; therefore, smaller character sets are more likely to introduce visual errors. On the other hand, specific character sets have interesting effects on the SIRTS. Try character set 9, which uses only the line-drawing characters. Figure 6-5 is a hand-assembled SIRTS containing three lines from each character set.

## High and Low ASCII

*Low ASCII* is the basic U.S. IBM-PC English-language character set. It contains only the 52 upper- and lowercase letters, the ten digits, and some punctuation. It's referred to as low ASCII because your computer represents all these characters internally with numbers less than 127.

The *high ASCII* character set, also known as the *extended* or *graphic character set*, consists of the characters your computer represents with the numbers 127 to 255. You can type these characters in most programs by holding down the (ALT) key while pressing (0) followed by three more digits on the numeric keypad, for example, (ALT) 0169. What character actually appears onscreen depends on the software you're running. Some programs use high ASCII slots for line-drawing characters, math symbols, italic characters, or letters with diacritics in languages other than English.

High ASCII characters are not universally supported in all printers and fonts. None of the standard Windows fonts support them very well. Also, many e-mail and BBS (computer bulletin board) services have difficulty handling high ASCII. CompuServe may refuse to accept messages that contain high ASCII characters.

You may get unexpected results in printed or e-mailed SIRTS that use character sets 6, 7, 8, and 9, because they contain high ASCII characters. If portability is a concern for your SIRTS, it's best to stick with character sets 1, 2, 3, and 4.

So why does SIRTSER give you the option of using high ASCII characters? Because they look neat! Check out all the weird little squiggles and bars in Figure 6-5. You can see them onscreen in DOS, and you can probably print them on your printer, if you set it correctly. See your printer manual for details on its fonts and character sets. None of SIRTSER's character sets contain any of the ASCII characters commonly used for printer control commands, so you can print an .RTS file without worrying about inadvertently form-feeding all your paper.

Character set 5, containing numbers only, is something of a special-purpose curiosity. SIRTSER limits character set 5 to convergence strip widths from 3 to 9, because there are only ten digits to choose from. This also effectively limits you to depths from 0 to 4, because depth values greater than half the convergence strip width may cause you to converge the wrong points.

```
        o              o              o              o
aztgfwpnhukiomaztgfwpnhukiomaztgfwpnhukiomaztgfwpnhukiomazt
usjrcqgidpxaozusjrcqgidpxaozusjrcqgidpxaozusjrcqgidpxaozusj
deoincklfbagtsdeoncklfbagtsdeoncklfbagtsdeoncklfbagtsdeonuc
xowhrzivbmkytqxowrzivbmkytqxowrzivbmkytqxowrzivbmkytqxowrez
otxmchajzknqygotxchajknqygotxchajknqygotxchajknqygobtxchauj
yboaqxrmctngjhyboqxrmtngjhyboqxrmtngjhyboqxrmtngjhykboqxrfm
jazrwevuhyoiscjazwevuyoisjazwevuyoisjazwevuyodisjazrwevuyno
qlhegswjczrdinqlhgswjzrdiqlhgswjzrdiqlhgswjzrmdiqlhugswjzcr
nhvdxilbwftagrnhvxilbftagnhvxlbftagnhvxklbftaygnhvxpklbftma
ouwgkzbxaypqjvouwkzbxypqjouwkbxypqjouwkibxypqdjouwkhibxypcq
iwulyhnrvkmcqgiwuyhnrkmcqiwuynrkmcqiwuyfnrkmcsqiwuydfnrkmtc
rtzfnmuawdveiyrtznmuadveirtznuadveirtznfuadveqirtznpfuadvse
mkcavisxzhtfyemkcvisxhtfymkcvisxhtfymkcvisxhtufymkcpvisxhet
vjxgpbfwrcodqevjxpbfwcodqvjxpbfwcodqvjxpbfwcoldqvjxspbfwcto
zmaylgnbjhfecuzmalgnbhfecuzmalgnbhfecuzmalgnbhfecuzymalgnrb
scgatlyrxfwndqscgtlyrfwndqscgtlyrfwndqscgtlyrfwndqskcgtlyur
zwghvnidesryabzwgvnidesryabzwgvnidesryabzwgvnidesryabzwgvkn
jdagwypnbzmltujdawypnbzmltujdawypnbzmltujdawypnbzmltujdawoy
vvwnelcmidszpoxvwnelcmidszpoxvwnelcmidszpoxvwnelcmidszpoxvwn
vzaomiglwrjyenvzaomiglwrjyenvzaomiglwrjyenvzaomiglwrjyenvza
```

*Figure 6-4* SIRTS pyramid composed of lowercase letters

6#JB3Tt8H2L}P4F6#JB3Tt8H2L}P4F6#JB3Tt8H2L}P4F6#JB3Tt8H2L -c1
EX]JOM#NAH306%REX]JOM#NAH306%REX]JOM#NAH306%REX]JOM#NAH3 -c1
7Y@9[JGb5KUDtd27Y@9[JGb5KUDtd27Y@9[JGb5KUDtd27Y@9[JGb5KU -c1
6,UYjS#k9!)x|PsV7@6,UYjS#k9x|PsV7@6,zRUYjS#k9x|PsV7@6,zR -c2
5[{yE8Iafi)rcG#vCu5[{yE8IafrcG#vCu5[?]{yE8IafrcG#vCu5[?] -c2
{F5K`jJx[76l)CZHEb{F5K`jJx[l)CZHEb{FzB5K`jJx[l)CZHEb{FzB -c2
MGIAXKPNLQRVUETBYMGIAXKPNLQVUETBYMGIWAXKPNLQVUETBYMGIWAX -c3
UGZIMAKBYXHPCJODNUGZIMAKBYXPCJODNUGZVIMAKBYXPCJODNUGZVIM -c3
UIPMBLTGESROXCAJKUIPMBLTGESOXCAJKUIPWMBLTGESOXCAJKUIPWMB -c3
cihzdkyowbagetjrsmcihzdkyowgetjrsmcilahzdkyowgetjrsmcila -c4
vhdebgkwtijlnxmscavhdebgkwtlnxmscavhfodebgkwtlnxmscavhfo -c4
saczotfphybeidkxursaczotfpheidkxursagbczotfpheidkxursagb -c4
15076359281432915076359281432915076359281432915076359281 -c5
26187450392543026187450392543026187450392543026187450392 -c5
48309672513765248309672513765248309672513765248309672513 -c5
íñ}pfóz4_Müë!Ñb¬Ajíñ}pfóz4_ë!Ñb¬Ajíñxô}pfóz4_ë!Ñb¬Ajíñxô -c6
}@ma#\1êewªïJ&jPâÖ}@ma#\1êeïJ&jPâÖ}@|[ma#\1êeïJ&jPâÖ}@|[ -c6
æAfh!Gvaô£6ªLÆHDë[æAfh!GvaôªLÆHDë[æAd]fh!GvaôªLÆHDë[æAd] -c6

***Figure 6-5*** SIRTS with three lines of each SIRTSER character set

The –C5 section of Figure 6-5 actually has a convergence strip width of 18, but it was produced by hand. This demonstrates the fact that SIRTS are simple ASCII text. You can load them into your editor after generating them, and tinker to your heart's content. You can even produce a SIRTS entirely by hand, but it's not a task for the fainthearted.

## Changing the Output Width

SIRTSER defaults to creating a SIRTS that is 79 characters wide, so that you can display it on a standard 80-column computer screen without line wrapping. You can specify a different total width with the –W (output Width) option. SIRTSER accepts –W output width values from 10 to 999. For example, to set an output width of 40 columns, type these commands:

```
SIRTSER PYRAMID.TXT PYRAMID3.RTS -W40 (ENTER)
TYPE PYRAMID3.RTS (ENTER)
```

As shown in Figure 6-6, some of the image is lost on the right side, because SIRTSER throws away anything remaining in the source image beyond the specified output width.

```
            O                   O
%41}f{LNR!85GB%41}f{LNR!85GB%41}f{LNR!85
}[]l4bUYXWKS5I}[]l4bUYXWKS5I}[]l4bUYXWKS
58!}|3l{]W12JM58!|3l{]W12JM58!|3l{]W12JM
tkD9J{Z6G%NKFXtkDJ{Z6G%NKFXtkDJ{Z6G%NKFX
G][Ed|FHM8K2BVG][d|FH8K2BVG][d|FH8K2BVG]
%8}NIKtfPBk#UO%8}IKtfBk#UO%8}IKtfBk#UO%8
65E|}SJD8Wdkt465E}SJDWdkt65E}SJDWdkt65E}
NMJ]At6OV#%F@TNMJAt6O#%F@NMJAt6O#%F@NMJA
8C]Ja%}3WSOKPD8C]@%}3SOKP8C]@}3SOKP8C]@A
%lBbU5Qt]IZERO%lBU5QtIZER%lBUQtIZER%lBU3
}?4]&KdZUtO[D7}?4&KdZtO[D}?4&dZtO[D}?4&E
CH9GIUVK1fba@k{CH9IUVKfb@kCH9IVKfb@kCH9I#
J95K{?TYFM6#G%J95{?TYM6#GJ95{?TYM6#GJ95{
OTW2UkNSO6VBh#OTWUkNS6VBhOTWUkNS6VBhOTWU
[7FLhAT2#1{]4d[7FhAT21{]4d[7FhAT21{]4d[7
9Zh2GPO5VWO4TB9ZhGPO5WO4TB9ZhGPO5WO4TB9Z
E&190@T{Q[35Y7E&1O@T{Q[35Y7E&1O@T{Q[35Y7
ROM%l2]#WNUIV!ROMl2]#WNUIV!ROMl2]#WNUIV!
V#AXBQTU{WhDPZV#AXBQTU{WhDPZV#AXBQTU{WhD
GEL%f&BDIt41SNGEL%f&BDIt41SNGEL%f&BDIt41
```

***Figure 6-6*** A skinny, 40-column SIRTS

# Changing the Margins

Any single-image stereogram is easier to see if it's surrounded by a flat background. This gives your eyes a reference plane, a place to rest, as well as helping to define the outline of any objects hidden in the stereogram. If the background uses the convergence strip width for a repetition interval, then it produces what is known as a zero depth level. The rest of the image will be closer to a parallel viewer, or farther from a cross-eyed viewer.

Three options control the margins of the SIRTS. SIRTSER adds two zero-depth-level rows to the beginning and end of your source file, unless you tell it otherwise. It also adds 4 character spaces to the left margin. You control the number of zero-depth-level rows at the beginning of the file with the –H (Header) option, and at the end with the –T (Tail) option. The left edge is specified with the –M (Margin) option. SIRTSER accepts values from 0 to 9 for all three margin options.

For example, to create a SIRTS with no zero-depth-level rows at the top, 4 zero-depth-level rows at the bottom, and a left margin of 4 character spaces, type the following commands:

```
SIRTSER PYRAMID.TXT PYRAMID.RTS –HO –M9 –T4 (ENTER)
TYPE PYRAMID.RTS (ENTER)
```

```
          0              0              0              0
k#FCD!BTLP|75{k#FCD!BLP|75{k#FCD!BLP|75{k#FCD!BLP|75{k#FCD
bYWMI5C3SQ7{#dbYWMI5C3Q7{#bYWMI5C3Q7{#bYWMI5C3Q7{#bYWMI5]C3
hML3BKA}!%Ik?OhML3BKA}%Ik?hML3BKA}%Ik?hML3BKA}%Ik?hML3BKfA}
&9dJfYS5bGN@H2&9dJfYS5GN@H&9dJYS5GN@H&9dJYS5GN@H&9PdJYS5CGN
XNJ6ZURFB&Od@}XNJ6ZURF&Od@XNJ6URF&Od@XNJ6URF&Od@XNLJ6URFV&O
OOF4fBXdQ?HM}3OOF4fBXd?HM}OOF4BXd?M}OOF4BXd?kM}OOFJ4BXd?EkM
|[k!EOJHTJd6&O|[k!EOJHJd6&|[k!OJHJ6&|[k!OJHJC6&|[kM!OJHJ%C6
k4?CYU9hS!{BdXk4?CYU9h!{Bdk4?CU9h!Bdk4?CU9h!2Bdk4?JCU9h!O2B
ZGbNY&O4CADlOUZGbNY&O4ADlOZGbN&O4AlOZGbN&O4A@lOZGbXN&O4AL@l
O3l#{BASCbV61FO3l#{BACbV6FO3l{BACbV6FO3l{BACbV6FOf3l{BA!Cb
W|Hd%CYLk#TRS4W|Hd%CYL#TRSW|Hd%CYL#TRSW|Hd%CYL#TRSW|Hd%CEYl
WTd03|M7ElODKCWTd03|M7lODKWTd03|M7lODKWTd03|M7lODKWTd03|}M7
Ft7LMCNO!1KWA%Ft7LMCNO1KWA%Ft7LMCNO1KWA%Ft7LMCNO1KWA%Ft7LMC
&O?A}kQfVF9T{7&O?A}kQfF9T{7&O?A}kQfF9T{7&O?A}kQfF9T{7&O?A}k
C}BQ9CK&h?VX!OC}BQ9CK&h?VX!OC}BQ9CK&h?VX!OC}BQ9CK&h?VX!OC}B
6!%RW|MC9E&45J6!%RW|MC9E&45J6!%RW|MC9E&45J6!%RW|MC9E&45J6!%
tJSG|KOXB3&ME8tJSG|KOXB3&ME8tJSG|KOXB3&ME8tJSG|KOXB3&ME8tJS
BJPOD2}GSVNf&5BJPOD2}GSVNf&5BJPOD2}GSVNf&5BJPOD2}GSVNf&5BJP
```

**Figure 6-7** SIRTS with large left margin and no top header

Look at how the placement of the pyramid has changed, as shown in Figure 6-7.

# Repeatable Randomness

SIRTSER produces different output from the same source file every time, because the program randomly chooses the individual characters. You can control this random number generator with the –R (Random) option. SIRTSER's random number generator seeds itself from the number you supply. SIRTSER accepts –R values from 0 to 9999. For instance, the command

`SIRTSER PYRAMID.TXT PYRAMID.RTS –R513` (ENTER)

produces exactly the same output every time you run it.

The command

`SIRTSER PYRAMID.TXT PYRAMID.RTS –R27` (ENTER)

produces output that is different from –R513, but still repeats predictably every time.

One value is different. If you type

`SIRTSER PYRAMID.TXT PYRAMID.RTS –R0` (ENTER)

you get the default behavior of different output every time.

Table 6-2 lists other SIRTSER options.

| Option | Range | Default | Explanation |
|--------|-------|---------|-------------|
| –Cn | 1 to 9 | 1 | Character set used to build SIRTS |
| –Snn | 3 to 99 | 14 | Strip width for a zero-level depth |
| –Hn | 0 to 9 | 2 | Number of zero-level lines as header |
| –Tn | 0 to 9 | 2 | Number of zero-level lines as tail |
| –Mn | 0 to 9 | 4 | Number of spaces added to left margin |
| –Wnnn | 10 to 999 | 79 | Total output width of generated SIRTS |
| –Rnnnn | 0 to 9999 | 0 | Repeatably seed the random number generator |
| | | | 0 seeds the random number generator from clock |

*Table 6-2* A summary of SIRTSER command-line options

# Source File Sorcery

Now that you know how to generate single-image random text stereograms from source files, it's time to learn how to make your own source files.

As you saw in Figure 6-1, a SIRTSER source file is a map of the apparent depth at each point in the hidden picture. The only characters that matter are the digits 1 to 9, and these correspond to how far away from the zero depth level you want that point in your picture to appear. Creating a SIRTSER source file means simply "drawing" a picture with numbers, and using larger numbers in the places that you want sticking out.

The examples in this section will introduce you to Ued. If you've got a text editor that suits you, you can go ahead and use it, but you may want to try Ued in either case. It's quite a useful tool.

## Running Ued

This book's Install program puts Ued in the same directory as SIRTSER (\STEREO3D\ TEXT3D). To start the program, type the command

**UED** (ENTER)

from this directory. Ued lists all the available commands at the bottom of the screen, as shown in Figure 6-8.

## Loading Files

Ued can edit up to nine files at once. There are several ways to load them. One way is to use the File command (F1). When the File menu appears, press (L) for Load. Ued asks you what filename you want to load. If you know the name of the file you want, you can type it in—but don't do that now. Just press (ENTER) instead. Ued then displays a list of the files in the current directory, known as a *picklist*. Find PYRAMID.TXT, and move the cursor to it using your keyboard arrow keys. Press (ENTER) again, and Ued loads the familiar pyramid example source file. You can load files from other directories, as well, by typing the directory and filename after the Load prompt.

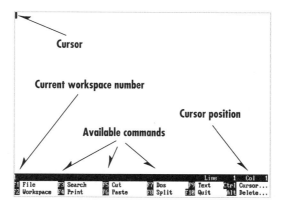

**Figure 6-8** Ued presents a clean and informative interface

You can also load up to nine files right from the command line. For example, to load three files named ONE.TXT, TWO.ASC, and THREE.DOC, you would type

`UED ONE.TXT TWO.ASC THREE.DOC` (ENTER)

## Switching Among Workspaces and Cursors

(F2) is the Workspace command. Press it, and the menu changes to show you the ten Ued workspaces. Workspace 0 is the Clipboard, and 1 through 9 are slots into which you can load files. The line above the workspace shows you the meaning of the symbols that appear beside the workspace numbers. For example, Figure 6-9 shows menu bar that is telling you

- ☺ The current workspace is number 2.
- ☺ There are files loaded in workspaces 1, 2, 3, and 4.
- ☺ The file in workspace 3 has been edited but not saved.

Use the cursor keys to move the arrow to number 2 now, and press (ENTER). Press (F1), then (L), then (ENTER) again to get to the file picklist. Highlight the file ALPHABET.TXT and press (ENTER). You will see some large letters on the screen, as shown in Figure 6-10. This is the top of a file containing two sample alphabets for use in your source files.

Now for one of Ued's most useful tricks. Notice the Ctrl Cursor... selection in the command menu. Ued has two independent cursors. Hold down the (CTRL) key and press (F) to flip back and forth between the two cursors. You can use this command to switch between two workspaces, or between two different points in one file. Try the other commands in the Ctrl Cursor menu, too. (CTRL)-(N) moves the cursor to the next higher workspace number, and (CTRL)-(B) to the next lower workspace number. (CTRL)-(→) and (CTRL)-(←)

**Figure 6-9** Ued's Workspace menu shows you what's what

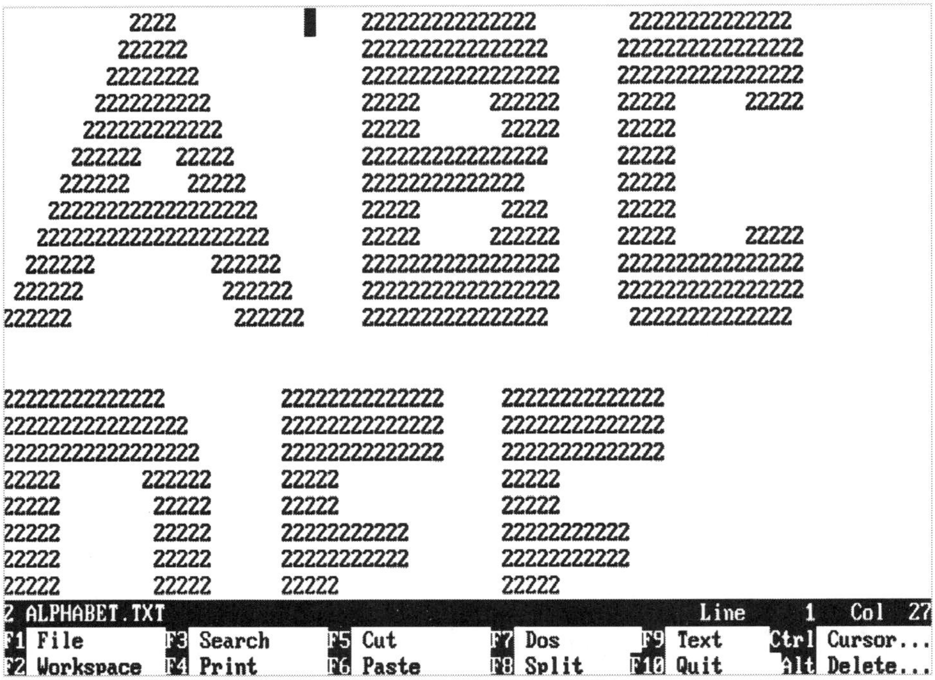

**Figure 6-10** Some letters from ALPHABET.TXT

move the cursor to the next word (right or left). These commands make it very easy to move quickly and precisely around in a file.

Use (CTRL)-(F) now to switch to the cursor in workspace 1, which contains PYRA-MID.TXT. Press (CTRL)-(N) twice or use (F2) to move that cursor to workspace 3, which is empty. Now (CTRL)-(F) switches you to ALPHABET.TXT in workspace 2. Hold down (CTRL) and press (→) twice to get to the top of the letter *B* in that file. You're going to copy this *B* into a new file.

# Block Copying

Press (F5) to get to the Cut menu. Notice that Ued highlights the first line of the file; this is *line marking*. Press (↓) so that two lines are highlighted. Line marking highlights an entire line at a time.

Now press the (R) key. The end of the first line and the beginning of the second line will be highlighted. This is *range marking*, from a starting to an ending point.

Now press (B). Two characters will be highlighted. This is *block marking*, which marks a rectangular column block.

Move the cursor around and switch among the three different marking modes until you have a clear understanding of how they work.

When you're ready, use block marking to highlight the entire letter *B*. The Copy command on the Cut menu is (C), so press it now. (CTRL)-(F) switches you to the other cursor, which is in the empty workspace number 3. Press (F6) to paste a copy of the letter *B* into this workspace.

## Search and Replace

The letter *B* you have copied is made of the character 2, so SIRTSER will put it two levels off the zero plane. Let's change it to one level off.

Press (F3) to get to the Search menu (see Figure 6-11). You're going to replace the pattern "2" with the pattern "1". Press (P) and Ued asks what pattern you want to search for. Press (2) and then (ENTER). Press (R) to get the Replacement prompt, and then press (1) and (ENTER). Press (G) to globally replace all the 2s with 1s, as shown in Figure 6-11. Press (ESC) to get back to the main menu.

## The Sample Alphabets

The file ALPHABET.TXT contains two different alphabets. You can copy and paste the letters from these alphabets into your source files.

ALPHABET.TXT ends with solid chunks of various numbers (use (CTRL)-(END) to get there). The Block Copy command makes it easy to grab columns and bars of whatever size and depth level you wish from these chunks. Bear in mind that vertical lines and spaces should be at least three characters wide to be clearly visible in the SIRTS. Horizontal lines and spaces should be at least two characters high. Thicker is better.

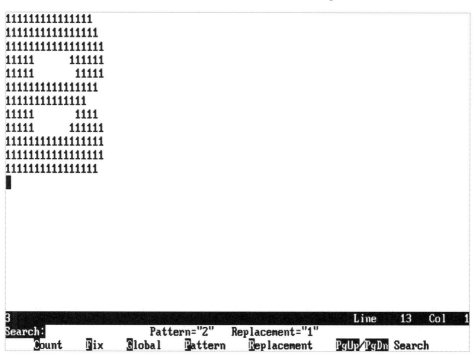

*Figure 6-11* Search and replace all the 2s with 1s

Copy some things into your new file. For instance, make a circle out of 1s, with a triangle of 2s inside it. Take care to keep everything left of column 62, because SIRTSER's default output width will truncate the source file after column 61. Ued displays the current line and column position of the cursor in the lower-right corner of the screen, above the menu, as you can see in any of the Ued screen shots in this chapter. This makes it easy to keep track of where you are in the file.

## Saving and Exiting

Now that you've created an enduring masterpiece, it's time to name and save your file. Press (F1) to get the File menu, and (N) to get the Name prompt. Notice that if you press (↑) at this point, Ued fills in the name of the last file it loaded or saved. Type a name for your file, such as FIGURE.TXT, using DOS filename conventions. Press (ENTER) to get back to the main menu.

Press (F1) again, and then to save the file under the name you've chosen. Press (F10) to exit back to DOS.

## Viewing and Printing from Ued

Generate a SIRTS from your source file, with the command

**SIRTSER FIGURE.TXT FIGURE.RTS** (ENTER)

Let's view this file in Ued, and learn a new way to load files into Ued.

Type the command

**UED FIGURE.RTS** (ENTER)

Ued will fire up and load your SIRTS. Press (F10) to exit, and try the command

**UED *.RTS** (ENTER)

Ued will load the first nine files with the extension .RTS in the current directory, and you can move among them with (CTRL)-(N) or the (F2) workspace selector.

You can also print from Ued by pressing (F4). This sends the file in the current workspace to any conventional printer attached to your computer's parallel port, LPT1. Because Ued doesn't do any formatting or font selection, this should work with any common printer, except a PostScript printer.

By the way, there's nothing magical about the .RTS extension used in this chapter. It can help you identify your Random Text Stereograms, but you can use any filename extension you like.

## More About Ued

You've only used a few of Ued's many functions in this section, and you may wish to explore it further. It's a very powerful little tool. It can split the screen and display two files at once. If you have a VGA video card, Ued can switch video modes to put twice as many lines on the screen. (ALT) gets you to a menu that will let you delete a whole line, the next word, or everything from the cursor to the beginning or end of the line—with a single keystroke. You can set most of the program's defaults just the way you want them by running the configuration program UEDCFG. This controls such things as screen color, video mode, word wrap on/off, insert/overtype, and cut/copy style. For more information, see the file UED.DOC.

# Printing SIRTS

You can print SIRTS on almost any printer, from Ued or any word processor. You can even print directly from MS-DOS. For example, to print the file PYRAMID2.RTS on a standard printer attached to your parallel port, just type the command

**COPY PYRAMID.RTS PRN** (ENTER)

## Fonts

SIRTS must be printed and viewed in a monospaced font. Monospaced fonts give each character the same amount of space. Proportional fonts give each character only the amount of space it needs. Here in the word *swim*, the proportional *w* needs much more space than the *i*.

`This sentence says swim in a 10-point monospaced font.`

This sentence says swim in a 10-point proportional font.

Proportional fonts don't maintain the regular grid spacing required by the single-image stereogram principle. Most printers default to monospaced fonts.

As noted previously, some programs, printers, and fonts may not support the high ASCII characters used in SIRTSER's −C character sets 6, 7, 8, and 9. Character sets 1 through 5 use only the ANSI standard, low ASCII characters for maximum compatibility.

## Landscape and Tile Printing

SIRTSER can generate images up to 999 characters wide, much wider than can be viewed on any video screen. You can print these out if you have a reasonably adept word processor or text file printing program. Your spell checker will doubtless find them fairly amusing along the way. Wide-carriage, 132-column dot matrix printers are great for printing out big SIRTS.

Many programs can print a file in landscape mode. This rotates the text ninety degrees and prints it sideways on the page. This allows you to print an image ten inches wide on an ordinary sheet of paper, instead of being limited to the usual seven inches. Turn the page sideways to view the stereogram. All of the Gallery images in this book are printed in landscape.

Another useful feature is tile printing, which splits a big file up into page-sized chunks and prints them a page at a time. You paste them together afterward to make as large an image as you'd like. Most spreadsheet and database programs provide tile printing.

## Printing in Windows

Generally, Windows programs have better printing capabilities than most MS-DOS programs. The graphical nature of Windows easily accomodates scaleable fonts and WYSIWYG (What You See Is What You Get) previews of the printed page. These features are particularly useful in the somewhat peculiar task of printing out big SIRTS. To meet the requirement of using monospaced fonts for SIRTS, as discussed earlier in this chapter, Windows comes with one monospaced TrueType font—Courier New—and you can buy others. If you're using Adobe Type Manager (ATM), monospaced PostScript fonts are also available.

# Tips and Pitfalls

Here are some tips to help you produce good single-image random-text stereograms:

- ☺ Features are difficult to distinguish if they're less than 3 characters wide.
- ☺ Avoid large changes in depth level. A 2 next to an 8 will probably cause hyperconvergence and depth confusion in the SIRTS. Build up gradually to high levels.
- ☺ Adjust the convergence strip width for the size of your final intended output. This helps avoid hyperconvergence.
- ☺ Limit your maximum depth to less than half of the convergence strip width value. This helps avoid converging the wrong points.
- ☺ For a screen viewed with the MS-DOS TYPE command, the total SIRTS width must be less than 80, or else the word wrap'll get you.
- ☺ Source characters wider than the total output width minus the strip width get thrown away. With the default settings, that means SIRTSER ignores anything beyond column 61 in the source file. You can control this behavior with the -W option.
- ☺ Use spaces instead of tabs in your source file. SIRTSER treats each tab, zero, or other non-numeric character as one space. A source line such as

  ```
  123qsgtd000r222 3331111111D111
  ```

  will produce the same output as the line

  ```
  123      222 3331111111 111
  ```

# What's Next?

SIRTSER uses the power of your computer to combine text characters into single-image random-text stereograms containing hidden 3D images. In the next chapter, we'll substitute dots for the text, and up the ante by giving you a fully graphical drawing program to create the hidden image.

*Chapter 7*

# Creating SIRDS with RDSdraw

T  he RDSdraw program provides an excellent place to start exploring single-image random-dot stereograms (SIRDS). Within this single program, you can draw pictures with your mouse and turn them into SIRDS; view the SIRDS on your computer screen; save the pictures and the SIRDS as files for printing from other programs; and load files from other programs for conversion to SIRDS—easily, and all in a matter of a few minutes. This chapter shows you how.

## About RDSdraw

RDSdraw is a remarkably full-featured and nicely realized freeware SIRDS drawing program. It uses different colors in the drawing to represent the apparent 3D depths in the final SIRDS image. You decide how far in or out of the screen an object will be before you begin drawing it, and then draw with the color that corresponds to that level of depth. RDSdraw generates a random-dot image on the basis of your drawing (which is a depthmap of the SIRDS). The SIRDS can be displayed onscreen in black and white or in color, and it can be saved as a .TGA (Targa) file.

    RDSdraw's tools automate the drawing of several useful 3D objects by filling in all the successive layers of depth between two limits. These 3D tools make it possible to create some rather impressive SIRDS images with great ease.

## Licensing Information

RDSdraw is freeware, written by Johannes Schmid. You can reach the author by e-mail at the address Johannes_Schmid@m2.maus.de. Send postal mail to

Johannes Schmid
Rudliebstr. 50
81925 München, Germany

## System Requirements

RDSdraw requires a mouse and a VGA card, which it will run in 16-color, 640x480 mode. It does not require or use a math coprocessor.

## Starting RDSdraw

The book's installation program puts RDSdraw in the directory \STEREO3D\RDS-DRAW. From this directory, type the following at the DOS prompt:

**RDSDRAW** (ENTER)

RDSdraw will load and display its credit screen. After reading the screen, press any key on the keyboard to start the program.

# Creating SIRDS with RDSdraw

RDSdraw presents all of its tools on a toolbar on the left side of the screen, as shown in Figure 7-1. Below the toolbar is the palette, a column of bars displays 16 drawing colors. RDSdraw uses these colors onscreen to specify depths in a SIRDS. The number on each bar tells you the depth level the color represents. In the SIRDS generated from the image you create, objects painted in lower-numbered colors will appear farther away than objects painted with higher-numbered colors.

Below the palette, the active color bar reminds you which color-depth level you have assigned to each mouse button. This determines the depth of the object (or depth range, in the case of 3D objects) you draw. The Linear/Round toggle, in the lower-right corner of the screen, tells you whether RDSdraw will create 3D objects with straight (linear) or rounded sides. Between the active color bar and the Linear/Round toggle, the status line displays various instructions relating to the tool you are using.

## Drawing a 3D Crazy Quilt

A section at the end of this chapter discusses each of the RDSdraw tools in greater detail. For now, let's get started by drawing a crazy-quilt sampler. In the process, you'll use most of RDSdraw's tools. The SIRDS generated from this exercise is shown in Figure 7-2. Refer back to this figure as you draw each object, to see how the onscreen image relates to the 3D illusion you are creating.

### Drawing Guides

When you start RDSdraw, the drawing space is solid black. Since black is in the middle of the color-depth palette, the empty space starts as a middle depth. Objects drawn with the

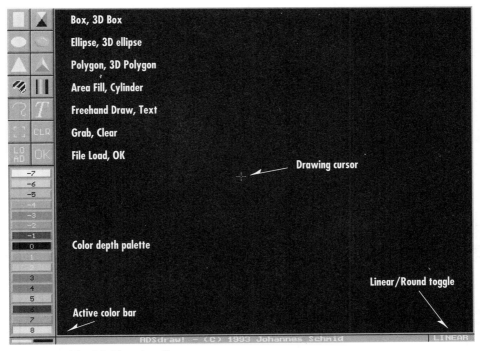

**Figure 7-1** The RDSdraw interface

colors above black in the palette (those with negative numerical values) appear deeper in the SIRDS.

The first step in this exercise divides the drawing area into nine rectangles of equal size.

1. Select depth level –6 by clicking on the light blue bar (second from the top in the palette) with the left mouse button. The left half of the active color bar, below the palette, changes from white to light blue.

2. Select the Box tool, which is the top-left button on the toolbar. You can select it with either mouse button, or with the left/right cursor keys.

3. Position the mouse cursor at the left edge of the drawing area, next to the bottom-right corner of the Text tool button. Click and hold the left mouse button. The status line now says, "You are drawing with the BOX-function!"

4. Without releasing the mouse button, drag the cursor down the screen. A rubber-band line tracks your mouse from the first click point to its new position. If you drag the mouse straight down the screen, you will have a single straight line; but if you move it to the right at all, the line breaks up into a series of segments. This makes it easy to tell whether you're directly in line with your first point. The program will not let you drag the cursor out of the drawing area.

5. Position the cursor at the left edge of the drawing area, next to the lower-right corner of the light gray –2 color bar in the palette, and release the mouse button. The

*Figure 7-2*  A crazy-quilt RDSdraw sampler

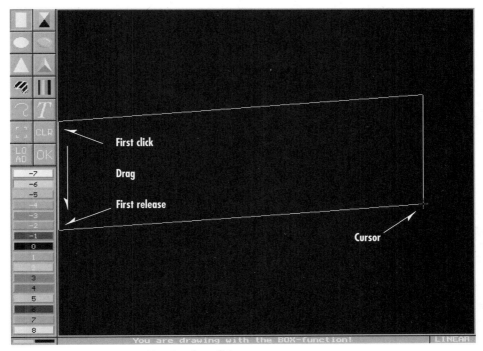

*Figure 7-3* Controlling a rubber-band parallelogram

rubber-band line disappears. When you next move the mouse, you have a complete rubber-band parallelogram under your control, as shown in Figure 7-3.

6. Position the mouse cursor straight across from the point of first release, at the right edge of the drawing area, and then click the left mouse button. The parallelogram fills with light blue, dividing the screen into thirds vertically.

7. Using the same color, draw a second rectangle, dividing the screen into thirds horizontally, as shown in Figure 7-4. The screen should now be divided into nine equal rectangles, which you will use as guides.

## Saving a Temporary File

Click on the OK tool with either mouse button. RDSdraw asks if you wish to save the file. Press Ⓨ for Yes. RDSdraw tells you it is using the image name NONAME. Press ⏎ENTER. and you have just saved the drawing area to a temporary file called NONAME.TGA. When RDSdraw returns the message "IMAGE SUCCESSFULLY SAVED," press any key on the keyboard to continue.

If you remember to save temporary files often, you reduce the amount of time you will spend starting over after a mistake, because you can reload the temporary file and continue drawing on it.

## Drawing Pyramids

The next step in this example replaces the upper-left sector of the quilt with a pyramid. The pyramid is a 3D object composed of concentric rectangles, ranging in depth from a

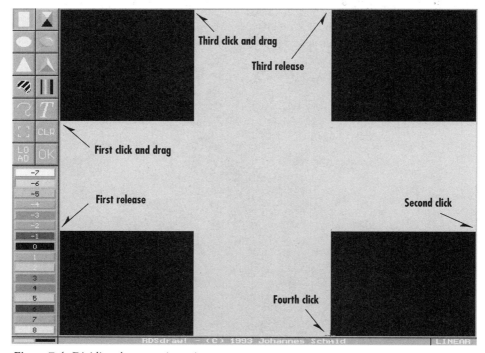

**Figure 7-4** Dividing the screen into nine sectors

value set by the color of the left mouse button, to a value set by the color of the right mouse button.

1. Select depth level –7, light blue, with the right mouse button. Select depth level 8, white, with the left mouse button.

2. Select the 3D Box tool. Since the color-depth level you want at the peak of the pyramid is active on the left mouse button, this is the button to draw with. (If you were to draw with the right mouse button, the pyramid would be inverted.)

3. Position the cursor in the upper-left corner of the drawing area. Click and drag straight down to the lower-left corner of the upper-left sector. Release the button, and move the cursor to the lower-right corner of the upper-left sector. Click and release the left mouse button.

The sector fills with a series of concentric rectangles, as shown in Figure 7-5. Each rectangle is one color level higher than the last, with the border being the light-blue color level of the right mouse button, and the center being the white color level of the left mouse button. Notice that each concentric rectangle has the same line width. This will give the appearance of straight sides in the SIRDS generated from this drawing.

4. Click on the word LINEAR in the lower-right corner of the screen. The toggle changes to read ROUND, indicating that RDSdraw will now make 3D objects with rounded sides.

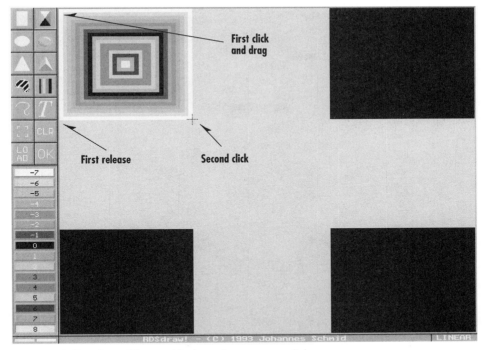

**Figure 7-5** Drawing a 3D pyramid takes only two mouse clicks

5. Draw another 3D box in the upper-middle sector. Just repeat step 3, drawing from the upper-left corner of the sector to its lower-right corner.

When RDSdraw fills in its concentric rectangles, the inner ones are thicker than the outer ones. This means the depth changes faster at the edges than in the middle, producing the appearance of rounded surfaces in the SIRDS. Figure 7-6 shows the rounded pyramid.

RDSdraw uses your choice of mouse buttons to determine the direction in which it fills 3D objects. You drew the first two pyramids with the left button. RDSdraw filled them with the right button color-depth level (–7) at the edge, and the left button color-depth level (8) in the center.

6. Draw a third 3D Box in the upper-right sector. This time, however, use the right mouse button for the final click. RDSdraw creates a receding pyramid, filled from 8 at the edges to –7 in the center.

Figure 7-7 shows all three pyramids.

## Drawing Cones with the Ellipse Tool

The next step in drawing the crazy-quilt sampler is to add three cones with various features.

1. Click on the Linear/Round toggle; it changes to LINEAR, activating straight-sided 3D objects. Select the 3D Ellipse tool.

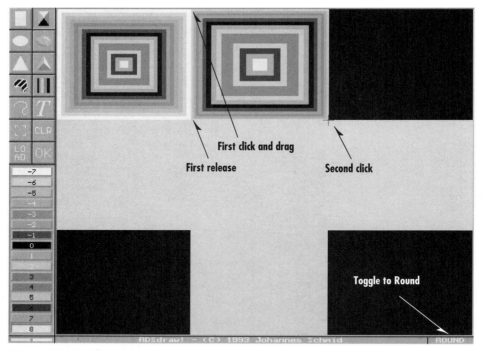

**Figure 7-6** Straight and rounded pyramids

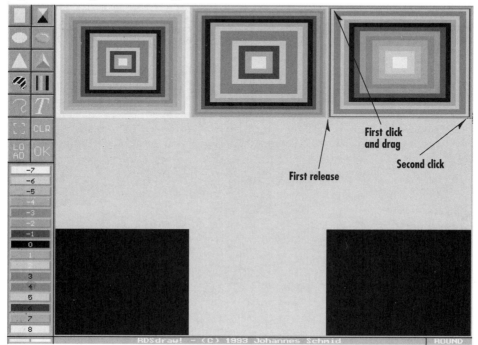

**Figure 7-7** Using the right mouse button for reverse depths

2. Position the cursor in the center of the left-middle sector, about at the height of the –7 palette block. Click and hold the right mouse button. The message on the status line says "You are drawing with the 3D-ELLIPSE-function!"

3. Move the cursor while still holding the mouse button. A rubber-band ellipse tracks your cursor position. Try making circles as well as vertical and horizontal ovals.

4. Drag the cursor to the lower-right corner of the sector. If your first click was off center, you can press (ESC) to cancel the operation and try again. Once you have an oval that neatly fills the sector, release the mouse button. The oval fills with a series of concentric ovals, as shown in Figure 7-8.

5. Click the Linear/Round toggle back to ROUND. Draw a 3D ellipse in the middle sector with the left mouse button.

6. Draw a third 3D ellipse in the right middle sector, this time using the right mouse button to invert the 3D fill. As you can see in Figure 7-9, these two ellipses have thinner rings at their outside edges, so they will appear rounded in the SIRDS generated from this drawing.

## Drawing a 3D Polygon

1. Click on the Linear/Round toggle, so it changes back to LINEAR. Select the 3D Polygon tool.

2. Position the cursor in the upper-left corner of the lower-left sector. Click and release the left mouse button to mark the first point.

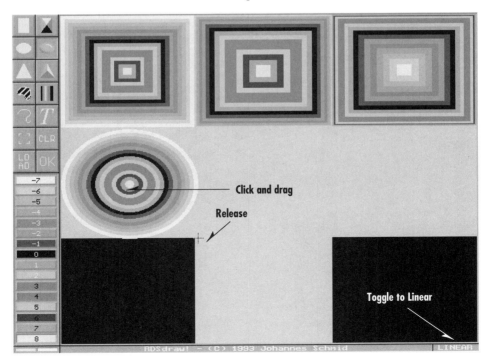

*Figure 7-8* One click and drag draws a cone

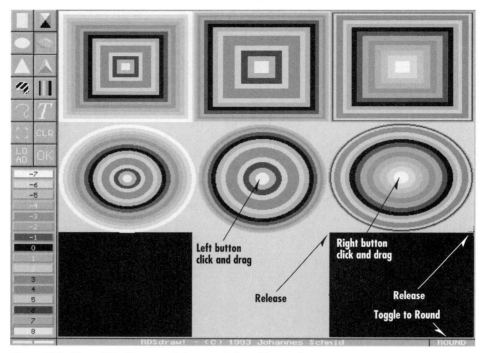

**Figure 7-9** Three 3D ellipses: straight, rounded, and inverted

3. Drag the mouse, and a rubber-band line follows your cursor.

4. Click and release in the upper-right and lower-right corners of the sector.

5. Click several more times to make a zigzag path back to the first corner, as shown in Figure 7-10.

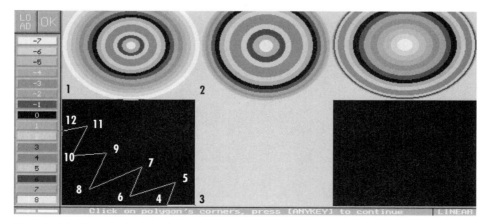

**Figure 7-10** First you draw the base...

6. Press the (SPACEBAR). (Actually, any key but (ESC) will do.) You now have mouse control of the tip of a rubber-band 3D polygon.

7. Position the cursor near the upper-right corner of the sector, as shown in Figure 7-11. Click and release the left mouse button. RDSdraw fills in the levels as shown in Figure 7-12.

This 3D polygon has straight sides, and your last click determines its highest level. If you had used the right mouse button for the last click, RDSdraw would have reversed the fill and created a receding polygon. If you had pressed a key instead of the last mouse click, RDSdraw would have calculated the center point of the base polygon and filled up to there, regardless of the cursor position.

## Drawing 3D Cylinders

Next, you'll fill the remaining two sectors with 3D cylinders.

1. Select the Cylinder tool, using your mouse or cursor arrows.

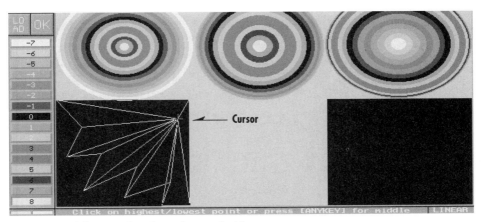

**Figure 7-11** Then you drag the peak around with your mouse

**Figure 7-12** And RDSdraw fills in the levels

2. Position the cursor in the upper-left corner of the lower-middle sector. Click and hold the left mouse button. The status line reports, "You are drawing with the CYLINDER-function!"

3. Drag the cursor straight across to the upper-right corner of the sector and release it. You now have control of a rubber-band parallelogram, just as with the Box and 3D Box tools.

4. Position the cursor in the lower-right corner of the sector, and click the left mouse button. Instead of concentric rectangles, RDSdraw fills your rectangle with parallel stripes. This fill creates a ridge across the middle of the rectangle, as shown in Figure 7-13.

5. Click on the Linear/Round toggle, setting it to ROUND. Position the cursor in the upper-right corner of the remaining sector.

6. Click and hold the left mouse button. Drag the cursor straight down to the lower-right corner and release it.

7. Position the cursor at the left edge of the sector, a little up from the bottom, so your rubber-band rectangle overlaps the 3D Ellipse in the sector above it. Click the left mouse button to fill the cylinder, as shown in Figure 7-14.

Notice that RDSdraw uses your first click-and-drag to determine the direction of the fill. The first cylinder contained horizontal stripes; this one uses vertical stripes. The first cylinder used the same width for each stripe. This cylinder uses smaller stripes at the edge for a rounded appearance, in accordance with the status of the Linear/Round toggle.

## Adding Text

Next you'll use the Text tool to write the program's name across the drawing. This is a good time to save a temporary file. It's not easy to predict how far text is going to reach across your drawing.

1. Select color level 4, the light orange bar in the palette, with the left mouse button.

2. Select the Text tool.

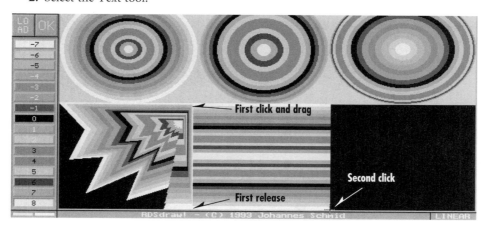

**Figure 7-13** The cylinder tool produces a horizontal ridge

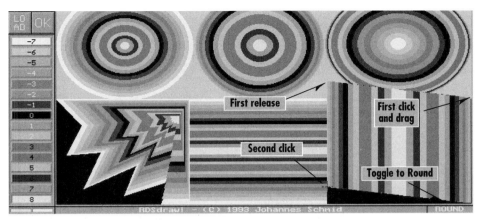

**Figure 7-14** A 3D ridge takes a couple of mouse clicks

3. Position the cursor just to the right of the top of the Text tool button. Click and release the left mouse button. The status line is now empty, waiting for your input.

4. Type in the name of the program, **RDSdraw**. The characters you enter appear on the status line. Press (ENTER) when done. Figure 7-15 shows how "RDSdraw" appears on the screen, with the upper-left corner located where you clicked the mouse.

**Figure 7-15** A mouse click places the upper-left corner of the text

The text, drawn in light orange at level 4, appears in the SIRDS floating in front of anything drawn at a lower level. The centers of the left two pyramids both reach higher levels. If your text overlaps these higher levels, it will appear to cut into them. If it overlaps one of the bands drawn in the same orange color, the text will be difficult to read because the overlapping area won't be seen.

## Drawing Freehand Lines

The final step in this example consists of drawing some freehand lines. This is another good point to save a temporary file. The Freehand Draw tool is a bit difficult to control, and, unfortunately, RDSdraw doesn't have an Undo function.

*1.* Select the Freehand Draw tool.

*2.* Position the cursor at the left edge of the drawing space, beneath the text. Press the left mouse button and drag the cursor to the right, stopping before the orange ring in the left ellipse. Release the button. (Move the mouse slowly, since the line you are drawing tends to lag behind. If you mess up, reload the image from your temporary file.)

*3.* Move the cursor to the right, past the orange ellipse. Click and drag to draw another line segment to the next orange ellipse, and release the mouse button.

*4.* Skip over the second orange ellipse, and draw a third line segment under the end of the text.

*5.* For a final touch, draw a U-shaped loop around the middle ellipse from one underline to the next, as shown in Figure 7-16. A bit of a smiley face livens up the image.

## Saving the Source File

Save this masterpiece as a source file, so you can bring it back and tinker with it. Select the OK tool in the toolbar. When RDSdraw asks if you want to save the image, press Ⓨ. You will next see the Save File dialog, with your directory and the default temporary filename, NONAME, highlighted in red. Backspace to erase the word NONAME, and type in whatever name you'd like, such as QUILT1. Don't enter an extension, because RDSdraw will add the .TGA suffix. Press (ENTER) to save the file. The word "Saving" appears in the dialog box and on the status line as RDSdraw writes the file to your hard disk. The dialog box disappears, and an "IMAGE SUCCESSFULLY SAVED" message box appears. Press any key to return to the drawing screen.

# Generating and Saving the SIRDS

Now it's time to generate your RDS so you can view this image in 3D. Click on the OK tool again, and answer Ⓝ when asked if you want to save the file. RDSdraw displays a dialog box presenting the three kinds of RDS images it can generate, with "Black/White RDS" highlighted in red. Use the keyboard's up/down cursor arrows to scroll through the list of RDS types. Find "4 Color RDS" and press (ENTER).

RDSdraw now removes the toolbar and generates a vertical strip of random dots on the left side of the screen. It then repeats this strip across the screen, modulating it with depth information provided by your drawing. Next, it draws two convergence dots at the top of the screen to help you lock onto the image. Finally, you see a dialog box asking if you want to save the completed RDS image. Press Ⓨ.

***Figure 7-16*** Draw with the mouse using the Freehand Draw tool

RDSdraw presents the Save .TGA (Targa) dialog box again. Notice that the name you typed for the source file is still highlighted. If you don't change the name, the program will overwrite the source file you just saved! So backspace and type a new name, such as RDS1, and press (ENTER). RDSdraw saves the file to your hard disk, and a dialog box tells you when it is done. Press any key to clear it and there you are. Your RDS image is onscreen in all its multicolored glory. (It was shown in grayscale earlier as Figure 7-2.)

Look at the rather subtle difference between the straight and rounded 3D objects. The free-hand-drawn lines are more distinct than RDSdraw's text, which is a bit small. You might do better making text using the Freehand Draw tool.

Also notice the few areas where you didn't draw over the default black opening screen. The lower-left corner of the image stayed black. Now it floats at midlevel in the SIRDS, as if it covered part of the 3D polygon. It's an interesting effect.

When you finish viewing the 3D image, press any key and RDSdraw will unceremoniously dump you back to MS-DOS. Don't worry—this is the program's normal behavior. If you wish to continue, simply restart RDSdraw.

## Importing a .TGA File

Not only does the RDSdraw program draw pictures and turn them into RDS images, it also imports pictures from other sources. This function permits you to edit an RDSdraw source file in another graphics application. You can also generate a different type of RDS from an RDSdraw source file using another SIRDS application, such as RDSGEN or

SHIMMER (Chapters 8 and 9). You can import an image for editing as an RDSdraw source file, or import an image and just turn it straight into a SIRDS.

## Limitations

RDSdraw does have a few simple limitations. It can read only some flavors of .TGA files. They must be either 8-bit grayscale or 24-bit RGB color, and they must be uncompressed.

There are no apparent file size limitations; even 1024x768 .TGAs load fine. However, whatever you load gets clipped off at 572x465 (or scaled down if you select the Load In Box option), so there's no reason to try to load a really large file.

Few normal images are immediately suitable for direct conversion to SIRDS. Color in the source image has no real meaning, since RDSdraw only looks at pixel intensity or brightness. If you use a viewer that can show a grayscale version of an image, it should give you a good idea of what RDSdraw will see. Large areas of similar intensity are good, as are smooth gradients. Fine detail tends to generate meaningless noise in the RDS. If you have the programs Fractint, Polyray, or POV-Ray, you can generate wonderfully suitable images; follow the tips in Chapters 9, 10, and 11.

## Let's Do It

Ready to import a neat source file? Click on the Load tool. RDSdraw presents a dialog box in which you can enter the filename of the .TGA you wish to load. Backspace to erase the default, NONAME, and type **WAVES**. Do not type the extension, because RDSdraw will add .TGA to whatever filename you give it. Press (ENTER). The LOAD IN BOX: NO item will now be highlighted in red. Press (ENTER). A dialog box announces that it is loading a 572x465, 8-bit grayscale image. Press (ENTER) again to proceed. RDSdraw loads the file and displays it. Click on the OK tool and generate an RDS from this .TGA.

# RDSdraw Tools Reference

This section discusses each of RDSdraw's tools. If you need to, refer back to the entire workspace illustration in Figure 7-1. The button icons are shown here, next to the description of each tool.

## Color and Depth Controls

RDSdraw uses the 16 screen colors to represent 16 depths in the final SIRDS. The lower half of the toolbar displays these colors and depths as a vertical palette. Light blue represents −7, the deepest level you can draw. White represents +8, the nearest level.

At the bottom of the palette is a rectangular color bar showing the active drawing colors. The left half of the bar displays the left mouse button's drawing color, and the right half displays the right mouse button's drawing color.

You can use the left and right mouse buttons to select colors, or use the keyboard arrow keys. (↑) and (↓) step the left mouse button through the palette. (CTRL)-(↑) and (CTRL)-(↓) step the right mouse button through the palette.

## The Drawing Tools

The upper third of the toolbar contains the drawing tools. Flat tools are on the left, and 3D tools are on the right. Select a tool by clicking on it with the mouse, or press the ⬅ and ➡ keys to step through the toolbox.

 ### The Box Tool

The Box tool draws filled parallelograms. The first mouse click marks the first vertex. Hold down the mouse button while you drag the cursor to the next vertex, and then release the mouse button. Then, as you move the mouse, a rubber-band parallelogram tracks your cursor position. Click and release the mouse to mark the third vertex. RDSdraw will draw and fill the parallelogram.

 ### The 3D Box Tool

The 3D Box tool draws pyramids with parallelogram bases. Click and drag to draw the first segment, just as with the Box tool. Position the rubber-band parallelogram. Click and release to complete the base, and RDSdraw builds the pyramid.

   The mouse button you use to make the second click determines whether the pyramid points into or out of the screen. The color level of the mouse button you click will color the peak of the pyramid. The base of the pyramid will be the color level of the other mouse button. RDSdraw fills in the levels between as a straight line or a curve, depending on the status of the Linear/Round toggle.

 ### The Ellipse Tool

The Ellipse tool draws ovals and circles on a single depth level. Click and hold either mouse button to mark the center. A rubber-band ellipse tracks your position as you drag the mouse away from the center. Release the mouse button to mark a corner and draw the ellipse. The mouse button used determines the color level of the ellipse.

 ### The 3D Ellipse Tool

The 3D Ellipse tool operates exactly as the Ellipse tool does, except that the mouse button you use determines the color at the center of the ellipse. The perimeter of the ellipse matches the color level of the other button. RDSdraw fills in the steps between with a linear or curved scale, depending on the status of the Linear/Round toggle.

 ### The Polygon Tool

The Polygon tool draws filled polygons having from 2 to 99 vertices (corners). A mouse click places each vertex in order, and pressing any key on the keyboard (except (ESC))

draws the polygon. The mouse button used for the first click determines the color level used to fill the polygon. Pressing (ESC) cancels the operation.

 ## The 3D Polygon Tool

The 3D Polygon tool draws 3D polygons. These are constructed from a polygon with 3 to 99 vertices on one color level, and a single point on another color level. Draw the base with either mouse button, using a click for each vertex. Complete the base by pressing any key on the keyboard. This gives you mouse control of a rubber-band pyramid. Position the peak where you want it. Click with the mouse button that has the color level you want at the peak. The perimeter of the base polygon matches the other mouse button's color level, and RDSdraw interpolates the levels between them according to the state of the Linear/Round toggle.

If you press a key instead of placing the peak with your mouse, RDSdraw calculates the center of the base and places the peak there automatically.

 ## The Area Fill Tool

The Area Fill tool is a little dangerous. It fills an area with the chosen color until it reaches a perimeter of the same color. Its chief use is to fill an arbitrary closed shape drawn with the Freehand Draw tool. You must fill with the same color as the drawn line.

The Area Fill tool can also flatten the top (or bottom) of a 3D gradient object such as a 3D Ellipse. Select the color level of one of the intermediate rings, and use that mouse button to click on the peak. The tool fills the center out to the color level you've chosen, flattening the top of the gradient object that appears in the SIRDS.

---

Be careful with the Area Fill tool! It can easily blot out your entire drawing if you use it in an unenclosed area. There is no undo. Frequent temporary file saving is strongly encouraged.

---

 ## The Cylinder Tool

The Cylinder tool draws ridges and valleys. It works just like the 3D Box tool, with one difference: Instead of filling up to a single peak, it fills the base parallelogram up to a ridge the length of the object. This ridge runs parallel to the first line segment drawn to define the parallelogram. The color level of the mouse button used for the last click determines the color-depth level of the central strip of the ridge. The sides of the base match the color level of the other mouse button. The walls of the object appear either straight or curved, depending on the status of the Linear/Round toggle.

 ## The Freehand Draw Tool

The Freehand Draw tool draws lines following your mouse as you drag it across the drawing space. RDSdraw colors the line according to which mouse button you hold down.

The width is not adjustable, and the tool will lag behind the mouse if you move too fast. You may find it useful to select the drawing color level with the left mouse button, and use the right button for the color level over which you're drawing. This enables you to use the right button as an eraser.

 ## The Text Tool

The Text tool creates characters. The type style, size, and orientation of this text are not adjustable. After you have selected the tool, you must click the mouse in the drawing area to mark the point where the upper-left corner of the text will be placed. The button you use for this click determines the color level of the text. As you type your text, it appears on the status line. Press (ENTER) to draw it.

The type may be a little small and hard to read, but the RDS medium doesn't do text very well, anyway. You can also create text with the Freehand Draw tool. A third approach is to draw text in a separate paint program, and import it using the Load tool with the In Box option set to Yes.

 ## The Grab Tool

The Grab tool copies a rectangular area so that you can use it as a rubber stamp. Marking the rectangle with the left button copies the area. Marking it with the right button cuts it from the screen and fills the area with the right button's color level. As you move the cursor around the screen, clicking the left mouse button pastes down a copy of the rectangular area. Clicking the right mouse button fills an area the size of the rectangle with the color assigned to the right mouse button. However, any areas in the source rectangle that were the same color as the right button behave differently: Any parts of the screen that are under these areas remain untouched. The copy remains on the Clipboard until you click on the Grab tool again with the right mouse button.

# The Control Buttons

Below the drawing tools are three control buttons: Clear, File Load, and OK.

 ## The Clear Button

The Clear button erases the drawing workspace by filling it with the right mouse button's color level. It also sets that color as the 0 level in the palette, and renumbers the palette up and down from there. This renumbering doesn't affect the final image, but it may help you to keep track of the depth level on which you are drawing.

 ## The File Load Button

The File Load button reads in a .TGA file, which can either be 8-bit grayscale or 24-bit RGB. The Load In Box option fits an image into a rectangle you mark onscreen. You can use this to load images larger or smaller than 572x465 and still fill the screen with them. You can also use it to fit an image into a part of your drawing.

Clicking on File Load displays a dialog box in which you enter the filename of the .TGA you wish to load. Backspace to erase the default filename (NONAME), and type in the name of the file you want. Do not type an extension; RDSdraw will automatically add .TGA to the filename. When you press (ENTER), the dialog remains onscreen, with LOAD IN BOX: NO highlighted in red. Your choices now are to press (Y), (N), (ENTER), or (ESC).

- ☺ Pressing (Y) and then (ENTER) chooses the Load In Box option. Click and hold the left mouse button to mark one corner of the box. Drag the rubber-band box to the shape you want, and release it. RDSdraw will then scale the .TGA file into the selected rectangle.

- ☺ If you press (N) (the default setting) and then (ENTER), you tell RDSdraw that you wish to load as much of the .TGA as will fit, pixel for pixel, beginning with the upper-left corner of the work area.

- ☺ When you press (ENTER), a message is briefly displayed, telling you how big the file is and whether it is 8-bit grayscale or 24-bit color. If the file is in an unsupported format, RDSdraw returns the message "UNKNOWN TYPE."

Press (ESC) if you wish to cancel the load operation.

RDSdraw loads the file and displays it. Black in the source file becomes depth –7, which is light blue in RDSdraw. White in the source file becomes depth 8, or white in RDSdraw. All other grays and colors get mapped in between, by pixel intensity.

 ## The OK Button

The OK button brings up a dialog that lets you save your drawing to a file or process your drawing into a SIRDS. When you select OK, RDSdraw asks whether you'd like to save the drawing as a source file. Choose Yes, and it prompts you for a filename. After saving the file, it returns you to the drawing screen. If you choose No, the program asks whether you want a color or black-and-white SIRDS, which is generated onscreen. You then have a chance to save the SIRDS to a file after generating it.

This tool saves your entire drawing area as a 572-by-465-pixel, 8-bit grayscale .TGA file, and your SIRDS as a 640x480, 24-bit RGB .TGA file. The SIRDS file can be printed from many different MS-DOS or Windows programs. The drawing file is suitable for reloading into RDSdraw for continued editing, or for loading into another SIRDS generator such as RDSGEN, MindImages, or SHIMMER.

# What's Next?

RDSdraw simplifies many 3D drawing operations with its palette control and flexible 3D object fills. It provides an excellent environment for learning about SIRDS. Since it generates the SIRDS onscreen with only a few options, the final output is somewhat limited. However, RDSdraw's saved source files work very well with more powerful SIRDS generators, because most programs use very similar source files.

As you will see in Chapter 9, you can use DTA (Dave's Targa Animator) to scale RDSdraw files to whatever size you like. Then you can use RDSGEN to make high-resolution SIRDS or image-mapped single-image stereograms, with all of RDSGEN's many options at your disposal.

In the next chapter, you will enjoy a wealth of SIRDS using two viewing programs, MindImages and SHIMMER. You will also learn how to use DTA to convert your own images, from RDSdraw and elsewhere, to the highly compact MindImages file format.

# Chapter 8

# MindImages
# .RLE SIRDS

*I*n 1992, subscribers to the Internet newsgroup, alt.3D, became interested in exchanging SIRDS. This was due, in part, to the release of Andrew A. Kinsman's TORUS.PS PostScript printer file. SIRDS files contain a lot of fine detail, so they do not compress well. This means they tend to be fairly large, which makes them slow to transfer by e-mail, and therefore expensive to share on the Internet. MindImages was written as an answer to this problem.

Many people realized that the hidden image inside a SIRDS tends to be quite simple. SIRDS are generated from a file that is a simple map of the depths in a picture (the depthmap). The source files for SIRTSER (Chapter 6) are numerical depthmaps. The drawing files that RDSdraw (Chapter 7) reads and writes are graphical depthmaps. Depthmaps can be much lower resolution than the SIRDS they turn into, and they always compress far better than their SIRDS.

MindImages is both a viewing program and a file format. Its authors created a compressed depthmap format for distribution, and a program to turn that depthmap into a SIRDS at viewing time. They specifically designed the file format to allow direct e-mail transmission across the Internet, so the format uses only ANSI standard ASCII characters. MindImages .RLE (Run Length Encoded) depthmap files are often less than one-tenth the size of their SIRDS.

This chapter presents two programs for viewing the many .RLE SIRDS included on this book's disk. The first program is MindImages itself; the second is SHIMMER, which allows you to view .RLE SIRDS through a bizarre but effective dot-animation technique.

You will also learn how to convert your own pictures to .RLE depthmaps with Dave's Targa Animator, better known as DTA.

# About MindImages

MindImages is a versatile and friendly SIRDS viewing program. It displays a menu of SIRDS for either cross-eyed or parallel viewing. It can even display them as anaglyphs for viewing with red/blue or red/green 3D glasses (for people who can't master the cross-eyed or parallel techniques). MindImages can write SIRDS to a PostScript file for printing. It can also display the depthmap used to generate a SIRDS, to help with viewing and troubleshooting.

MindImages comes with 32 excellent SIRDS .RLE files, and more are regularly available on the Internet alt.3D Usenet newsgroup.

## Licensing Information

MindImages is public domain software, written by Eric Thompson, Rob Scott, and Gordon Flanagan. You can reach the authors by Internet e-mail at the following addresses: E.Thompson@newcastle.ac.uk, Robert.Scott@newcastle.ac.uk, and G.J.Flanagan@ newcastle.ac.uk.

## System Requirements

MindImages requires a PC-compatible computer equipped with a VGA video card, which the program will run in 640x480x16 mode.

## Installation

There is no setup required. If you used the default installation settings, this book's installation program put MindImages in the directory \STEREO3D\MINDIMAG.

# About SHIMMER

SHIMMER is a command-line program that displays SIRDS from MindImages .RLE files. It uses several enhancement techniques to make viewing easier.

## Licensing Information

SHIMMER is freeware, written by Stuart J. Inglis. You can reach the author by Internet e-mail at singlis@waikato.ac.nz. From CompuServe, the address is >INTERNET: singlis@waikato.ac.nz. Send postal mail (airmail is recommended) to

Stuart J. Inglis
Computer Science Department, Waikato University
Hamilton, New Zealand

Stuart Inglis is also coauthor (along with Harold W. Thimbleby and Ian H. Witten) of a very interesting paper on SIRDS algorithms. If you have Internet access, you can ftp a

PostScript version of this paper. It is located on wuarchive.wustl.edu in /mirrors/architec/ Documents/Sirds.tar.Z, and on ftp.cs.waikato.ac.nz in the /pub/papers directory.

## System Requirements

SHIMMER requires a PC-compatible computer with a VGA or SVGA video card. It prefers the 640x480x256 video mode. You also need some .RLE files, as distributed with this book or the MindImages package.

## Installation

This book's installation program put SHIMMER in the directory \STEREO3D\ MINDIMAG, along with a batch file you can use to run SHIMMER more conveniently. SHIMMER requires you to set an environment variable telling it where to find its video driver, SVGA256.BGI. Don't panic; that just means that you type

**SET BGIDIR=C:\STEREO3D\MINDIMAG** (ENTER)

from the DOS prompt at some point before running SHIMMER. If you've put SVGA 256.BGI in some other directory, substitute that directory name for C:\STEREO3D\ MINDIMAG in the preceding statement. You only need to set the environment variable once each time you reboot your computer, and SHIMMER will remind you if you've forgotten. You can also add this SET statement to your AUTOEXEC.BAT file.

We've made it even easier by including a batch file, called SHIM.BAT, that does the SET command and then calls SHIMMER for you. Run the batch file by changing to the \STEREO3D\MINDIMAG subdirectory, then typing the command

**SHIM** (ENTER)

to see the copyright and program information screen.

In the unlikely event that you get an Out Of Environment Space error when you type the SET command or run SHIM.BAT, you will have to modify your CONFIG.SYS file. Look for a line that says

**SHELL=C:\COMMAND.COM**

and edit it so that it says

**SHELL=C:\COMMAND.COM /E:288**

If your copy of COMMAND.COM is in a different directory, such as C:\DOS, substitute that directory for the C:\ in the SHELL statement. If your CONFIG.SYS has no SHELL statement, add one. If your SHELL statement already has a /E parameter, increase the current value by 32.

# About DTA

DTA, Dave's Targa Animator, is a command-line graphics utility. Originally created to build .FLI animation files, it has since grown into a complete and powerful graphics tool kit. You can use it to create MindImages .RLE files from many different graphics file formats, including .TGA, .GIF, and .PCX.

DTA has far more capabilities than those explained here. More information is available in the files DTA.DOC and WHATSNEW.DTA, as well as in the Waite Group books, *Making Movies On Your PC* (1993, ISBN 1-878739-41-7) and *Morphing On Your PC* (1994, ISBN 1-878739-53-0).

## Licensing Information

DTA is a shareware program. If you use it regularly, you are requested to send a $35 registration fee to

David K. Mason
P.O. Box 181015
Boston, MA 02118

You can also reach the author on CompuServe at 76546,1321, or from the Internet, at 76546.1321@compuserve.com.

## System Requirements

DTA requires a PC-compatible computer with a minimum 2 MB of RAM, configured as XMS or raw extended memory. DTA will not use EMS memory. It does not require any graphics display capabilities.

## Installation

This book's installation program put DTA and its runtime files in the directory \STEREO3D. You should add this directory to your PATH statement, since the material in several chapters uses DTA from various directories. If you don't want to modify your AUTOEXEC.BAT, you can move all the files in \STEREO3D to a directory already in your path. No other setup is needed.

DTA requires two support files, DPMI16BI.OVL and RTM.EXE. These make up the protected-mode drivers for Borland Pascal 7.0, the compiler used to build DTA. DTA must find these in its directory or in a directory in your path.

There is a third file, DPMIINST.EXE, which you may need the first time DTA runs on a 286 PC. DTA will tell you if you need to run this program, and DPMIINST.EXE provides its own instructions when it is run. PCs using 386s, 486s, or better do not need this program. You can delete it from your hard disk after running DTA once.

Once you have added the directory in which DTA resides to your path, you can type the command

**DTA** (ENTER)

from any directory to see the copyright and command-line information screens.

# Viewing MindImages .RLE SIRDS

In this section you'll learn to run MindImages and view some inspired SIRDS using the various MindImages display modes and option settings. You will also learn how to save images to PostScript printer files.

***Figure 8-1*** The MindImages main menu offers many viewing options

## Running MindImages

First, make sure you're in the MindImages directory (\STEREO3D\MINDIMAG). Type the command

**MINDIMG2** (ENTER)

MindImages will load, display its copyright information, and ask you which drive holds your .RLE files. Press ⓒ for the C: drive (or a letter designating another drive, as appropriate). This brings you to the main menu, shown in Figure 8-1.

Press (F2). MindImages brings up its file selection screen, listing all the .RLE files in the current directory. Use the cursor arrows to highlight the filename SEASINES.RLE. Press (ENTER). MindImages clears the screen and generates the SIRDS. View it parallel. Rob Scott created this image, which demonstrates remarkable depth and very smooth gradients. Press any key to return to the main menu.

Table 8-1 lists the nine commands available on the menu. You execute these commands by pressing the indicated function key. You can also press any cursor arrow key until MindImages highlights the command you want, and then press (ENTER). To return to the main menu, press any key.

| F-Key | Command | Function |
| --- | --- | --- |
| (F1) | View RLE - Red/Green | Displays SIRDS for 3D anaglyph glasses |
| (F2) | View RLE - White/Black | Displays SIRDS for parallel or cross-eyed viewing |
| (F3) | Generate PostScript File | Makes .PS file for printing |
| (F4) | Change Drive | Used to view .RLE files on a floppy drive |
| (F5) | Normal | Toggles (F2) between parallel and cross-eyed |
| (F6) | Toggle Screen Colors | Toggles (F1) between red/green and red/blue |

*continued on next page*

*continued from previous page*

| F-Key | Command | Function |
|-------|---------|----------|
| (F7) | Adjust Density 125 | Sets (F2) black-to-white ratio, from 5 (nearly black) to 255 (nearly white) |
| (F8) | View Shape | Displays .RLE depthmap with false color substituted for the various gray levels |
| (F9) | Exit to DOS | Exits MindImages |

***Table 8-1*** MindImages main menu commands

## Try Cross-Eyed and Parallel Viewing

Press (F2), cursor to ARROWS.RLE, and press (ENTER). This Rob Scott image, shown in Figure 8-2 has a very deep, flat background with triangular arrows reaching forward. View this image parallel. Return to the main menu.

Press (F5), and notice that the (F5) menu item toggles from Normal to Inverted. Press (F2) to view ARROWS.RLE again. Figure 8-3 shows this image. If you view it parallel now, the arrows recede from a foreground plane. However, if you view it cross-eyed, you will see the same image you saw before. When you're ready to continue, return to the main menu. Press (F5) to switch the toggle back from Inverted to Normal.

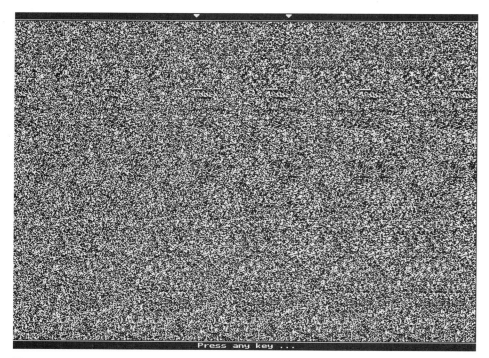

Press any key ...

***Figure 8-2*** ARROWS.RLE: A particularly deep and clear stereogram (© Rob Scott 1992)

*Figure 8-3* ARROWS.RLE, displayed inverted for cross-eyed viewing

## More White, More Black

You can adjust the ratio of black to white pixels in the image. MindImages calls this *density*. Press (F7) several times until the menu reads Adjust Density 200 instead of the default 125. Press (F2) and bring up ARROWS.RLE again. Notice that more of the pixels are white, as shown in Figure 8-4. Return to the main menu, and press (F7) several more times until the menu reads Adjust Density 50. Press (F2) and display ARROWS.RLE again. The higher black-to-white ratio means that many more of the pixels are black, as shown in Figure 8-5.

You may be surprised to discover just how few pixels it takes to create a 3D illusion. Try viewing SEASINES.RLE at a density of 250. Figure 8-6 shows this image.

You can use the (F7) density setting to match your personal viewing preference. You can also use it to control the density of your printed output if you have a PostScript printer available. When you're ready, press (F7) to return the setting to 125. This generates SIRDS with equal amounts of black and white pixels.

## Printing to PostScript

If you have access to a PostScript printer, MindImages does a great job of printing. Make sure you have set the F5 and F7 toggles the way you want. Press (F3), select the file you want to print, and press (ENTER). MindImages generates a PostScript printing file in the same directory. This file has the same root name as the .RLE file you selected, with the extension .PS.

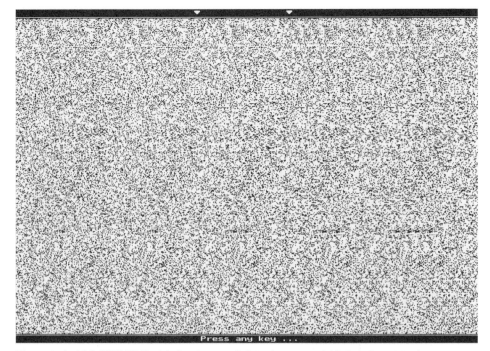

***Figure 8-4*** ARROWS.RLE with density 200, lighter than normal (© Rob Scott 1992)

***Figure 8-5*** ARROWS.RLE with density 50, darker than normal (© Rob Scott 1992)

**Figure 8-6** SEASINES.RLE displays well even with very few pixels (© Rob Scott 1992)

You can print this file to a PostScript printer from MS-DOS, with a command such as

**COPY ARROWS.PS LPT1** (ENTER)

or you can print it on a non-PostScript printer with a PostScript emulator, such as GhostScript.

## 3D Anaglyph Glasses

MindImages also displays the 3D illusion for people who can't master either cross-eyed or parallel viewing. With a pair of colored-lens 3D glasses, anyone can see the SIRDS. It doesn't matter if the glasses use red/green or red/blue lenses; MindImages supports both combinations. These glasses are available from Reel 3D. See References at the back of this book for their address.

Press (F6) to toggle the appropriate lens colors into menu command F1, and make sure you have set the F5 toggle back to Normal. Press (F1) and again display ARROWS.RLE. Look at it through your 3D glasses. The 3D illusion may not be as pronounced as when you view it parallel or cross-eyed, and it will certainly be much darker.

## Viewing SIRDS with SHIMMER

MindImages was developed fairly early in the short popular history of SIRDS. The algorithm used by the program to generate SIRDS from .RLE files has a few problems with echoes. These are visible as repeated distortion in the image which worsens as you look from left to right. Some people have reported difficulty viewing with MindImages.

However, the MindImages authors have designed it to be flexible and portable. They documented the .RLE file format well. Anyone can write their own .RLE viewer, using whatever algorithms or computer platform they prefer. You will find this .RLE file documentation in the file README.TXT in the \MINDIMAG subdirectory.

Stuart Inglis wrote his .RLE viewer, SHIMMER, to demonstrate both a new SIRDS algorithm that eliminates echoes, as well as an interesting dot-animation technique that makes SIRDS viewing easier for some people.

## Running SHIMMER

SHIMMER loads and displays one file each time you run it, but you have to know the name of the file first. To see a list of all the MindImages .RLE files in your directory, type the command

**DIR *.RLE /W** (ENTER)

Then view any of them by entering SHIM followed by the name of the file. (The MS-DOS command-line history TSR, DOSKEY, is a real labor saver with any program like this. See your MS-DOS manual for more information.)

Let's try one. Make sure you're in the directory \STEREO3D\MINDIMAG, then start SHIMMER by typing the following command:

**SHIM HELIX.RLE** (ENTER)

*Figure 8-7*  HELIX.RLE: A difficult SIRDS that SHIMMER handles well (© Rob Scott 1992)

SHIMMER first shows you the HELIX.RLE depthmap of a Rob Scott SIRDS image of a spiral and then generates the SIRDS. It beeps after completing the screen. This SIRDS causes real problems for MindImages, but SHIMMER displays it with no echoes at all, as shown in Figure 8-7.

Press (TAB) to see the convergence dots. They appear in the middle of the image, where it's easiest to lock onto them. You can toggle them on or off at any time by pressing (TAB).

## Shimmering

Now for the fun part. Press the (SPACEBAR). SHIMMER animates the screen, producing something that looks very much like an untuned TV if you look at it normally. This shimmering image, viewed parallel, is easier for many people to lock onto than a still SIRDS.

Press and hold the (+) key, and the rate of shimmering will speed up. Press and hold the (-) key, and it will slow back down again. Press the (SPACEBAR) again at any time to freeze the shimmering. Press (ESC) to exit back to MS-DOS.

# Working with DTA

Dave's Targa Animator (DTA) is a tool of many blades. DTA can read .GIF, .PCX, and .TGA files, and write MindImages .RLE files from any of them. This allows you to turn any suitable graphics image into a SIRDS depthmap and view it with MindImages or SHIMMER. In this section, you will convert an RDSdraw source file to .RLE format. Then you'll convert an .RLE depthmap to a .GIF file and to an inverted .RLE file.

## Converting RDSdraw Depthmaps to MindImages .RLE Format

RDSdraw includes a sample depthmap file called WAVES.TGA. This book's installation program puts this file in the directory \STEREO3D\RDSDRAW. Make sure that you are in the directory \STEREO3D\MINDIMAG, and type the command

**DTA \STEREO3D\RDSDRAW\WAVES.TGA /SC512,256 /FR /OWAVES.RLE** (ENTER)

This DTA command does all of the following:

- ☉ Reads the file \STEREO3D\RDSDRAW\WAVES.TGA
- ☉ Scales the file to 512x256 pixels (as MindImages requires)
- ☉ Writes it to an .RLE file called WAVES.RLE in the current directory

View the .RLE file with the command

**SHIM WAVES.RLE** (ENTER)

Figures 8-8 and 8-9 show WAVES.TGA and SHIMMER's display of the .RLE version, converted by DTA.

## Converting .RLE Files to Other Graphics Formats

DTA can also read .RLE files and write them to .TGA, .GIF, and grayscale .TIF.

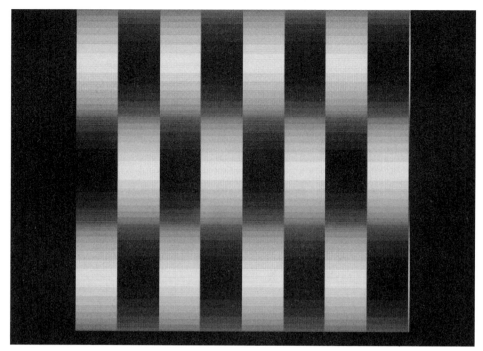

*Figure 8-8* WAVES.TGA: A depthmap from RDSdraw

*Figure 8-9* WAVES.RLE, converted by DTA, displayed by SHIMMER

To convert WHORL.RLE to an uncompressed .TGA file called WHORL.TGA, suitable for loading into RDSdraw (see Chapter 7), type the command

`DTA WHORL.RLE /FT /NC` (ENTER)

To copy all of your .RLE files to .GIF files so that you can view or edit the depthmaps in other programs, type the command

`DTA *.RLE /FG` (ENTER)

## Parallel vs. Cross-Eyed Viewing in SHIMMER

If you'd like to invert an .RLE for cross-eyed viewing in SHIMMER, DTA can do that, too. The command

`DTA WHORL.RLE /INV /FR /OWHORL2` (ENTER)

reverses all the depths in WHORL.RLE and writes a new file called WHORL2.RLE. Then you can type

`SHIM WHORL.RLE` (ENTER)

for normal parallel viewing and

`SHIM WHORL2.RLE` (ENTER)

for cross-eyed viewing.

## DTA Command Summary

DTA has many, many functions. Most of these relate to creating animation. The basic format of a DTA command line is as follows:

`DTA` *inputfilename parameters*

Table 8-2 summarizes the DTA command-line parameters that are of particular interest for converting SIRDS depthmaps.

| Parameter | Function |
|---|---|
| /F*t* | Specifies what kind of output file to write: |
| | /FG     .GIF file |
| | /FR     .RLE file |
| | /FT     .TGA file |
| /NC | Specifies no compression on .TGA files; useful for compatibility. |
| /B*n* | Number of bits per pixel in .TGA files; default is 24. Valid values for *n* are 8, 16, 24, and 32. |
| /O*n* | Specifies the name of the output file. DTA defaults to writing a file with the same root name as the source file. /OFILENAME writes a file called FILENAME instead. The file extension is taken from the /F*t* parameter. |

*continued on next page*

*continued from previous page*

| Parameter | Function |
|---|---|
| /SCx,y | Specifies the size, in pixels, of the output file. /SC512,256 writes a file 512 pixels wide and 256 pixels tall; .RLE files must be no larger than 512x256, and each dimension must be one of these values: 64, 128, 256, or 512. |
| /Gn | Converts a color image to grayscale with specified number of levels. Valid values for *n* are 4, 8, 16, 32, 64, and 128. /G without a number makes a 256-level grayscale image. |
| /INV | Inverts all the colors in the output file. Black becomes white, light gray becomes dark gray, red becomes cyan, etc. |

**Table 8-2** Selected DTA commands

## Tips and Pitfalls

MindImages .RLE files were designed, as a compact way to transfer files for onscreen viewing. Its developers limited the resolution to 512 by 256 pixels and the depth to 64 levels. This means there's no particular reason to use high-resolution images as sources for .RLE files. Programs can extrapolate higher-resolution SIRDS from these files. MindImages does this when it writes a PostScript printer file.

The general rules for all single-image stereogram depthmaps apply to MindImages .RLE files, as well. Chapter 9 discusses these guidelines in greater detail.

## What's Next?

In this chapter, you learned about the MindImages .RLE depthmap file format. You met two programs, MindImages and SHIMMER, that view this format. You also learned how to use DTA to convert your own graphics files to the compact and portable .RLE format.

In the next chapter you will learn how to generate high-resolution single-image stereograms from your own files, using RDSGEN.

*Chapter 9*

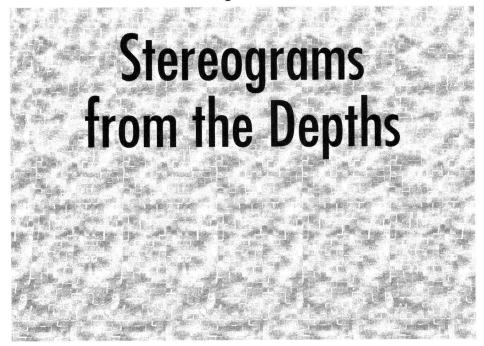

# Stereograms from the Depths

**M**ost computer pictures contain information representing the color at each point in the image. Depthmaps, however, are a special class of computer pictures. In a depthmap each point in the image represents the distance from the viewer, forming a map of depths. A typical depthmap is simply a picture in which the near areas of the scene are lighter than the far areas. You can create a depthmap with almost any graphics program. That's the easy part. Turning a depthmap into a single-image stereogram is the hard part. That's where RDSGEN comes in.

There is no one "right way" to generate a single-image stereogram from a depthmap. Each method has its strengths and flaws, and each image has its own special needs. A wide selection of tools comes in very handy. Using them is a trial-and-error process of tweaking parameters and changing options.

In this chapter you'll find examples using RDSGEN to make SIRDS and image-mapped single-image stereograms. Image-mapped stereograms are composed of imaginative color and grayscale patterns instead of random dots. These are the stereograms that are sold commercially in poster shops, and in books such as *Magic Eye: A New Way of Seeing the World* (Andrews and McMeel, 1993).

The chapter also includes an RDSGEN command-line reference section, and a discussion of how to create depthmaps with paint programs.

# About RDSGEN

RDSGEN is a command-line program that produces single-image random-dot stereograms (SIRDS) and image-mapped single-image stereograms from .TGA and .GIF files. The program includes four different algorithms for stereogram creation, and many options.

The C source code for this program is freely available, making RDSGEN a good test bed for new ideas and algorithms if you're interested in programming. The archived file RDSGEN.ZIP contains the original source, documentation, and examples for RDSGEN, as well as the source for the modified version of RDSGEN included with this book and used in this chapter. This version of RDSGEN incorporates a few bug fixes and a cleaned-up information screen. This book's installation program puts the file RDSGEN.ZIP in the directory \STEREO3D\RDSGEN.

## Licensing Information

RDSGEN is free software written by Frederic N. Feucht. You can reach the author on CompuServe at address 74020,407. From the Internet, use 74020.407@compuserve.com.

## System Requirements

RDSGEN runs on any MS-DOS PC. It does not require graphics hardware or a math coprocessor. It can use a CGA, EGA, or VGA video card to display images of specific sizes while processing.

## Installation

This book's installation program puts the RDSGEN program in the directory \STEREO3D. You should add this directory to your PATH statement so you can use RDSGEN from various directories. If you don't want to modify your AUTOEXEC.BAT, you can move all the files in this directory to a directory already in your path. No other setup is needed.

# SIRDS from Depthmaps

This section walks you through the process of creating SIRDS from a depthmap, using various RDSGEN parameter settings. You'll be able to observe the results as you go, because RDSGEN can display SIRDS as it creates them, as long as the source file is a suitable size. The examples in this section require a VGA video card.

---

**Please note:** In order for you to view stereograms in RDSGEN, its video driver file (EGAVGA.BGI or CGA.BGI) must reside in the current directory. This means that you must copy these files into the current directory from the \STEREO3D directory. Before you try the examples in this section, change to the drive where you have installed \STEREO3D, then type these commands at the DOS prompt:

```
CD \STEREO3D\RDSGEN  (ENTER)
COPY \STEREO3D\*.BGI  (ENTER)
```

---

The command-line history TSR, DOSKEY, is highly recommended for the exercises in this chapter. See your MS-DOS manual for details.

## Make a SIRDS

Change to the directory where the RDSGEN example files are located. This book's installation program put them in \STEREO3D\RDSGEN. Type the command

```
RDSGEN OVAL.GIF TEST1.GIF –V –I ENTER
```

RDSGEN reads the file OVAL.GIF, makes a SIRDS from it, and writes it to the file TEST1.GIF. The –V tells RDSGEN to display the image onscreen as it is created, and the –I tells the program to put convergence marks at the top of the image. The rest of RDSGEN's settings remain at their default values.

The depthmap shown in Figure 9-1 was easily created with oval-shaped gradient fills in a paint program. (This chapter ends with a discussion of paint program depthmaps.)

RDSGEN sounds a tone when the SIRDS is completed, and pauses. When you've finished examining this image, any keypress clears the screen and takes you back to DOS.

## Make a Smoother SIRDS

Now let's run the same depthmap through RDSGEN with a few different parameters. (Here's where DOSKEY comes in real handy: If you're running DOSKEY, you can simply press ⤊ and edit the last line. Sure beats typing it all over again.) Type

```
RDSGEN OVAL.GIF TEST2.GIF –V –I –A1 –F6 –D20 ENTER
```

This SIRDS, written to the file TEST2.GIF, uses algorithm 1 (–A1), shallower depth (–F6), and fewer black dots (–D20). The shallower depth isn't as spectacular, but it results in smoother contours and easier viewing, as you can see in Figure 9-2.

***Figure 9-1*** OVAL.GIF: A depthmap from simple gradient fills in a paint program

***Figure 9-2*** RDSGEN SIRDS from OVAL.GIF

***Figure 9-3*** SEE3D.GIF: A depthmap with extreme level changes

## Try One with Some Text

The smooth gradients in OVAL.GIF make a good SIRDS. Hard contours, on the other hand, and large changes in adjacent levels present more difficulties for SIRDS programs. For instance, Figure 9-3 shows the depthmap SEE3D.GIF.

To generate the SIRDS, type

```
RDSGEN SEE3D.GIF TEST3.GIF -V -I -A1 (ENTER)
```

***Figure 9-4***  The SIRDS from SEE3D.GIF: too deep and off-center

The SIRDS that appears (shown in Figure 9-4), contains extreme combinations of depth, which make difficult viewing. It's almost impossible to hold the letter *D* and the background behind it in focus at the same time. Also notice that the left edge of the letter *S* is cut off.

You can fix these problems by typing

```
RDSGEN SEE3D.GIF TEST4.GIF -V -I -A1 -F4 -Y40 (ENTER)
```

As shown in Figure 9-5, the shallower depth (–F4) makes more comfortable viewing. Shifting the depthmap 40 pixels (–Y40) centers it, and rescues the letter *S* from oblivion.

# Image Mapping

Have you had enough fun with random dots? Want to make pictures like those posters in the bookstores and the mall? It's time to try image mapping.

You need to have a way to produce .GIF files to use this feature, so we assume here that you have some kind of graphics file viewing software.

## Noisy Words of Cork

In this next set of exercises, you will generate stereograms from two .GIF files using a number of different parameters. Start by typing the command

```
RDSGEN SEE3D.GIF TEST5.GIF -I -A1 -F4 -Y40 -MCORK.GIF (ENTER)
```

***Figure 9-5***  The SIRDS from SEE3D.GIF with depth and position corrected

Instead of creating its own random dots, RDSGEN reads from the file CORK.GIF (–MCORK.GIF), and uses the pixels it finds there to make the new image.

In your favorite image viewer, load up the output image, TEST5.GIF, and take a look. TEST5.GIF is presented here in grayscale as Figure 9-6.

The left edge of this image shows a nice cork texture. RDSGEN works progressively across the depthmap. When depth levels remain constant or increase, it copies previous pixels according to the algorithm in use. When depth levels decrease, it gets new pixels from the image map file as needed. By the time it reaches the right edge, enough inappropriate new pixels have been included so that all trace of the cork texture is gone, except at the top and bottom edges. One of the reasons RDSGEN has so many parameters is to help you defeat this type of noise in a stereogram.

## Cleaner Cork

Fix the noise by typing this command:

```
RDSGEN SEE3D.GIF TEST6.GIF –I –A2 –F4 –MCORK.GIF –O370  (ENTER)
```

Algorithm 2 (–A2) produces a little less depth than algorithm 1, but handles extreme level changes more gracefully. RDSGEN begins processing in the middle of the image (–O370 means 370 pixels into the 640-pixel-wide file), and works both left and right from there. This alone cuts introduced noise in half, because the noise accumulates dur-

***Figure 9-6*** Image-mapped stereogram with bad noise

ing the process. Beginning in the middle means the program only has to process half as far before reaching the edge. Algorithm 2 also centers the depthmap itself, so the depthmap offset (–Y) got dropped, as well.

View the results in the output file TEST6.GIF, shown in Figure 9-7. The noise has decreased tremendously. Now, however, you may detect some echo artifacts. The letter *S* is marked by stripes echoing the left edge of the letter *E*. The background trailing the *3* and the *D* show echoes of those characters, as well.

A side effect of the algorithm offset (–O) is that it also offsets the starting position in the image map. In this case, it uses a less interesting area of the CORK.GIF file. CORK.GIF was scanned from the author's bulletin board with a hand scanner, and the center is somewhat washed out.

## Cleaner Still

Now beat all these bugs by typing

```
RDSGEN SEE3D.GIF TEST7.GIF -I -A2 -F6 -MCORK.GIF -O370 -X300 -E -W7 ENTER
```

This shifts CORK.GIF to the right 300 pixels (–X300) before mapping, so the best section of the image map is back in action.

Instead of bringing in new, unrelated pixels for receding surfaces, RDSGEN uses pixel extrapolation to stretch copied pixels over the new areas (–E). This produces yet another

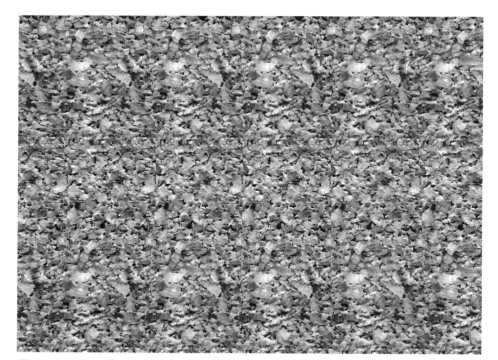

***Figure 9-7*** Better, but now it's got some echoes

***Figure 9-8*** The image-mapped cork stereogram, all cleaned up

artifact, pixel streaking, but not too badly. The streaking is visible at the edges of the output file TEST8.GIF, shown in grayscale as Figure 9-8. This RDSGEN command line also widens the convergence strip width by telling RDSGEN the monitor is smaller (–W7). This reduces the number of times pixels get copied across the image, which further minimizes all the artifacts.

# RDSGEN Reference

Here is the RDSGEN command-line syntax:

```
RDSGEN depthmapfilename outputfilename options
```

You can press (ESC) to bail out of the program early.
Table 9-1 defines the various options.

| Command | Default | Range | Explanation |
|---|---|---|---|
| –An | 2 | 1 to 4 | Choice of algorithm |
| –C | B/W | | Color dots instead of black and white |
| –Dn | 50 | 0 to 100 | Dot density; percentage of black pixels |
| –E | | | Extrapolate missing pixels (except with –A3) |
| –Fn | 2 | 1 to 16 | Depth scaling; lower values make greater depth |
| –I | | | Include indexing triangles at convergence strip width |
| –Mfilename | | *.GIF | Image mapped, must be .GIF with same dimensions as depthmap |
| –N | | | Negative depthmap, where black is closest |
| –On | 0 | 0 to width –1 | Offset origin of algorithm by n pixels (not with –A3) |
| –Rn | 1 | 1 to 32767 | Seed random generator; produces different dot patterns |
| –Sn | 8 | 1 to width | Number of strips; sets convergence strip width (only with –A1) |
| –T | | | 24-bit .TGA type 2 output, instead of .GIF |
| –V | | | Show preview display, specific sizes only, dots only |
| –Wn | 10 | 2 to 120 | Output width in inches; sets convergence strip width (not with –A1) |
| –Xn | 0 | 0 to width | Offset background map file by n pixels |
| –Yn | 0 | 0 to width | Offset depthmap source file, use ½ strip width with –A1 |

*Table 9-1* RDSGEN command-line options

# Tips and Pitfalls

The only way to really learn the ins and outs of RDSGEN is to supply it with lots of depthmaps and image maps and observe the results. Here's a collection of notes about some of the program's quirks and strengths.

## Algorithm 1 is Different

RDSGEN includes a choice of four algorithms for creating stereograms from depthmaps. The behavior of algorithm 1 is different from 2, 3, and 4 in several ways. Algorithm 1 produces more depth for a given –F (depth scale) setting. A command line such as

```
RDSGEN FOO.GIF BAR.GIF -A1 -F4 ENTER
```

produces the same apparent depth as

```
RDSGEN FOO.GIF BAR.GIF -A2 -F3 ENTER
```

Table 9-2 is a conversion chart that will help adjust depth settings when you switch between algorithms.

| –A1 | –A2, –A3, –A4 | |
| --- | --- | --- |
| –F2 | no match | |
| –F3 | –F2 | ↑ |
| –F4 | –F3 | Increasing |
| –F5, F6 | –F4 | depth |
| –F7 | –F5 | ↑ |
| –F8 | –F6, F7 | |

*Table 9-2* Key to depth settings of algorithms

## Specifying Convergence Strip Width

You have learned that the maximum distance between repetitions in an image is called the convergence strip width—the widest spread that your eyes have to converge to view this image. Pixels making up the deepest possible level repeat at this interval, and index marks are usually this distance apart. If the convergence strip width is too wide, you may not be able to converge the image and view the 3D illusion. If it is too small, you will tend to hyperconverge the image, which also makes it difficult to view. The ideal width for parallel viewing varies from person to person, depending on the distance between your eyes.

RDSGEN initially assumes that you are viewing a 10″-wide image on a 12″ computer monitor, and that you want a convergence strip width of 1.2″. Obviously, however, images can be any dimensions, and you may find 1.2″ spacing a bit narrow. The author likes convergence strip widths between 1.5″ and 2″. Everyone's comfortable range is different, and many variables affect the ease of viewing an image. Also, your particular output needs may not allow an ideal strip width. For instance, the images in Figures 9-9 and 9-10 can't use a 2″ convergence strip width because they're only 2.5″ wide. Even with a

.75″ strip, they view well and are not particularly prone to hyperconvergence. Trial and error is the rule here; viewing the completed image is the final test.

If you want to specify the convergence strip width directly, there are two different procedures depending on your choice of algorithms.

Algorithm 1 uses the –S setting to set the convergence strip width. You tell RDSGEN how many convergence strip widths fit across the image. The default, –S8, 8 strips on a 10″ image, makes a convergence strip width of 10/8 or 1.2″. In understanding these values, bear in mind that your convergence strip width equals the width of the image divided by the –S strip number. An 1,800-pixel-wide depthmap called BIGMAP.GIF, for example, going to a 300-dpi laser printer produces an image that is 1,800/300 or 6″ wide. If you want a 1.5″ convergence strip width in this 6″ print, you need 6/1.5 or 4 strips. So you type this command:

**RDSGEN BIGMAP.GIF PRINTME.GIF –A1 –S4** (ENTER)

Algorithms 2, 3, and 4 use –W for the same purpose. You tell RDSGEN the width of your physical output (monitor or printed page) in inches. RDSGEN produces an image that will have a 1.2″ convergence strip width when displayed at the size you specify. Your convergence strip width, in pixels, equals 1.2 divided by the –W value, times the width of the image in pixels.

Thus, to get RDSGEN's default 1.2″ convergence strip width in the printed output described above, you type this command:

**RDSGEN BIGMAP.GIF PRINTME.GIF –A2 –W6** (ENTER)

To get a larger convergence strip width, you tell RDSGEN that you have a smaller output in mind. For a 1.8″ convergence strip width, you say your output is (1.2/1.8)*6, or 4″. The new command line is

**RDSGEN BIGMAP.GIF PRINTME.GIF –A2 –W4** (ENTER)

Table 9-3 lists equivalent settings for the different algorithms on various output sizes.

| Choice of Algorithm | | Convergence Strip Width for Output Width of: | | |
| --- | --- | --- | --- | --- |
| –A1 | –A2, –A3, –A4 | 8″ (Printed Page) | 10″ (14″ Monitor) | 12″ (17″ Monitor) |
| | –W2 | 5.4″ | 6″ | 8″ |
| –S2 | | 4″ | 5″ | 6″ |
| | –W3 | 3.2″ | 4″ | 4.8″ |
| –S3 | –W4 | 2.7″ | 3″ | 4″ |
| –S4 | –W5 | 2″ | 2.5″ | 3″ |
| –S5 | –W6 | 1.6″ | 2″ | 2.4″ |
| –S6 | –W8 | 1.2″ | 1.5″ | 2″ |
| –S7 | –W9 | 1.1″ | 1.3″ | 1.7″ |
| –S8 | –W10 | 1″ | 1.2″ (default) | 1.5″ |

*continued on next page*

*continued from previous page*

| Choice of Algorithm | | Convergence Strip Width for Output Width of: | | |
|---|---|---|---|---|
| **–A1** | **–A2, –A3, –A4** | **8″**<br>**(Printed Page)** | **10″**<br>**(14″ Monitor)** | **12″**<br>**(17″ Monitor)** |
| –S9 | –W11 | .9″ | 1.1″ | 1.3″ |
| –S10 | –W12 | .8″ | 1″ | 1.2″ |
| –S11 | –W13 | .7″ | .9″ | 1.1″ |
| –S12 | –W15 | .7″ | .8″ | 1″ |
| –S13 | –W17 | .6″ | .7″ | .9″ |

*Table 9-3* Convergence strip width chart

Algorithm 1 is the only one of the four that doesn't center the depthmap automatically. Center it yourself by using the –Y parameter, set to half of the image's convergence strip width as measured in pixels. For instance, the –A1 –S4 BIGMAP.GIF example has a strip width of 1,800/4 or 450 pixels. You would center it with this command:

```
RDSGEN BIGMAP.GIF PRINTME.GIF –A1 –S4 –Y225  (ENTER)
```

## Algorithmic Quirks

Algorithms 2 and 4 produce nearly identical output. There are mathematical differences in the way the geometry is interpreted from the depthmap, but they're pretty subtle.

Algorithm 3 does not take advantage of pixel extrapolation (–E) or depthmap offset (–O). Also, it processes from right to the left. You can run the other algorithms right to left, too, by using an origin offset (–O) equal to the image width minus 1. So, for an 1800-pixel-wide depthmap, the command line

```
RDSGEN BIGMAP.GIF PRINTME.GIF –A2 –W4 –O1799  (ENTER)
```

tells RDSGEN to start processing at the right edge and proceed from right to left.

Pixel extrapolation (–E) fails with extreme depth-level changes and low depth-scaling (–F) values. The symptoms of failure are solid horizontal lines across sections of the image.

SIRDS display (–V) works only with dots and a few specific image sizes. With a VGA display, RDSGEN can preview images that are exactly

- ✪ 320x200
- ✪ 640x200
- ✪ 640x350
- ✪ 640x480

Colored dots (–C) don't use the dot density value (–D). As noted earlier, the –V parameter will work only if the appropriate RDSGEN video driver (EGAVGA.BGI or CGA.BGI) is in the current directory. You can copy the driver from the \STEREO3D directory.

## File Format Considerations

RDSGEN can read .GIF and uncompressed .TGA files. It generates .GIF files by default, and 24-bit type-2 .TGA files if you use the –T parameter.

Image mapping (–M) requires a .GIF file map image the same dimensions as the source depthmap.

DTA, as discussed in Chapter 8, proves very useful for converting other file formats to meet RDSGEN's requirements. It's also handy for resizing imagemap files to match depthmap files. For example, the command

```
DTA FOO.TGA /SCF640,480 /DF /FG /OIMAGE.GIF  ENTER
```

reads a file called FOO.TGA and turns it into a 640x480 256-color file named IMAGE.GIF, suitable for use as an RDSGEN image map. FOO.TGA can be 16-, 24-, or 32-bit color, or 8-bit grayscale, compressed or uncompressed. DTA will perform the same conversions from .PCX, .GIF, and .BMP files.

# Depthmaps from Paint Programs

In one sense, depthmaps are just pictures. There's no difference between the file format of OVAL.GIF, a depthmap used in one of the earlier examples, and any other .GIF picture. Yet, in another sense, they're entirely different because each point in a depthmap is colored according to its depth.

In this section, you'll see how depthmaps work, and how you can create your own depthmap using any paint or draw program.

## Depthmap Formats

The most common depthmap format uses 256 shades of gray, from white (nearest the viewer) to black (farthest away). This is not universal, however. Other formats reverse the order so that black is nearest. Some software may expect a .GIF depthmap in which the color map index of a pixel, rather than the color itself, indicates how deep a pixel should appear. Polyray (Chapter 11) can output a .TGA depthmap file that uses the red byte and the green byte to hold the integer and fractional parts of a 16-bit depthmap. However, 16 bits holds 65,000 levels, far more than any SIRDS can use, so this format is overkill for our purposes.

RDSGEN accepts several depthmap formats. The 256-gray format is the most easily read and interpreted visually, and holds plenty of levels. Your author recommends it exclusively.

## Creating Depthmaps by Hand

Think of a depthmap as simply a gray picture. You can make a depthmap in nearly any graphics program, including paint programs, fractal programs, renderers, ray tracers, image editors, even charting and graphing programs. If a program only produces color output, you can convert it to gray with DTA's /G switch.

Many paint programs provide an effect called a gradient fill, which produces beautiful depthmaps. In its simplest form, the gradient fill covers a selected area with a smooth transition from one color to another. Figure 9-9 shows a very simple depthmap and the

***Figure 9-9*** A simple depthmap and SIRDS using a linear fill

SIRDS it produces. This depthmap started with a solid black fill. A linear gradient fill from white down to black, applied to a selected rectangle, becomes a ramp in the SIRDS.

In many paint programs you have access to circular, rectangular, elliptical, or polygonal fills. Even vector-based drawing programs such as CorelDRAW and Microsoft PowerPoint can be used. For instance, draw an object, use CorelDRAW's powerful shading and gradient tools, and export it as a .GIF file at whatever size you need. You can take a cue for another approach from the separate levels drawn in RDSdraw. Draw solid-colored objects in shades of gray, and keep in mind that darker is deeper. If you have Windows, you have Windows Paintbrush, which is fine for this style of drawing. Paintbrush also gives you access to the TrueType fonts available on your system.

Gaussian Blur, Blur Heavily, Blur More, Smooth: These tools are all friends of the depthmap creator. Figure 9-10 shows a depthmap and SIRDS that began as a black background with three identical white rectangles. The top one was left alone, and it appears in the SIRDS as a flat plate floating in front of the background. Picture Publisher's Image|Effects|Smooth tool was applied several times to the middle rectangle, resulting in the 3D object sitting on the background. Then the Image|Effects|Gaussian Blur tool was applied several times to the the bottom rectangle. This produced the illusion of a rounded mound pushed up from the background. Simple tools, simple objects...very different effects.

## Depthmaps from RDSdraw

RDSdraw (Chapter 7) provides several tools for drawing objects with gradients. These gradients appear in various colors onscreen. However, when you save a drawing file in

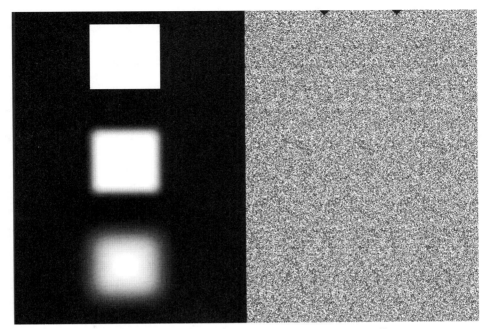

***Figure 9-10*** Picture Publisher's Smooth and Blur tools produce interesting effects

RDSdraw, it actually writes a grayscale depthmap. This depthmap, written as a 572x465, 8-bit .TGA file, makes a perfect source file for RDSGEN. You can resize it as needed with DTA. For instance, to create a 640x480 file called DEPTH.GIF from an RDSdraw saved file, you use the command line

```
DTA NONAME.TGA /SCF640,480 /FG /ODEPTH ENTER
```

This file's dimensions work with RDSGEN's preview display. As a side benefit, the file size typically reduces from 265K to 15K!

Generate a SIRDS from the new file with a command line such as

```
RDSGEN DEPTH.GIF TEST.GIF -V -I -A1 -F3 -D30 ENTER
```

A SIRDS generated with this command line appears deeper than the SIRDS that RDSdraw produces from the same file.

# What's Next?

RDSGEN is complex and powerful, but once you master it, you can easily perform the task of turning depthmaps into stereograms. You can also make interesting depthmaps with any paint or draw program. But what if you want something really wild and organic? What if you're not so good at drawing with a mouse? No problem. The next chapter shows you how to create depthmaps using the popular freeware fractal program, Fractint.

*Chapter 10*

# Fractint Depthmaps

*A*s Chapter 9 demonstrated, it's easy to make single-image stereograms from depthmaps. *Fractals*, which are intricate pictures generated from simple mathematical formulae, make excellent depthmaps. Before you tackle this chapter about fractals, make sure you understand the concept of depthmaps described in Chapter 9, and how RDSGEN turns them into single-image stereograms.

Fractint is a delightful fractal-generation program. This chapter assumes that you already have Fractint and are somewhat familiar with it. Fractint is not included with this book, but it is freeware and easy to find. Although the examples used here are for Fractint version 18.2, the principles we discuss apply to any DOS version. Be aware that the Windows version of Fractint doesn't have the palette editor used in this chapter.

Even if you have never heard of fractals, you should flip to the end of this chapter now and look at the minigallery of examples. They may inspire you to seek out your own copy of Fractint. Some of the images in the Chapter 4 Gallery use Fractint depthmaps, as well.

## About Fractint

Fractint is written by The Stone Soup Group. This dedicated group of programmers meets on CompuServe in the Graphic Developer's forum (where the POV-Ray developers also hang out). At the time of this writing, Fractint lives in library 4 of Go GRAPHDEV under the filename FRAINT.EXE. You can also find it on many BBSs.

If you'd like to get a copy of Fractint, with complete documentation and a CD full of the best fractal GIFs, Tim Wegner and Bert Tyler, two of Fractint's authors, have written a wonderful book called *Fractal Creations, Second Edition* (Waite Group Press, 1993, ISBN 1-878739-34-4). Although it gives the program the in-depth treatment it deserves, the book does not discuss the use of Fractint to produce depthmaps for SIRDS generation. This chapter fills that gap.

Fractint is freeware, copyrighted by The Stone Soup Group. You can reach the primary authors on CompuServe at the following addresses: Bert Tyler 73477,433; Timothy Wegner 71320,675.

# Formulae, Types, .PARs, and .MAPs

Fractint generates fractal images from mathematical formulae. You don't need to know those formulae, because you can pick them off a list in the program. This list is the Fractal Types menu, activated by pressing (T) within the program. Each of the examples in this chapter mentions what formula the fractal came from, in case you want to go hunting for similar images.

When you find a fractal that you want to save, you have two choices. If you want to use the fractal as a depthmap or view it in another program, press (S) to save the entire onscreen fractal image to a .GIF file. If you just want to return to that same point in Fractint at another time, you can press (B) to save a .PAR file. This small text file contains all the parameters that Fractint needs to re-create the fractal at whatever resolution you choose.

Finding an interesting fractal is only half of the Fractint game. You can color a fractal in various ways to produce wildly different effects. Once you've made a color scheme that you like, you can save it independently of the fractal, so that you can apply it to other fractals. This color map file is called a .MAP and is saved and loaded from inside the (E) palette editor.

# Palette Editing

This section walks through two examples in which you load a suitable fractal from a .PAR file and modify its color map to produce a good depthmap. The next section presents examples of fractals that make good and bad depthmaps, with a discussion of the reasons why.

## Installing the Example Files

This book includes 17 .PAR and .MAP files used in the examples in this chapter. The book's installation program puts these files in the directory \STEREO3D\FRACTINT. If your Fractint directory is in your DOS PATH, then you can run these examples in \STEREO3D\FRACTINT. Otherwise, you'll need to change to the directory where you keep Fractint, and copy the book's example .MAP and .PAR files into your Fractint directory. To do this, type these commands from your Fractint directory:

```
COPY \STEREO3D\FRACTINT\*.PAR (ENTER)
COPY \STEREO3D\FRACTINT\*.MAP (ENTER)
```

If your copy of Fractint lives on a different drive than the one in which you installed the book's files, you'll need to specify the installed drive in the preceding commands. For example, if your Fractint directory is D:\FRACTINT and you installed the book's files to drive C, you need to change to the directory D:\FRACTINT, and type

```
COPY C:\STEREO3D\FRACTINT\*.PAR (ENTER)
COPY C:\STEREO3D\FRACTINT\*.MAP (ENTER)
```

The examples require the Fractint formula file FRACTINT.FRM that comes with Fractint.

## Loading an Image from a .PAR File

To load the first example fractal, fire up Fractint with the command

```
FRACTINT (ENTER)
```

Then perform the following steps:

1. Press (@) to bring up the Load .PAR screen.
2. Press (F6) to select a new .PAR file. Select the file RDSMAPS.PAR.
3. Press (ENTER) to load the .PAR file. Select the .PAR called Example01.
4. Press (ENTER) to get to the main menu.
5. Press (ENTER) again to bring up the Video Mode Selection Screen.
6. Choose a good 256-color video mode for your system, such as 640x480 with 256 colors.
7. Press (ENTER) to generate the fractal.

**Note:** These example screens all use 1024x768, 256-color mode, but that may take too long on some computers. If this is your first encounter with Fractint, see your Fractint documentation for help with video modes.

This first image, shown in Figure 10-1, is a few zooms deep in the Phoenix formula. Imagine this picture in 3D. Can you tell which points are highest?

## Loading a .MAP

Fractint's default colors are nice to look at, but they offer you little clue as to how they will map to depth values. The 16 .MAP files provided with this book contain only shades

***Figure 10-1*** Where's the highest point in this picture?

of gray in various arrangements. Mapping a fractal in gray produces an image in which you can visually interpret shade as depth, in the same way the stereogram software will. The gray maps provided with the book are discussed in detail at the end of this chapter.

Press Ⓔ now to enter Palette Editing mode. Fractint shows the outline of the palette-editing frame in its default position, in the upper-left corner of the screen. This position works well for this image. You can move the frame with your mouse or cursor arrows if it ever obscures an interesting part of the image. Press ⒺⓃⓉⒺⓇ now to display the editing frame with the default palette.

Press Ⓛ to load a .MAP file. Select RDS04CLB.MAP, which is a file you copied from the directory \STEREO3D\FRACTINT. Press ⒺⓃⓉⒺⓇto load this gray map. The results, shown in Figure 10-2, are gray but not very satisfying as a depthmap. The lighter a pixel, the closer to the viewer it appears in the stereogram. Thus the white spiral would stand out alone from a deep background, essentially producing two levels. The busy white spirals that are off the main one contribute small details that would become distracting noise in the stereogram, without adding any interest.

## Using the Palette Editor

The procedure for making an interesting depthmap from this fractal involves a few simple manipulations of the palette.

*1.* Use your mouse or cursor arrows to position the palette cursor in the lower-left corner of the image. The active register (in the upper-left corner of the palette-editing frame) should be a light gray with values R57, G57, B57. The eighth index in the palette should be highlighted as in Figure 10-2.

*2.* Rotate the palette with the Ⓒ (comma) and Ⓒ (period) keys on the keyboard until the eighth index and the active register are white, with the values R63, G63, B63, as shown in Figure 10-3. This will be the highest point in the map and the nearest level in the SIRDS. Now, wrapped around the spiral, you have a lovely smooth gradient from white to black.

*3.* The original white spiral, which at first seemed to be the focus of the image, clearly belongs in the background. To put it there, you just need to change its color and

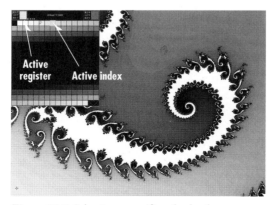

*Figure 10-2* Selecting a specific color level

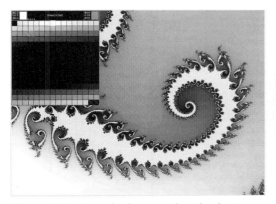

**Figure 10-3** Rotated palette, so selected index is brightest

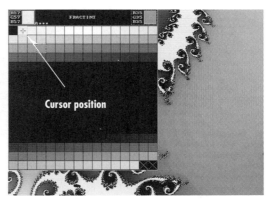

**Figure 10-4** Selecting the background index

position the palette cursor on the second index in the palette frame. The active register should show the values R57, G57, B57, as shown in Figure 10-4.

4. Set the active register to black as shown in Figure 10-5, by pressing (R), (0), (G), (0), (B), (0). There you are: The original white spiral is now black and will appear on the background depth level of the SIRDS. As a bonus, the busy edges of the main spiral now blend nicely into the dark areas around them.

5. Press (ESC) to leave Palette Editing mode. Press (X) to bring up the Options screen, then change the default save filename from FRACT001 to DEPTH001. Press (ESC) to return to the image.

6. Press (S) to save this image, shown in Figure 10-6, as a .GIF depthmap file.

Figure 10-7 shows a SIRDS produced from this depthmap by RDSGEN. As described in Chapter 9, the actual command line you feed to RDSGEN depends on the resolution of your Fractint .GIF and the final displayed size of the SIRDS you want to generate.

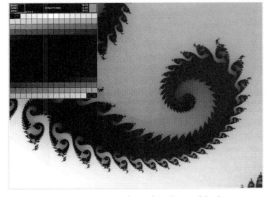

**Figure 10-5** Setting a selected index to black

**Figure 10-6** Example01 with a good gray depthmap palette

***Figure 10-7*** SIRDS generated from Example01 depthmap

# Range and Gamma

The .MAP files included with this book are a good place to start, but most images' palettes require fine-tuning to produce the best output. The Fractint palette editor's Range and Gamma functions aid this tweaking tremendously.

Range, applied to a gray map, creates a smoothly shaded range of grays between the two active registers in the palette editor. This behaves somewhat like the 3D objects in RDSdraw (Chapter 7) or the gradient fills discussed in Chapter 9. The end result is a smooth level change in the depthmap.

Gamma helps you control exactly how the levels change. With the default gamma value, 1, Fractint divides up the range equally, producing a mathematically linear gradient. Higher or lower gamma values shift the middle of the gradient toward one end of the range, so that levels change faster in one area and slower in another. By adjusting gamma, you can control the curve of slopes in your stereogram.

This next example applies three different gamma values to the same range in a fractal.

1. Press (@) to bring up the Load .PAR screen. Select and load the .PAR called EXAMPLE02 in the file RDSMAPS.PAR. This image, shown in grayscale in Figure 10-8, is generated from the Formula AltMTet type.

2. Press (E) and (ENTER) to enter Palette Editing mode. Press (L) to bring up the Load Map screen, and select RDS02CLF.MAP. Press (ENTER) to load this gray palette, shown in Figure 10-9.

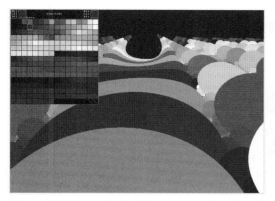

**Figure 10-8** Example02: A Formula AltMTet fractal with the default palette

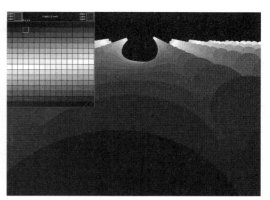

**Figure 10-9** The Example02 fractal with RDS02CLF.MAP

3. Move the cursor to the bottom of the image. Press Ⓙ to rotate the palette until the active index is white, values R63, G63, B63. Press (SPACEBAR) to mark the high end of the active palette range, as shown in Figure 10-10.

4. Move the cursor to the white background at the top of the image. Set it to black, as shown in Figure 10-11, by pressing Ⓡ, Ⓞ, Ⓑ, Ⓞ, Ⓖ, Ⓞ.

5. Move the cursor into the palette-editing frame, to the black index in the first column of the ninth row. Press the (SPACEBAR) to mark the low end of the active palette range, as shown in Figure 10-12.

Figure 10-13 shows the SIRDS produced from the image at this point. Later, to generate this yourself, you can press (ESC) to leave Palette Editing mode, Ⓢ to save the image, and (ESC) to quit Fractint. Then you can run RDSGEN on the saved image. Don't do that right now, though: The fun part is coming up.

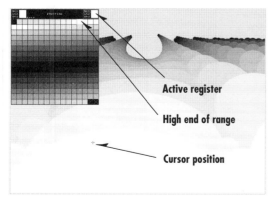

**Figure 10-10** Rotated palette, with high end of range marked

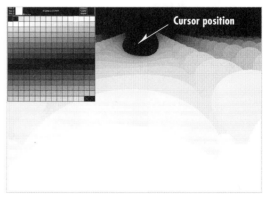

**Figure 10-11** Setting the background to black

Now let's set a higher gamma value. Press Ⓜ to bring up the Gamma Editing dialog and enter 1.5. Press (ENTER) to return to the image, then press ⊜ to create a smooth gradient in the active palette range you marked.

Notice, as shown in Figure 10-14, that the palette shifts. The marked ends of the range don't change, but the steps become larger at the white end and smaller at the black end. For comparison, press Ⓤ to undo the smoothing and ⊜ to redo it.

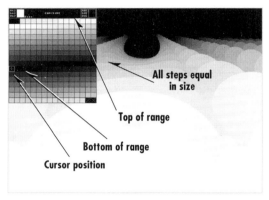

*Figure 10-12*   Marking the low end of range

*Figure 10-13*   SIRDS produced from Figure 10-12

Figure 10-15 shows the SIRDS produced by the image at this point. The near levels have much more separation than those in Figure 10-13, but the positions of the nearest and farthest levels are unchanged.

Next, set a lower gamma value. Press (M) and enter a new gamma value of 0.6. Press (ENTER) to return to the image, and (=) to smooth the active range with gamma 0.6. The palette, as shown in Figure 10-16, shifts back the other way. The white levels are now very close and there are more of them.

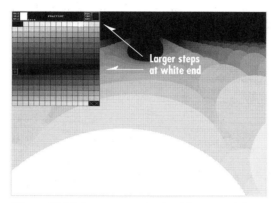

*Figure 10-14* Separate near levels with gamma 1.5

*Figure 10-15* SIRDS produced from Figure 10-14

Figure 10-17 shows the SIRDS produced by the image at this point. The near gradients are much smoother, with a faster and steeper fall-off at the back of the image. Compare this to Figures 10-13 and 10-15.

# Fractint Minigallery

This section reproduces some example fractals and the SIRDS they create. This by no means covers the full range of suitable fractal types, however. Fractint yields up something

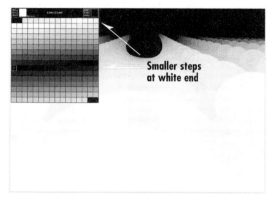

***Figure 10-16*** Smooth near levels with gamma 0.6

***Figure 10-17*** SIRDS produced from Figure 10-16

new to everyone who explores it. RDSMAPS.PAR includes all of these fractals, with their gray palettes. You can use Fractint's @ function to load and examine any of them on your computer.

Example03, (Figures 10-18 and 10-19) contains a single smooth curve. This image is a good test for a SIRDS-generating program, since the extreme change of level to the point is difficult to produce. If your software's not up to the task, you'll see repeated copies of the level change, off to the right. These echoes are one of the most common failings of

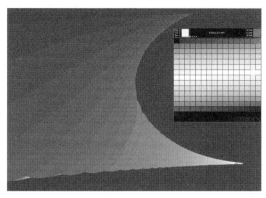

**Figure 10-18** Example03: A Formula FnDog fractal resulting in a simple gradient

**Figure 10-19** SIRDS produced from Example03

single-image stereogram algorithms. You can see echoes in many commercially produced stereograms.

Example04 (Figures 10-20 and 10-21) is a good example of a fractal made of simple shapes. As you can see in the palette, there are few different levels, but the SIRDS gives an impression of complex depth.

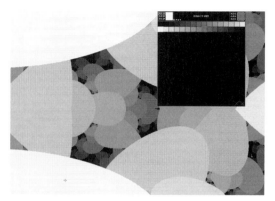

**Figure 10-20**  Example04: A Formula JTet fractal showing complex depth from few levels

**Figure 10-21**  SIRDS produced from Example04

Example05 (Figures 10-22 and 10-23) uses shapes very similar to those in the previous example but produces a much simpler effect. The sections are a little too far apart for this image to really be successful. Also, notice how easy it is to hyperconverge the brightest, nearest points, making them appear to be holes instead of protrusions. This demonstrates the problem with using small white areas near large dark ones.

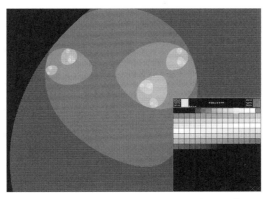

**Figure 10-22**  Example05: A Formula DeltaLog fractal that is a little too sparse

**Figure 10-23**  SIRDS produced from Example05

Example06 (Figures 10-24 and 10-25) is a very tough job for the SIRDS-generating program. The repetitive spacing and hard-edged level changes are very prone to echo artifacts.

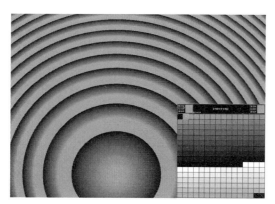

***Figure 10-24*** Example06: A Circle fractal that is a tough test for the software

***Figure 10-25*** SIRDS produced from Example06

Example07 (Figures 10-26 and 10-27) has a pleasing tactile quality. It's important, with a fractal like this one, to use the palette editor to trim some of the busy details away from the edges. The next example shows why.

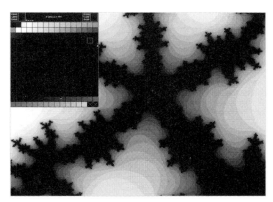

***Figure 10-26*** Example07: A Formula HyperMandel fractal with busy edges trimmed

***Figure 10-27*** SIRDS produced from Example07

Example08 (Figures 10-28 and 10-29) would be nice if it weren't so busy. The clusters of pixels with many different values all together translate into confusing noise in the SIRDS. As you can see in the palette, the same few shades are used in all sections of this fractal. There isn't any way to make one general area deeper than another.

**Figure 10-28** Example08: A Formula Jm_02 fractal that's much too noisy

**Figure 10-29** SIRDS produced from Example08

Example09 (Figures 10-30 and 10-31) is simple and interesting. The simplest sources often produce the most pleasing SIRDS.

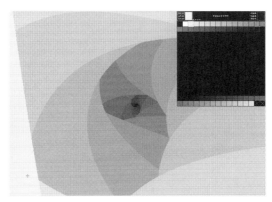

**Figure 10-30**  Example09: A Formula Jm_05 fractal showing that simple is often best

**Figure 10-31**  SIRDS produced from Example09

Example10 (Figures 10-32 and 10-33) depicts a latticework of spidery arms arching over a flat background.

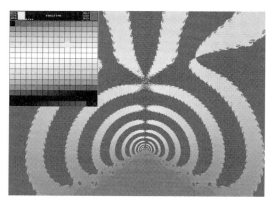

***Figure 10-32*** Example10: A Spider Fractal with arching latticework

***Figure 10-33*** SIRDS produced from Example10

Example11 (Figures 10-34 and 10-35) is the same fractal as Example10. Reversing the palette has produced a flat latticework over a smoothly curving background.

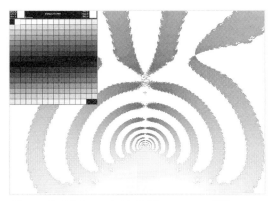

**Figure 10-34** Example11: Different map, different SIRDS

**Figure 10-35** SIRDS produced from Example11

Example12 (Figures 10-36 and 10-37) too, starts with Example10. By zooming in on the lower-left corner and trimming the palette, we create an entirely different effect. A single simple fractal can yield a variety of interesting SIRDS.

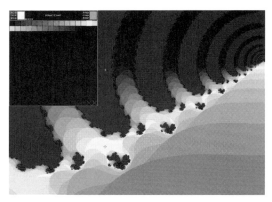

**Figure 10-36**  Example12: A Spider fractal detail

**Figure 10-37**  SIRDS produced from Example12

# A .MAP to the Kingdom

Palette maps are the key to quickly and easily producing good depthmaps in Fractint. The disk enclosed with this book includes a number of .MAP files designed to help you create suitable palettes for your fractal depthmaps. The book's installation program puts them in the directory \STEREO3D\FRACTINT, and the instructions at the start of this chapter had you copy them to your Fractint directory. Let's take a look at the various .MAP files.

They all begin with the letters RDS, so they're easy to spot in the Load Map screen. The rest of the name tells you something about each .MAP file's values for the 256 indices in a .GIF file palette, as follows:

- ☻ The two digits after RDS indicate how many times that .MAP covers the range from white to black. For instance, a 64-step scale can repeat 4 times in 256 indices.

- ☻ The sixth character in each name is *A*, *D*, or *C*. *A*, for Ascending, means the values go from black up to white. *D*, for Descending, means the values go down from white to black. *C*, for Cycling, means the values cycle from white to black and then back to white.

- ☻ The next character is an *L* or a *B*. *L*, for Linear, means each step in the .MAP is the same size. *B*, for Biased, means the .MAP is skewed with smaller steps between values at the white end and larger steps between values at the black end. This produces smoother gradients at the front, and still gets all the way to black in the specified range.

- ☻ The last character of the name is *F*, *B*, or *W*. *F*, for Full-range, means the palette repeats in the .MAP file as many times as needed to fill all 256 indices. *B*, for Black, means the palette ranges from black to white and then back to black, once. The rest of the palette indices are black. *W*, for White, means the palette ranges from white to black and then back to white, once. The rest of the palette indices are white.

Table 10-1 describes the .MAP files included in the \STEREO3D\FRACTINT directory.

| Filename | Description |
|---|---|
| RDS01ALF.MAP | 256 levels, from black up to white |
| RDS01DLF.MAP | 256 levels, from white down to black |
| RDS02CBB.MAP | 118 levels, from black to white and back to black, filled with black, biased towards white |
| RDS02CBW.MAP | 118 levels, from white to black and back to white, filled with white, biased towards white |
| RDS02CLF.MAP | 128 levels, from white to black and back to white |
| RDS04CBB.MAP | 58 levels, from black to white and back to black, filled with black, biased towards white |
| RDS04CBW.MAP | 58 levels, from white to black and back to white, filled with white, biased towards white |

*continued on next page*

*continued from previous page*

| Filename | Description |
|---|---|
| RDS04CLB.MAP | 64 levels, from black to white and back to black |
| RDS04CLF.MAP | 64 levels, from white to black and back to white, repeating |
| RDS04CLW.MAP | 64 levels, from white to black and back to white, filled with white |
| RDS08CLB.MAP | 32 levels, from black to white and back to black |
| RDS08CLF.MAP | 32 levels, from white to black and back to white, repeating |
| RDS08CLW.MAP | 32 levels, from white to black and back to white, filled with white |
| RDS16CLB.MAP | 16 levels, from black to white and back to black |
| RDS16CLF.MAP | 16 levels, from white to black and back to white, repeating |
| RDS16CLW.MAP | 16 levels, from white to black and back to white, filled with white |

*Table 10-1*  .MAP files included in the \STEREO3D\FRACTINT directory

# Tips and Pitfalls

This section lists some things to bear in mind while hunting depthmaps among the fractals. Once you've found an area in a fractal that looks like good depthmap material, it's up to you to turn it into a meaningful depthmap. These ideas and resources are guidelines, not hard-and-fast rules.

## Choose Suitable Fractals

Many fractal types are simply not well suited to life as a depthmap. The ifs, lorenz, cellular, gingerbread, and others lack the areas of solid color that translate clearly into depth levels in the SIRDS. Any of the fractal types used in the minigallery in this chapter make good starting places, as do most of Fractint's formulae.

## Stay Gray

With Fractint, you are creating depthmap source files—not finished images. A SIRDS generator doesn't care if the colors you use in your fractals look nice. In fact, it may misinterpret them. It reads either the pixel intensity or the palette index. Is full blue brighter than full red? Are they the same? Especially if a program is reading the palette index, instead of the color values, it may interpret the depthmap in ways that are difficult to predict.

Do yourself a big favor. Work with palette maps containing only shades of gray, and convert your files from palette-mapped to grayscale before using them. This approach allows you to accurately predict how the SIRDS generator will interpret your depthmap, because the pixel intensity, palette index, and visual brightness will all agree with one another.

## White to Black

Try to spread your palette across the full range from white to black. This lets you work with the maximum depth resolution and creates the smoothest possible steps between levels in the SIRDS. It also gives you more control over the relative size of level steps at various points in the palette. Using levels that are close together at the light end and farther apart at the dark end produces images that have smooth contours up close and still reach all the way to maximum black depth. If you want a stereogram that isn't so deep, you're better off reducing the level with the depth of field parameter in the SIRDS generator.

## Trim Noisy Edges and Avoid Noisy Areas

Busy detail containing a variety of colors becomes confusing noise in the SIRDS. Much of this can be cleaned up by making all the busy levels a single color. Sometimes, however, the colors in the small details are also used in the parts you want to emphasize in the SIRDS. In this case it's best to look for a more suitable fractal. Figures 10-28 and 10-29 in the minigallery illustrate one form of this problem. The colors in the broad, interesting areas also appear as random pixels in the noisy areas. There's no way to use one without fighting the other unless you want to edit the fractal in a paint program.

## Use Appropriate Scaling

Successful stereograms often contain one large object. You need to fill the entire image as much as possible. Placing a small object in a large area of solid color wastes the limited resolution of the average video monitor.

## Avoid Large Steps

Smooth gradients provide more comfortable and stable stereogram viewing. If you have difficulty seeing an image you're working on, try reducing the depth scale in your stereogram-generating program.

Small white levels in dark areas can lead to hyperconvergence. This confuses all the levels and disrupts viewing.

## Watch the Edges

Design your depthmaps with a specific SIRDS generator in mind. If this isn't possible, avoid putting important detail at the left and right edges. The SIRDS generation process requires that the final image be one strip width wider than the depth information it contains, and the various programs deal with this in their own ways.

JRDS, John Swenson's unreleased program that produced this book's cover stereogram from a Fractint depthmap, cuts a strip width off the right side of the depthmap image. ENC, another SIRDS generator, cuts a strip width off the left side. RDSGEN centers the depthmap and trims some off both sides. John M. Olsen's SIRDS generation code adds a strip width and produces a bigger image than what it starts with. RDSdraw does this, too. This method preserves the entire source image at the risk of producing nonstandard image sizes.

## Disk Video for Printing

Higher resolution makes smoother SIRDS. Laser printers typically output 300 dpi which is a much higher resolution than what video monitors display. A full 8-inch by 10-inch page at 300 dpi requires an image 2,400 by 3,000 pixels. Fractint can create images that large, and RDSGEN can process them.

Fractint's disk video modes are found at the end of the Video Mode ((DEL)) selection menu. Instead of displaying the fractal onscreen as it's generated, disk video writes the fractal to a buffer while displaying the number of the line it's working on. Don't forget to save ((S)) the fractal when it's complete.

You can add custom disk video modes of any size up to 2048x2048 to your FRACTINT.CFG file. This makes a 7-inch square on a 300-dpi laser printer. The SIRDS in this chapter were generated from fractals 1,500 by 1,125 pixels, using this technique.

Above 2,048 pixels, you need to use Fractint's Divide-And-Conquer feature. You access this from the Save Parameter File screen ((B)). Enter values in the X and Y Multiples lines, and Fractint writes out a batch file that you can run to generate enormous fractals in separate pieces. See your Fractint documentation for details.

## Not Just for Fractals Anymore

You can use the controls in Fractint's palette editor to polish up depthmaps you've drawn in other programs, too. Load any .GIF file with (R), call up Fractint's palette editor, and have at it.

# What's Next?

Fractint does a great job of producing wild, organic, abstract depthmaps. But what if your tastes run more to the geometric? Perhaps you want to make stereograms that hide representational pictures of rockets and cars, or horses and trees. And what if you still aren't so good at drawing with a mouse? No problem. The next chapter explores depthmap creation with the ray tracers POV-Ray and Polyray.

# Chapter 11

# Ray Tracing Depthmaps

*A*n experienced ray-tracing artist can create an image of almost anything, without drawing at all. Even a novice can create wonderful pictures of surprisingly complex objects in a short time. Ray-tracing programs build a mathematical model of a 3D scene in the computer's memory. They use this model to produce an image of what you would see if you could look at that scene. This common use of ray tracing is called *photorealistic rendering.*

Ray tracers can also use this mathematical model to produce depthmaps. Chapter 9 explains how to use RDSGEN to process a depthmap into a stereogram.

In this chapter you'll learn two approaches to creating stereogram depthmaps, using the popular ray-tracing programs POV-Ray and Polyray. These excellent progrms are not included with this book, but they are easy to find. The examples here use POV-Ray version 2.2, and Polyray 1.7. The chapter assumes that you are somewhat familiar with either POV-Ray or Polyray, but experience with a programming or rendering language will allow you to understand at least how the scene files work.

The principles explored in this chapter apply to nearly any ray tracer or renderer. Stephen Coy's ray tracer Bob, Pixar's RenderMan, Impulse's Imagine, and Autodesk's 3D Studio can all produce depthmaps for single-image stereograms.

# About POV-Ray

The POV-Ray ray tracer reads text descriptions of objects written in its scene language and builds a model of the objects in the computer's memory. It then draws the described image, using math to trace the path that light rays take through the model.

## Where to Find It

You can find POV-Ray on CompuServe in the Graphic Developer's forum, Go GRAPHDEV. Several of POV-Ray's authors collaborated on the Waite Group's books *Ray Tracing Creations: Generate 3-D Photorealistic Images on the PC* (1993, ISBN 1-878739-27-1) and *Ray Tracing Worlds with POV-Ray* (1994, ISBN 1-878739-64-6).

## Licensing Information

POV-Ray is a copyrighted freeware program written by a team of programmers in the Graphic Developer's forum (Go GRAPHDEV) on CompuServe. You can reach the head of the POV-Ray team, Chris Young, on CompuServe at address 76702,1655. From the Internet, use 76702.1655@compuserve.com.

# About Polyray

Polyray is both a ray tracer and polygon renderer. A little more flexible and a little less friendly than POV-Ray, Polyray has particular strengths in animation and math function rendering.

## Where to Find It

Look for Polyray on CompuServe in the Graphic Developer's forum, Go GRAPHDEV. Alexander Enzmann, Polyray's author, collaborated with David Mason, the author of DTA, on a Waite Group book about Polyray and DTA called *Making Movies On Your PC* (1993, ISBN 1-878739-41-7). Jeff Bowermaster's *Animation How-To CD* (Waite Group Press, 1994, ISBN 1-878739-54-9) also includes Polyray.

## Licensing Information

Polyray is a shareware program written by Alexander Enzmann. A registration fee of $35 is requested if you use this program regularly. You can reach the author on CompuServe at address 70323,2461. Use 70323,2461@compuserve.com from the Internet.

# Ambient Plus Fog Equals Depthmap

Most ray tracers include an effect called *fog* or *haze*, which mixes a specified color into a scene. The farther away from the viewpoint a pixel is, the more the ray tracer will color that pixel with the fog color. This feature is all that's needed to get a depthmap from a ray tracer.

The procedure for using fog to trace a depthmap is, in theory, quite simple. You begin by using only the color white and only *ambient texture* (self-illumination) on all the objects in your scene. Don't use any lights, reflection, or refraction. This ensures that everything starts out white, fully lit, and without shadows. Then you add black fog. Proper tweaking of the fog parameters produces an image in which the background is black. All the objects are colored lighter and lighter as they get nearer to the viewpoint, emerging from the fog.

Several example scenes for POV-Ray (.POV files) and Polyray (.PI files) come on the disk included with this book. The book's installation program puts them in the directory

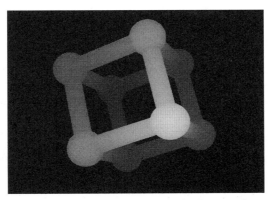

***Figure 11-1*** Depthmap of a skeletal cube using fog

***Figure 11-2*** Cube SIRDS from Figure 11-1

\STEREO3D\RAYTRACE. These scene files use no lights, and they use a single texture for all objects.

Our first example image, a skeletal cube, demonstrates the use of fog in POV-Ray and haze in Polyray. The files FOGCUBE.POV and FOGCUBE.PI produce the same image from their respective ray tracers, shown in Figure 11-1. Figure 11-2 shows a SIRDS created from this depthmap.

# POV-Ray 2.2 Fog Syntax

Since POV-Ray uses an exponential formula for fog, the density of the fog increases more rapidly as the distance from the viewpoint increases. You must begin the fog very early to get the full range of density change within the depth of an object. In other words, you must adjust the fog so it gets fairly dense close to the camera.

POV-Ray's fog always begins at the camera (see Listing 11-1). The distance value in the fog statement allows you to control how fast the fog density increases by specifying the distance from the camera at which the fog reaches 37% density. In this example that distance is 10 units. The object starts 45 units from the camera. This makes it deeply buried in the fog, so the ambient value in the texture must be raised artificially high. This compensates for the extreme fog density by making the object, technically, whiter than white. As they say, "ray tracing ain't reality." In a sense, the ambient value is a setting for self-illumination. An object deep in dense fog must glow brightly to be visible. Ambient 1 approximates an evenly lit surface painted perfectly white. Ambient values greater than 1 can be considered glowing, although they can't light up any other objects.

**Listing 11-1** FOGCUBE.POV, POV-Ray code for Figure 11-1

```
//Depthmap for RDS, demonstrates the use of POV-Ray's fog

camera {  location  <0, 0,-50>          //camera specs
          direction <0, 0, 2.2>
          up <0, 1, 0> right <4/3, 0, 0>
          look_at <0, 0, 0> }

          // NO LIGHTS!

#declare AllWhite = texture {              //define texture with
      pigment {color rgb < 1.0, 1.0, 1.0 > }   // color white
      finish { ambient 50 diffuse 0 }          // and very high ambient
}                                               // with no normal modifiers

fog { color rgb <0,0,0> distance 10 }       // black fog
                                            // reaching 37% density
                                            // 10 units from camera

union {              // combine for texturing and positioning the following
  sphere { < -5, -5, -5 >, 2 }             //cube corners
  sphere { < -5,  5, -5 >, 2 }
  sphere { < -5,  5,  5 >, 2 }
  sphere { < -5, -5,  5 >, 2 }
  sphere { <  5, -5, -5 >, 2 }
  sphere { <  5,  5, -5 >, 2 }
```

```
sphere { <  5,  5,  5 >, 2 }
sphere { <  5, -5,  5 >, 2 }            // and cube edges
cylinder { <  5,  5,  5 >, <  5,  5, -5 >, 1 }
cylinder { <  5,  5,  5 >, <  5, -5,  5 >, 1 }
cylinder { <  5,  5,  5 >, < -5,  5,  5 >, 1 }
cylinder { <  5, -5,  5 >, < -5, -5,  5 >, 1 }
cylinder { <  5,  5, -5 >, <  5, -5, -5 >, 1 }
cylinder { <  5, -5,  5 >, <  5, -5, -5 >, 1 }
cylinder { < -5,  5,  5 >, < -5, -5,  5 >, 1 }
cylinder { < -5,  5, -5 >, <  5,  5, -5 >, 1 }
cylinder { < -5,  5, -5 >, < -5,  5,  5 >, 1 }
cylinder { < -5, -5, -5 >, <  5, -5, -5 >, 1 }
cylinder { < -5, -5, -5 >, < -5,  5, -5 >, 1 }
cylinder { < -5, -5, -5 >, < -5, -5,  5 >, 1 }
texture { AllWhite }     // use the texture defined above
rotate < 20, 20, 20>     // position for visual interest
}
```

# Polyray 1.7 Haze Syntax

The effect produced by haze in Polyray is very similar to the effect produced by fog in POV-Ray. Haze color is mixed with the surface color, depending on how far from the camera a pixel appears. The density of the haze increases faster as distance from the camera increases. Polyray gives you finer control over density of haze than POV-Ray gives you over the density of fog. This means your textures can use a normal full ambient value of 1, instead of raising the ambient value artificially high as you must do to compensate for POV-Ray's extreme fog density.

Haze power values (the first parameter in the haze statement) range from 0 to 1. Higher haze power causes haze density to increase more slowly. Haze distance (the second parameter) specifies how far in front of the camera the haze begins.

In the Polyray version of this example, shown in Listing 11-2, the haze increases slowly (power = .92) and begins 38 units from the viewpoint. The closest part of the object is located 45 units from the camera, which Polyray calls the viewpoint. The depthmap produced from this listing is identical to Figure 11-1.

**Listing 11-2** FOGCUBE.PI, Polyray code for Figure 11-1

```
//Depthmap for RDS, demonstrates use of Polyray's haze

viewpoint { from <0, 0,-50>      // camera specs
            at <0, 0, 0>
            up <0, 1, 0>
            angle 25
            resolution 640,480  // image resolution
            aspect 4/3
          }

          // NO LIGHTS!
```

*continued on next page*

*continued from previous page*

```
define AllWhite texture { surface {
      color < 1.0, 1.0, 1.0 > // color white
      ambient 1.0              // full ambient
      diffuse 0.0
} }                            // no normal modifiers

haze 0.92, 38, <0,0,0>  // black fog building slowly (.92)
                        // starting 38 units from camera

object { // combine for texturing and positioning the following
  object { sphere < -5, -5, -5 >, 2 } + // cube corners
  object { sphere < -5,  5, -5 >, 2 } +
  object { sphere < -5,  5,  5 >, 2 } +
  object { sphere < -5, -5,  5 >, 2 } +
  object { sphere <  5, -5, -5 >, 2 } +
  object { sphere <  5,  5, -5 >, 2 } +
  object { sphere <  5,  5,  5 >, 2 } +
  object { sphere <  5, -5,  5 >, 2 } + // and cube edges
  object { cylinder <  5,  5,  5 >, <  5,  5, -5 >, 1 } +
  object { cylinder <  5,  5,  5 >, <  5, -5,  5 >, 1 } +
  object { cylinder <  5,  5,  5 >, < -5,  5,  5 >, 1 } +
  object { cylinder <  5, -5,  5 >, < -5, -5,  5 >, 1 } +
  object { cylinder <  5,  5, -5 >, <  5, -5, -5 >, 1 } +
  object { cylinder <  5, -5,  5 >, <  5, -5, -5 >, 1 } +
  object { cylinder < -5,  5,  5 >, < -5, -5,  5 >, 1 } +
  object { cylinder < -5,  5, -5 >, <  5,  5, -5 >, 1 } +
  object { cylinder < -5,  5, -5 >, < -5,  5,  5 >, 1 } +
  object { cylinder < -5, -5, -5 >, <  5, -5, -5 >, 1 } +
  object { cylinder < -5, -5, -5 >, < -5,  5, -5 >, 1 } +
  object { cylinder < -5, -5, -5 >, < -5, -5,  5 >, 1 }
  AllWhite                   // use the texture defined above
rotate < 20, 20, 20>         // position for visual interest
}
```

## Incorrect Fog Range Adjustment

A critical step in producing an effective ray-traced depthmap using fog or haze is adjusting the range over which the fog or haze is applied. Correct adjustment will cause the entire depth of the 3D object to be visible in the stereogram. Incorrect adjustment results in clipping of the near or far parts of the object. The following examples show the results of incorrect near and far adjustments in POV-Ray.

Figures 11-3 and 11-4 show the results of incorrect *near* adjustment. The same .POV file shown in Listing 11-1 produced the image in these figures, except that this one used a fog distance of 5 units instead of 10. This caused the fog to reach 37% density closer to the camera, which resulted in the density of the fog increasing more rapidly as it reached distant parts of the cube. This made the gradient at the cube much steeper, but also made the fog around the cube much denser. To compensate, the ambient value in this image was boosted to 13,000. This value was too high and resulted in the entire near corner of the cube being absolute white. This white area in the depthmap produces a single level in the SIRDS, with the near corner of the cube clipped off.

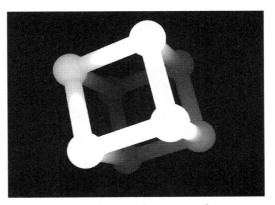

**Figure 11-3** Depthmap with overexposed near corner

**Figure 11-4** SIRDS with clipped near corner

Figures 11-5 and 11-6 show the results of incorrect *far* adjustment. Again, the same .POV file produced this image, except it used a fog distance of 4 units, for an even shorter working range with even denser fog. The ambient value was set to 20,000, which didn't quite succeed in pulling the object out of the fog. As a result, the far corner of the cube faded to black. This depthmap produces a SIRDS with the cube embedded into the background.

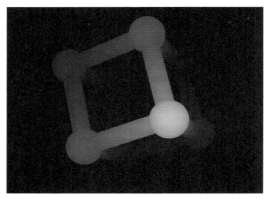

***Figure 11-5*** Depthmap with underexposed far corner

***Figure 11-6*** SIRDS with cube embedded in background

# Color Me White to Black

Many ray-tracing programs include the ability to color a surface from a colormap. This allows you to make a specific point one color and another point a second color, and the program shades the object between those two points with a smooth gradient from the first color to the second.

The depth direction, pointing toward and away from the viewer, is commonly known as the $z$ axis. If your program can rotate and scale a colormap so that it colors each pixel by how far along the $z$ axis it should appear to be, you can use the $z$ *gradient* feature to produce a depthmap.

In theory, this procedure is very simple. Position all of the objects in your scene, and then combine (union) them into one large, single object for texturing. Define a texture

**Figure 11-7** Depthmap of tripod using $z$ gradient

**Figure 11-8** Tripod SIRDS from Figure 11-7

with full ambient and a colormap from white to black. Rotate and scale the texture so that the nearest point in your scene is white and the farthest point is black. Apply the colormap to the entire scene. Don't use any lights.

This book's disk includes the POV-Ray and Polyray files GRADTRI.POV and GRADTRI.PI. Both of these scene files produce the same image from their respective ray tracers. Figures 11-7 and 11-8 show the depthmap and SIRDS produced from these files.

# POV-Ray 2.2 Syntax

In its pigment toolbox, POV-Ray provides a gradient along the $z$ axis. You simply need to specify the end values of the colormap as black and white. This strategy is implemented in GRADTRI.POV, shown in Listing 11-3. Next, you scale the gradient so that it's as long as the extent of all the objects in your scene. Finally, you translate it into place.

**Listing 11-3** GRADTRI.POV, POV-Ray code for Figure 11-7

```
//Depthmap for RDS demonstrating POV-Ray's z gradient

camera {   location  <0, 0,-50>          // camera specs
           direction <0, 0, 2.2>
           up <0, 1, 0> right <4/3, 0, 0>
           look_at <0, 0, 0> }

           // NO LIGHTS!

#declare DepthTexture = texture {
       pigment {                          // color by position
       gradient z                         // on z axis, colors
       color_map {                        // interpolated from
       [0.0 color rgb < 1.0, 1.0, 1.0 > ] // white at the origin
       [1.0 color rgb < 0.0, 0.0, 0.0 > ] // to black at 1 unit z
       } }
       finish { ambient 1.0 diffuse 0.0 } // full ambient
}                                         // no normal modifiers

union {  // combine everything in the scene for coloring
union {  // combine the tripod parts for positioning
  sphere { < 0, 8, 0 >, 3 }                      // head
  cylinder { <  0, 7.7, 0 >, < 0, 8.3, 0 >, 6 } // disks
  cylinder { <  0, -3,   0 >, < 0, -2, 0 >, 10 }
  cylinder { <  0, -9, -12 >, < 0, 10, 0 >, 1.2 // legs
      rotate < 0,   0, 0 > }
  cylinder { <  0, -9, -12 >, < 0, 10, 0 >, 1.2
      rotate < 0, 120, 0 > }
  cylinder { <  0, -9, -12 >, < 0, 10, 0 >, 1.2
      rotate < 0, 240, 0 > }
  rotate < 0, -9, 0>         // position for visual interest
}
  box { < -100, -8, -14 >, < 100, -9, 14> }    // floor

texture { DepthTexture       // use the texture defined above,
```

```
scale <1, 1, 28.1>        // size and position the gradient so
translate <0, 0, -14> }   // it covers the scene exactly once
}
```

# Polyray 1.7 Syntax

Polyray includes a gradient along the *x* axis in its noise surface options. If you rotate it around the *y* axis before applying it to an object, it becomes a *z* gradient. Scale and translate this texture so it covers your entire scene exactly once, with white at the near end and black at the far end. This procedure is shown in Listing 11-4.

**Listing 11-4** GRADTRI.PI, Polyray code for Figure 11-7

```
//Depthmap for RDS

viewpoint { from <0, 0,-50>          // camera specs
            at <0, 0, 0>
            up <0, 1, 0>
            angle 25.5
            resolution 640,480       // image resolution
            aspect 4/3
          }

          // NO LIGHTS

define DepthTexture texture { noise surface {
     position_fn 1            // according to the x coordinate,
     color_map( [ 0, 1,       // color the object with a gradient
       < 1.0, 1.0, 1.0 >,     // from white at 0
       < 0.0, 0.0, 0.0 > ] )  // to black at 1
     ambient 1.0              // with full ambient
     diffuse 0.0              //
     }                        // and no normal modifiers
rotate < 0, -90, 0 >     // rotate texture to make a z gradient
scale <1, 1, 28.0>       // size and position the gradient so
translate <0, 0, -14>    // it covers the scene exactly once
}


object {           // combine all objects in scene for texturing
object {           // combine tripod parts for positioning
  object { sphere < 0, 8, 0 >, 3 } +     // head and disks
  object { cylinder < 0, 7.7, 0 >, < 0, 8.3, 0 >, 6 } +
  object { disc     < 0, 7.7, 0 >, < 0, -1, 0 >, 6 } +
  object { disc     < 0, 8.3, 0 >, < 0, 1, 0 >, 6 } +
  object { cylinder < 0, -3, 0 >, < 0, -2, 0 >, 10 } +
  object { disc     < 0, -3, 0 >, < 0, -1, 0 >, 10 } +
  object { disc     < 0, -2, 0 >, < 0, 1, 0 >, 10 } +
  object { cylinder < 0, -9, -12 >, < 0, 10, 0 >, 1.2
           rotate < 0, 0, 0 > } +      // legs
  object { cylinder < 0, -9, -12 >, < 0, 10, 0 >, 1.2
```

*continued on next page*

*continued from previous page*

```
                rotate < 0,  120,  0 > } +
    object { cylinder <  0,  -9,  -12 >, <  0, 10,   0 >, 1.2
                rotate < 0, 240, 0 > }
    rotate < 0, -9, 0>       // position tripod for visual interest
    } +
object { polygon 4,       // floor
   < -100, -08, -15 > ,
   <  100, -08, -15 > ,
   <  100, -08,  14 > ,
   < -100, -08,  14 > }
   DepthTexture             // use texture defined above
}
```

# Tips and Pitfalls

Ray tracing depthmaps involves considerable tweaking and experimentation before you start to get it right. There is no substitute for experience. However, the following hints will help you avoid trouble and hasten you on your way.

## Render at Low Resolution

The higher the output resolution of a SIRDS, the more depth levels it can contain. The more levels it contains, the smoother its contours, and the easier it is to avoid most artifacts. Since the size of the SIRDS is directly related to the size of the depthmap, large depthmaps produce smoother SIRDS. Unfortunately, large depthmaps can take a long time to ray-trace.

In the SIRDS, much of the detail available in the depthmap gets thrown away. SIRDS use several pixels to display each point, so the effective resolution is much lower than in the original depthmap. This means the extra information gained in the longer trace time is wasted. Happily, there's a better way.

What's actually needed is more pixels, not more detail. Render your depthmap at about one-third the final size, and scale it up with DTA's /SCF command. The command

```
DTA SMALL.TGA /FT /SCF1024,768 /OBIG.TGA
```

scales the image SMALL.TGA, which might be 320x200, up to 1,024x768. The final SIRDS usually exhibits no loss of resolution. Do not use DTA's /SC smooth scaling command, because the intermediate colors generated by /SC may confuse the SIRDS software.

## Don't Anti-Alias

Anti-aliasing improves the look of a conventional ray-traced image by smoothing jagged edges. It does this by mixing the colors of each anti-aliased pixel with the pixels around it. When ray tracing depthmaps, however, there's absolutely no benefit to anti-aliasing; in fact, you should avoid it. The intermediate colors created by anti-aliasing may confuse the SIRDS software. A nearly white edge anti-aliased with a black background produces a range of grays. The SIRDS software interprets this range of grays as a range of depths and creates a false contour along the edge of the anti-aliased object.

Anti-aliasing also slows the ray-tracing process considerably, in case you need further incentive for not using it on depthmaps.

## Watch the Right and Left Edges

The SIRDS process produces output that is one strip width beyond the depth information it contains. Most SIRDS programs, including RDSGEN, throw away some of the source image from one or both ends, in order to end up with an output image the same dimensions as the input image. The exact amount lost depends on the convergence strip width and other parameters, and is difficult to predict. If you keep your objects away from the left and right edges, you won't have to worry about it.

## Stay Away from Absolute White and Black

Be careful not to let your object go completely to white or black, unless you want the front or back trimmed off, as seen in Figures 11-3 to 11-6.

## Move the Object, Not the Fog

Small changes in fog (haze) distance can make big changes in your depthmap. Begin by setting the fog distance as a rough estimate, and then fine-tune the image with the ambient level setting in POV-Ray, or the haze power setting in Polyray. If you don't get the desired range, change the fog distance and try again.

You may find it easier to use a basic scene including fog settings that work, and then scale your scene into it. Fog tweaking is not intuitive. This chapter's example scenes make a good starting point.

# What's Next?

You have seen demonstrated here the use of POV-Ray and Polyray for depthmap creation, and Chapter 9 explained how to use RDSGEN to create SIRDS from these depthmaps. Together, these two chapters show you how to make hidden-picture single-image stereograms of anything you can model on your computer. Icon-based single-image stereograms, on the other hand, present all their elements right out front. Parallel or cross-eyed viewing shows you a new, three-dimensional arrangement of parts you can already see. Chapter 12 explains how to create these images directly with your ray tracer.

# Ray Tracing Icon-Based Stereograms

*I*con-based stereograms are the graphical analogue of normal text stereograms, as seen in Chapter 5. Their name comes from the fact that icon-based stereograms are often composed of small pictures such as the program icons in Windows. Icon-based stereograms are based on the same basic principles as other stereograms. Similar objects arranged in horizontal rows take on the illusion of depth when viewed parallel or cross-eyed. The spacing between the objects produces the various apparent depths. The apparent depth of any single element in a stereogram depends on the distance from it to the similar element on each side. Increasing the interval between successive objects moves them deeper; decreasing the interval moves them toward the viewer.

You can draw icon-based stereograms with a paint program, by copying a small picture and pasting it down in a larger picture at regular intervals. This is tedious and difficult to control, however, and even minor adjustments usually require starting over. Commercial drawing programs such as CorelDRAW make the task somewhat easier, because they offer control over the placement of picture elements. Even so, a fair bit of hand work is required, and you are limited to two-dimensional elements in your 3D image.

Ray-tracing programs, on the other hand, allow you to precisely position objects in a scene by simply changing descriptions in a text file. Image mapping, a ray tracing feature that lets you attach an image to an object as if it were a decal, lets you use two-dimensional elements in your picture. You can also use 3D elements, since rendering 3D objects is actually the intended use for ray tracers. Changing the elements in a stereogram can be as simple as substituting a filename in the scene file and re-rendering the image.

***Figure 12-1*** Icon-based stereogram using image mapping (POV-Ray output)

In Chapter 11 you learned how ray tracers make depthmaps that you can use to generate hidden picture stereograms. Ray tracers can also produce several kinds of stereograms directly, without any additional postprocessing. One of these is the conventional *stereo pair*, just like the images Wheatstone popularized in the 1800s (see Chapter 3). Another is the icon-based single-image stereogram. This chapter shows you two approaches to creating icon-based stereograms, using examples created with POV-Ray or Polyray, which were first discussed in Chapter 11, although the principles and ideas presented here apply to any ray tracing or rendering program.

The examples here use POV-Ray version 2.2 and Polyray version 1.7. This book's installation program put the scene and imagemap files for these examples in the directory \STEREO3D\RAYTRACE.

# Using Imagemaps

This first example demonstrates the use of image mapping to create an icon-based stereogram. Image mapping projects a picture onto an object in the ray-traced scene, as if from a slide projector.

POV-Ray and Polyray handle image mapping rather differently, but their two scene files still produce nearly the same image. The POV-Ray output is shown in Figure 12-1, and the POV-Ray and Polyray scene files are presented in the sections that follow.

## POV-Ray 2.2 Syntax

To create the picture in Figure 12-1, POV-Ray read in six .GIF files, projected them onto invisible boxes, and arranged the boxes in rows. Listing 12-1 contains most of the POV-Ray 2.2 scene file, ICON2D.POV, that produced this image.

**Listing 12-1** ICON2D.POV, POV-Ray code for Figure 12-1

```
camera { location  <0, 0, -30> direction <0, 0, 3.0>
         up <0, 1, 0> right <4/3, 0, 0> look_at <0, 0, 0> }

#declare Spacer1 = 3.0     // distance between adjacent elements
#declare Spacer2 = 3.2     // edit for different depths
#declare Spacer3 = 3.3     // larger spacer = deeper
#declare Spacer4 = 3.4     // be sure to match larger
#declare Spacer5 = 3.5     // Spacers with larger Depths
#declare Spacer6 = 3.6     // in the next declare block

#declare Depth1 = .1       // these make overlaps work
#declare Depth2 = .2       // by placing "deeper" objects
#declare Depth3 = .3       // behind "forward" objects
#declare Depth4 = .4       //
#declare Depth5 = .5       // Depth1 is always used with Spacer1
#declare Depth6 = .6       // and Depth2 with Spacer2, etc

#declare Height1 =   0.2 // row placement on the screen
#declare Height2 =   1.4 //
#declare Height3 =   2.6 // edit as desired
#declare Height4 =   0.8
#declare Height5 =  -1
#declare Height6 =  -2.5
#declare Height7 =  -2
#declare Height8 =  -3
#declare Height9 =  -.5

#declare Shift1 =   1.5 // adjustable row shift so the rows
#declare Shift2 =   2.0 // don't all line up vertically
#declare Shift3 =   1.0 //
#declare Shift4 =   0.5 // edit as desired
#declare Shift5 =   0.8
#declare Shift6 =  -1.0
#declare Shift7 =  -2.0
#declare Shift8 =  -0.5
#declare Shift9 =  -2.5

#declare Thing0 = object { // box to image map on
    box { <0, 0, 0 >, < 1, 1, .001 > }
    finish { ambient 1 diffuse 0 }
    }

#declare Thing1 = object { Thing0
    pigment { image_map { gif "1.gif"
            map_type 0 interpolate 2
            filter 255, 1 } } } //color white, transparent

#declare Thing2 = object { Thing0
    pigment { image_map { gif "2.gif"
```

*continued on next page*

173

*continued from previous page*

```
                    map_type 0 interpolate 2
                    filter 255, 1 } } }

// declares for Thing3 - Thing6 with the images
// "3.gif" - "6.gif" deleted for brevity

union { // combine elements in 1 row for positioning
object { Thing1 translate <(-2*Spacer1), 0, 0> }
object { Thing1 translate <(-1*Spacer1), 0, 0> }
object { Thing1 translate <( 0*Spacer1), 0, 0> }
object { Thing1 translate <( 1*Spacer1), 0, 0> }
object { Thing1 translate <( 2*Spacer1), 0, 0> }
translate < Shift1, Height1, Depth1 >} // position the row

union {
object { Thing2 translate <(-2*Spacer2), 0, 0> }
object { Thing2 translate <(-1*Spacer2), 0, 0> }
object { Thing2 translate <( 0*Spacer2), 0, 0> }
object { Thing2 translate <( 1*Spacer2), 0, 0> }
object { Thing2 translate <( 2*Spacer2), 0, 0> }
translate < Shift2, Height2, Depth2 >}

// 7 more unions using Shift3 - Shift9, Height3 - Height9
// with Thing1 - Thing6 and Spacer1 - Spacer6
// deleted for brevity
```

POV-Ray draws this image in several steps. First, it creates a simple flat box, called *Thing0*. Then it makes six versions of that box, *Thing1* to *Thing6*, with a different .GIF file projected on each one. The .GIF files, 1.GIF to 6.GIF, contain the individual icons you see in Figure 12-1. Finally, POV-Ray arranges copies of the boxes *Thing1* to *Thing6* in rows according to the *Spacer*, *Depth*, *Height*, and *Shift* variables. Clustering all these placement variables together at the head of the scene makes it more convenient to edit the position of the objects in the scene.

Notice how the hearts overlap the faces. The .GIF picture containing the heart icon is rectangular, but the *pigment* statement tells POV to treat certain colors in the file as if they were clear. POV-Ray 2.2 uses the *filter* keyword to specify transparent parts of the image map. Let's dissect this statement:

```
#declare Thing2 = object { Thing0
    pigment { image_map { gif "2.gif"
            map_type 0 interpolate 2
            filter 255, 1 } } }
```

The *#declare* line tells POV-Ray to create an object for later use. It starts by copying another object, called *Thing0*. The *pigment* line tells POV to color the object according to the image found in the file 2.GIF, which is a picture of a gray diamond on a white background. *Map_type 0* is a planar image map, like a slide projector shining on the object. *Interpolate 2* tells POV to blend the edges of the imagemap's pixels together. The *filter* line tells POV to treat the color at index 255 in the .GIF file as transparent. Index 255 in 2.GIF is the color white. As you can see in the lower-right corner of Figure 12-1, the area around the diamond is transparent. You can see the bomb behind it.

When you make your own imagemaps for POV-Ray, remember that only the color white with filter 1 is truly transparent. Also, POV-Ray 2.2's *filter* statement uses the palette index of the imagemap, not the actual color. Most .GIF images use index 255 for white, but any other index may be used instead.

The finish textures in this example use an *ambient* value of 1 and no lights. This eliminates any shadows that might provide contradictory cues as to the actual geometry of the scene.

## Polyray 1.7 Syntax

As with the POV-Ray scene, the general strategy for Polyray is to read image files (in this case .TGA) and create a series of horizontal rows. Polyray 1.7 understands 32-bit image file formats, so you have better control over transparency. However, you must create the transparency externally. DTA can help.

To generate a 32-bit alpha transparent .TGA file from the file 1.GIF, enter the command

**DTA 1.GIF /CK255,255,255 /FT /B32** (ENTER)

If there aren't any other .GIFs in the directory you are using, you can process all six .GIFs for this image at once with the command

**DTA *.GIF /CK255,255,255 /FT /B32** (ENTER)

DTA converts the color white (color 255,255,255) into transparent black (color 0,0,0,0). Polyray uses this transparency when ray tracing the scene. A significant advantage of this method is that DTA reads the color value; you don't need to know the palette index in the image file.

Listing 12-2 contains excerpts from the Polyray scene file ICON2D.PI.

**Listing 12-2** ICON2D.PI, Polyray code for Figure 12-1

```
viewpoint { from <0, 0,-30>      // camera specs
            at <0, 0, 0>
            up <0, 1, 0>
            angle 19
            resolution 320,240
            aspect 4/3
          }

define Spacer1 3.0    // distance between adjacent elements
define Spacer2 3.2    // edit for different depths
define Spacer3 3.3    // larger spacer = deeper
define Spacer4 3.4    // be sure to match larger
define Spacer5 3.5    // Spacers with larger Depths
define Spacer6 3.6    // in the next define block

define Depth1  0.1    // these make overlaps work
define Depth2  0.2    // by placing "deeper" objects
define Depth3  0.3    // behind "forward" objects
define Depth4  0.4    //
```

*continued on next page*

*continued from previous page*

```
define Depth5   0.5    // Depth1 is always used with Spacer1
define Depth6   0.6    // and Depth2 with Spacer2, etc

define Height1   0.2   // row placement on the screen
define Height2   1.4   //
define Height3   2.6   // edit as desired
define Height4   0.8
define Height5  -1
define Height6  -2.5
define Height7  -2
define Height8  -3
define Height9  -0.5

define Shift1   1.5    // adjustable row shift so the rows
define Shift2   2.0    // don't all line up vertically
define Shift3   1.0    //
define Shift4   0.5    // edit as desired
define Shift5   0.8
define Shift6  -1.0
define Shift7  -2.0
define Shift8  -0.5
define Shift9  -2.5

define Thing1 object { // box to image map on
    box <0, 0, 0 >, < 1, -0.001, 1 >
    texture { special surface {
    color planar_imagemap ( image ("1.tga"), P )
    ambient 1 diffuse 0
    } }
    rotate < -90, 0, 0 > }

define Thing2 object {
    box <0, 0, 0 >, < 1, -0.001, 1 >
    texture { special surface {
    color planar_imagemap ( image ("2.tga"), P )
    ambient 1 diffuse 0
    } }
    rotate < -90, 0, 0 > }

//defines for Thing3 - Thing6 with 3.TGA - 6.TGA
//deleted for brevity

object { // combine the elements in 1 row for positioning
object { Thing1 translate <(-2*Spacer1), 0, 0> } +
object { Thing1 translate <(-1*Spacer1), 0, 0> } +
object { Thing1 translate <( 0*Spacer1), 0, 0> } +
object { Thing1 translate <( 1*Spacer1), 0, 0> } +
object { Thing1 translate <( 2*Spacer1), 0, 0> }
translate < Shift1, Height1, Depth1 >} // position the row

object {
object { Thing2 translate <(-2*Spacer2), 0, 0> } +
object { Thing2 translate <(-1*Spacer2), 0, 0> } +
```

```
object { Thing2 translate <( 0*Spacer2), 0, 0> } +
object { Thing2 translate <( 1*Spacer2), 0, 0> } +
object { Thing2 translate <( 2*Spacer2), 0, 0> }
translate < Shift2, Height2, Depth2 > }

// 7 more objects using Shift3 - Shift9, Height3 - Height9
// with Thing1 - Thing6 and Spacer1 - Spacer6
// deleted for brevity
```

The only real difference between this listing and the POV-Ray listing is that here, each *define Thing* statement includes the box, instead of declaring the box once as *Thing0* and calling it each time.

# Using 3D Objects

Ray tracers are great for precisely positioning two-dimensional elements. The reason that ray tracers exist, however, is to render 3D objects. And, indeed, you can use 3D elements in your icon-based stereograms. Instead of imagemaps, all the objects in this next scene are built right inside the ray tracer. The stereogram shown in Figure 12-2 demonstrates several techniques, including alternating objects within a single row, and object rotation to create binocular disparity.

If you have difficulty holding the upper and lower halves of this image steady at the same time, relax and concentrate on the ball in the center of the image. This image is designed for parallel viewing. The middle of the upper half should appear deeper than the lower half.

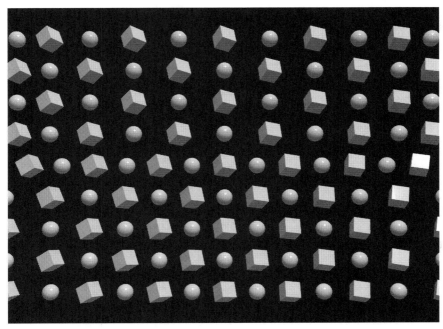

***Figure 12-2*** Icon-based stereogram for parallel viewing (POV-Ray output)

# Alternating Objects

Squeezing more than six repetitions into a 4-inch-wide image makes the image very prone to hyperconvergence. On the other hand, an image with only four or five elements in a row can look sparse and empty. This example solves both problems, by alternating objects within each row. This allows twice as many objects, each with a decent spacing. The objects in a given row must be different enough for you to keep from visually confusing them, however. If you were to change the cubes in this example to the same size as the spheres and re-render the image, it would become very difficult to view.

# Rotation for Binocular Disparity

When you view an actual physical object, your left eye sees more of the object's left side and your right eye sees more of the right side. This slightly differing view, known as binocular disparity, provides some of the information your brain uses to understand the shape of the object. When you parallel-view an icon-based single-image stereogram, your left eye is looking at one picture element while your right eye is looking at the next similar element to the right. If you want the individual elements in your stereogram to appear to have 3D shapes, each element must be slightly different. If you begin in the center, each element to the left must display a little more of its left side than the last one did. Each element to the right must display a little more of its right side.

The *Spin* variable in both the POV-Ray and Polyray scene files accomplishes this by rotating each object in toward the center of the screen. Objects farther from the center get rotated more. Figure 12-3 shows the same scene file rendered without the *Spin* variable. The cubes will appear inside out when parallel-viewed.

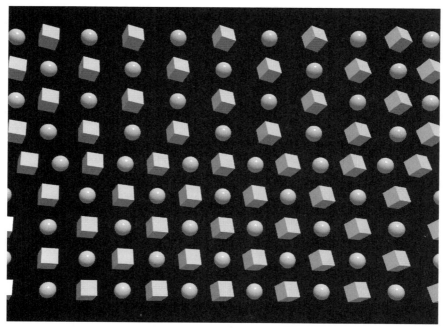

***Figure 12-3*** Parallel viewing inverts unrotated objects

Another way to grasp this concept is to consider any pair of adjacent objects in the example. The *Spin* variable rotates the individual objects, moving their near edges closer together and their far edges wider apart. Parallel viewing interprets "closer together" as "nearer to the viewer," and so you perceive the objects in 3D.

A limitation of any stereogram incorporating 3D elements is that it must be designed with a specific viewing method in mind. The binocular disparity and perspective cues that aid a parallel image can severely disrupt it when it's viewed cross-eyed. This clash of information tends to make objects appear as negative spaces or holes in the picture.

# POV-RAY 2.2 Syntax

The scene file for Figure 12-2 produces white objects arranged in rows. The rows in Figure 12-1 used consistent spacing so that all the objects in a given row appeared at the same depth. Here, though, the scene file tweaks the position of every single object. Each row contains objects with a wide range of depths.

Listing 12-3 shows excerpts from the scene file that produced Figure 12-2. The entire scene file, ICON3D.POV, is on this book's disk; the book's Installation program put it in the directory \STEREO3D\RAYTRACE.

**Listing 12-3** ICON3D.POV, POV-Ray code for Figure 12-2

```
//Icon based Stereogram, ICON3D.POV

camera { location  <0, 0, -30> direction <0, 0, 1.5>
        up <0, 1, 0> right <4/3, 0, 0> look_at <0, 0, 0> }

light_source { <10, 40, -30> color rgb <1,1,1> }

#declare Thing0 = object {         // a ball
    sphere { <0, 0, 0>, 0.5 }
    pigment {color rgb < 1.0, 1.0, 1.0 > }
    finish { ambient 0.2 diffuse 0.7 phong 1 phong_size 80 } }

#declare Thing1 = object {         // a box
    box { <-0.5, -0.5, -0.5 >, < 0.5, 0.5, 0.5 > }
    pigment {color rgb < 1.0, 1.0, 1.0 > }
    finish { ambient 0.2 diffuse 0.7 phong 1 phong_size 80 }
    rotate < 45, 45, 45 > }

#declare Spacer = 2   // default distance between objects
#declare Spin   = 8   // creates binocular disparity

#declare Height1 =  8 // position each row vertically
#declare Height2 =  6
#declare Height3 =  4
#declare Height4 =  2
#declare Height5 =  0
#declare Height6 = -2
#declare Height7 = -4
#declare Height8 = -6
```

*continued on next page*

*continued from previous page*

```
#declare Height9 = -8

union {  // Combine objects in 1 row for vertical positioning.
         // The decreasing spaces at the ends make this
         // row's ends curve toward the camera.
object { Thing0 rotate < 0, -5*Spin, 0 >      // a ball
                translate <(-5*Spacer*1.28), 0, 0> }
object { Thing1 rotate < 0, -4*Spin, 0 >      // a box
                translate <(-4*Spacer*1.34), 0, 0> }
object { Thing0 rotate < 0, -3*Spin, 0 >
                translate <(-3*Spacer*1.38), 0, 0> }
object { Thing1 rotate < 0, -2*Spin, 0 >
                translate <(-2*Spacer*1.39), 0, 0> }
object { Thing0 rotate < 0, -1*Spin, 0 >
                translate <(-1*Spacer*1.40), 0, 0> }
object { Thing1 rotate < 0,  0*Spin, 0 >      // center of row
                translate <( 0*Spacer*0.00), 0, 0> }
object { Thing0 rotate < 0,  1*Spin, 0 >
                translate <( 1*Spacer*1.40), 0, 0> }
object { Thing1 rotate < 0,  2*Spin, 0 >
                translate <( 2*Spacer*1.39), 0, 0> }
object { Thing0 rotate < 0,  3*Spin, 0 >
                translate <( 3*Spacer*1.38), 0, 0> }
object { Thing1 rotate < 0,  4*Spin, 0 >
                translate <( 4*Spacer*1.34), 0, 0> }
object { Thing0 rotate < 0,  5*Spin, 0 >
                translate <( 5*Spacer*1.28), 0, 0> }
translate < 0, Height1, 0 >} // position this row vertically

//three rows deleted here for brevity at Heights 2, 3 and 4

union { // This row maintains a constant depth.
object { Thing1 rotate < 0, -6*Spin, 0 >
                translate <(-6*Spacer*1.00), 0, 0> }
object { Thing0 rotate < 0, -5*Spin, 0 >
                translate <(-5*Spacer*1.00), 0, 0> }
object { Thing1 rotate < 0, -4*Spin, 0 >
                translate <(-4*Spacer*1.00), 0, 0> }
object { Thing0 rotate < 0, -3*Spin, 0 >
                translate <(-3*Spacer*1.00), 0, 0> }
object { Thing1 rotate < 0, -2*Spin, 0 >
                translate <(-2*Spacer*1.00), 0, 0> }
object { Thing0 rotate < 0, -1*Spin, 0 >
                translate <(-1*Spacer*1.00), 0, 0> }
object { Thing1 rotate < 0,  0*Spin, 0 >
                translate <( 0*Spacer*1.00), 0, 0> }
object { Thing0 rotate < 0,  1*Spin, 0 >
                translate <( 1*Spacer*1.00), 0, 0> }
object { Thing1 rotate < 0,  2*Spin, 0 >
                translate <( 2*Spacer*1.00), 0, 0> }
object { Thing0 rotate < 0,  3*Spin, 0 >
                translate <( 3*Spacer*1.00), 0, 0> }
object { Thing1 rotate < 0,  4*Spin, 0 >
```

```
                translate <( 4*Spacer*1.00), 0, 0> }
object { Thing0 rotate < 0,  5*Spin, 0 >
                translate <( 5*Spacer*1.00), 0, 0> }
object { Thing1 rotate < 0,  6*Spin, 0 >
                translate <( 6*Spacer*1.00), 0, 0> }
translate < 0, Height5, 0 > }

union { // The increasing spaces at the ends make
        // this row's ends curve away from the camera.
object { Thing0 rotate < 0, -6*Spin, 0 >
                translate <(-6*Spacer*1.13), 0, 0> }
object { Thing1 rotate < 0, -5*Spin, 0 >
                translate <(-5*Spacer*1.07), 0, 0> }
object { Thing0 rotate < 0, -4*Spin, 0 >
                translate <(-4*Spacer*1.04), 0, 0> }
object { Thing1 rotate < 0, -3*Spin, 0 >
                translate <(-3*Spacer*1.02), 0, 0> }
object { Thing0 rotate < 0, -2*Spin, 0 >
                translate <(-2*Spacer*1.01), 0, 0> }
object { Thing1 rotate < 0, -1*Spin, 0 >
                translate <(-1*Spacer*1.00), 0, 0> }
object { Thing0 rotate < 0,  0*Spin, 0 >
                translate <( 0*Spacer*1.00), 0, 0> }
object { Thing1 rotate < 0,  1*Spin, 0 >
                translate <( 1*Spacer*1.00), 0, 0> }
object { Thing0 rotate < 0,  2*Spin, 0 >
                translate <( 2*Spacer*1.01), 0, 0> }
object { Thing1 rotate < 0,  3*Spin, 0 >
                translate <( 3*Spacer*1.02), 0, 0> }
object { Thing0 rotate < 0,  4*Spin, 0 >
                translate <( 4*Spacer*1.04), 0, 0> }
object { Thing1 rotate < 0,  5*Spin, 0 >
                translate <( 5*Spacer*1.07), 0, 0> }
object { Thing0 rotate < 0,  6*Spin, 0 >
                translate <( 6*Spacer*1.13), 0, 0> }
translate < 0, Height6, 0 > }

//three rows deleted here for brevity at heights 7, 8 and 9
```

To understand how the rows in this example curve in and out, look at Listing 12-3. Begin at the line that is commented "center of row" and proceed up and down from there. The *Spacer* variable defines the most shallow depth. Each object moves out from the center by a multiple of *Spacer* and then is hand-adjusted from there with another multiplier. Let's look at that in detail.

In the following code segment taken from the scene file for the top row of Figure 12-2, the first *Thing1* is in the center of the row; it's position is not translated at all. *Thing0* is positioned at a distance of *Spacer* * 1.4 away from the first object. The third object, another copy of *Thing1*, is positioned at a distance of 2 * *Spacer* * 1.39 away from the first object. This means the spacing between the second and third objects is a little smaller than the spacing between the first and second objects. As in any stereogram, smaller spacing between objects in this row makes each successive object out from the center appear a little nearer to the viewer.

```
object { Thing1 rotate < 0,   0*Spin, 0 >        // center of row
                translate <( 0*Spacer*0.00), 0, 0> }
object { Thing0 rotate < 0,   1*Spin, 0 >
                translate <( 1*Spacer*1.40), 0, 0> }
object { Thing1 rotate < 0,   2*Spin, 0 >
                translate <( 2*Spacer*1.39), 0, 0> }
```

# Polyray 1.7 Syntax

The Polyray 1.7 version of this scene file is nearly identical to the POV-Ray version, differing only in the syntax of the individual statements. Listing 12-4 shows excerpts from the Polyray file, ICON3D.PI.

**Listing 12-4** ICON3D.PI, Polyray code for Figure 12-2

```
//Icon based Stereogram, ICON3D.PI

viewpoint { from <0, 0,-30>       // camera specs
            at <0, 0, 0>
            up <0, 1, 0>
            angle 37
            resolution 640,480
            aspect 4/3
          }

light <10, 40, -30>

define Thing0 object {             // a ball
    sphere <0, 0, 0>, 0.5
    texture { surface { color < 1.0, 1.0, 1.0 >
              ambient 0.2 diffuse 0.7
              specular 0.6 microfacet Phong 5 } } }

define Thing1 object {             // a box
    box <-0.5, -0.5, -0.5 >, < 0.5, 0.5, 0.5 >
    texture { surface { color < 1.0, 1.0, 1.0 >
              ambient 0.2 diffuse 0.7
              specular 0.6 microfacet Phong 5 } }
    rotate < 45, 45, 45 > }

define Spacer 2   // default spacing for minimum depth
define Spin    8   // creates binocular disparity

define Height1  8 // position each row vertically
define Height2  6
define Height3  4
define Height4  2
define Height5  0
define Height6 -2
define Height7 -4
define Height8 -6
```

```
define Height9 -8

object { // Combine objects in 1 row for vertical positioning
         // The decreasing spaces at the ends make this
         // row's ends curve toward the camera
object { Thing0 rotate < 0, -5*Spin, 0 >
                translate <(-5*Spacer*1.28), 0, 0> } +
object { Thing1 rotate < 0, -4*Spin, 0 >
                translate <(-4*Spacer*1.34), 0, 0> } +
object { Thing0 rotate < 0, -3*Spin, 0 >
                translate <(-3*Spacer*1.38), 0, 0> } +
object { Thing1 rotate < 0, -2*Spin, 0 >
                translate <(-2*Spacer*1.39), 0, 0> } +
object { Thing0 rotate < 0, -1*Spin, 0 >
                translate <(-1*Spacer*1.40), 0, 0> } +
object { Thing1 rotate < 0,  0*Spin, 0 >     // center of row
                translate <( 0*Spacer*0.00), 0, 0> } +
object { Thing0 rotate < 0,  1*Spin, 0 >
                translate <( 1*Spacer*1.40), 0, 0> } +
object { Thing1 rotate < 0,  2*Spin, 0 >
                translate <( 2*Spacer*1.39), 0, 0> } +
object { Thing0 rotate < 0,  3*Spin, 0 >
                translate <( 3*Spacer*1.38), 0, 0> } +
object { Thing1 rotate < 0,  4*Spin, 0 >
                translate <( 4*Spacer*1.34), 0, 0> } +
object { Thing0 rotate < 0,  5*Spin, 0 >
                translate <( 5*Spacer*1.28), 0, 0> }
translate < 0, Height1, 0 >}

// The remaining code is functionally identical to
// the POV-Ray 2.2 version in Listing 12-3.
// deleted here for brevity
// The complete scene file is on the book's disk.
```

# Summary

Once you learn to create ray-tracer scene files like the ones in this chapter, you will have at your disposal a remarkably powerful and flexible tool for creating icon-based stereograms. Ray tracers allow you to automate the placement of images against a background, and to adjust the position and relative spacing of the objects by simply changing the values of variables. The images that you use can be either external files or 3D objects created internally by the ray tracer. The techniques described in this chapter can be applied to the use of any other text-based ray tracers and renderers, as well, including RenderMan, Bob, Vivid, and Rayshade.

# References

## Bibliography

Darrah, William Culp. *Stereo Views.* Times and News, 1964.

Dyckman, Dan. "Single Image Random Dot Stereograms." *Stereo World,* May/June 1990.

Ensanian, Armand. "3-D Video." *Video Review,* May/June 1993, Vol. 14, Issue 2.

Falk, D., Brill, D. and Stork, D.G. *Seeing The Light: Optics In Nature, Photography, Color, Vision and Holography.* Wiley, 1988.

Hermida, Alphonso. *Adventures in Ray Tracing.* Que, 1993.

Horibuchi, Seiji, ed. *Stereogram.* Cadence, 1994.

Julesz, Bela. "Binocular Depth Perception of Computer-Generated Patterns." *Bell Systems Technical Journal,* 1960, Vol. 39.

Julesz, Bela. "Binocular Depth Perception Without Familiarity Cues." *Science,* July 24 1964, Vol. 145, No 3630.

Julesz, Bela. *Foundations of Cyclopean Perception.* University of Chicago Press, 1971.

Julesz, Bela. "Texture and Visual Perception." *Scientific American,* February 1965, Vol. 212, No. 2.

Kinsman, Andrew A. *Random Dot Stereograms.* Kinsman Physics, 1992.

Lavroff, Nicholas. *Virtual Reality Playhouse: Explore Artificial Worlds on Your PC.* Waite Group Press, 1992.

Lipton, Lenny. *The CrystalEyes Handbook.* 1991, StereoGraphics Corporation, 1991.

Lipton, Leonard. *Foundations of the Stereoscopic Cinema.* Van Nostrand, 1982.

Marr, D. and Poggio, T. "Cooperative Computation of Stereo Disparity." *Science,* October 15 1976, Vol. 194, No. 4262.

Mason, David K. and Enzmann, Alexander. *Making Movies On Your PC: Dream Up, Design, and Direct 3-D Movies.* Waite Group Press, 1993.

N. E. Thing Enterprises. *Magic Eye: A New Way of Looking at the World.* Andrews and McMeel, 1993.

Pickover, Clifford A. *Computers, Pattern, Chaos and Beauty.* St. Martin's Press, 1990.

Sakane, Itsuo. "The Random-Dot Stereogram and its Contemporary Significance: New Directions in Perceptual Art." In *Stereogram.* Seiji Horibuchi, ed. Cadence Books, 1994.

Stork, David G. and Rocca, Chris. "Software for Generating Auto-Random-Dot Stereograms." *Behavior Research Methods, Intruments and Computers,* 1989, Vol. 21, No. 5.

Stampe, Dave; Roehl, Bernie; and Eagan, John. *Virtual Reality Creations: Explore, Manipulate, and Create Virtual Worlds on Your PC.* Waite Group Press, 1993.

Thimbelby, Harold W.; Inglis, Stuart; and Witten, Ian H. *Displaying 3D Images: Algorithms for Single Image Random Dot Stereograms.* Internet ftp from ftp.cs.waikato.ac.nz in /pub/papers, August 1993.

Tyler, Christopher W. "The Birth of Computer Stereograms for Unaided Stereovision." In *Stereogram,* Seiji Horibuchi, ed. Cadence Books, 1994.

Tyler, Christopher W. "Sensory Processing of Binocular Disparity." In *Vergence Eye Movements: Basic and Clinical Aspects,* Clifton M. Schor and Kenneth J. Ciuffreda. Butterworths, 1983.

Upstill, Steve. *The RenderMan Companion.* Addison-Wesley, 1990.

Valius, Nikolai Adamovich. *Stereoscopy.* Focal Library, 1966.

Watkins, Christopher D.; Coy, Stephen; and Finlay, Mark. *Photorealism and Ray Tracing in C.* M & T, 1992.

Wegner, Tim and Tyler, Bert. *Fractal Creations, Second Edition.* Waite Group Press, 1993.

Wells, Drew and Young, Chris. *Ray Tracing Creations: Generate 3-D Photorealistic Images on the PC.* Waite Group Press, 1993.

# Other Sources of Information

Internet Usenet newsgroup, alt.3D

National Stereoscopic Association, NSA, P.O. 14801 Columbus, OH 43214

International Stereoscopic Union, ISU, 508 La Cima Circle Gallup, NM 87301

Reel 3D, 3D supplies by mail order, P.O. 2368 Culver City, CA 90231

# Index

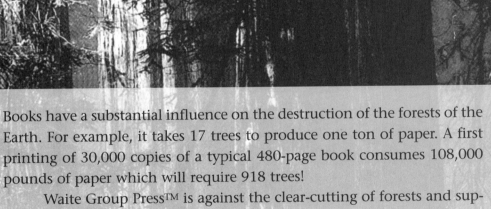

Books have a substantial influence on the destruction of the forests of the Earth. For example, it takes 17 trees to produce one ton of paper. A first printing of 30,000 copies of a typical 480-page book consumes 108,000 pounds of paper which will require 918 trees!

Waite Group Press™ is against the clear-cutting of forests and supports reforestation of the Pacific Northwest of the United States and Canada, where most of this paper comes from. As a publisher with several hundred thousand books sold each year, we feel an obligation to give back to the planet. We will therefore support and contribute a percentage of our proceeds to organizations which seek to preserve the forests of planet Earth.

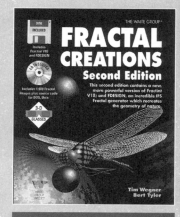

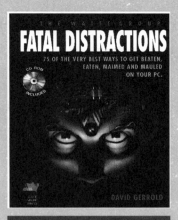

## LIMITED WARRANTY

The following warranties shall be effective for 90 days from the date of purchase: (i) The Waite Group, Inc. warrants the enclosed disk to be free of defects in materials and workmanship under normal use; and (ii) The Waite Group, Inc. warrants that the programs, unless modified by the purchaser, will substantially perform the functions described in the documentation provided by The Waite Group, Inc. when operated on the designated hardware and operating system. The Waite Group, Inc. does not warrant that the programs will meet purchaser's requirements or that operation of a program will be uninterrupted or error-free. The program warranty does not cover any program that has been altered or changed in any way by anyone other than The Waite Group, Inc. The Waite Group, Inc. is not responsible for problems caused by changes in the operating characteristics of computer hardware or computer operating systems that are made after the release of the programs, nor for problems in the interaction of the programs with each other or other software.

THESE WARRANTIES ARE EXCLUSIVE AND IN LIEU OF ALL OTHER WARRANTIES OF MER-CHANTABILITY OR FITNESS FOR A PARTICULAR PURPOSE OR OF ANY OTHER WARRANTY, WHETHER EXPRESS OR IMPLIED.

## EXCLUSIVE REMEDY

The Waite Group, Inc. will replace any defective disk without charge if the defective disk is returned to The Waite Group, Inc. within 90 days from date of purchase.

This is Purchaser's sole and exclusive remedy for any breach of warranty or claim for contract, tort, or damages.

## LIMITATION OF LIABILITY

THE WAITE GROUP, INC. AND THE AUTHORS OF THE PROGRAMS SHALL NOT IN ANY CASE BE LIABLE FOR SPECIAL, INCIDENTAL, CONSEQUENTIAL, INDIRECT, OR OTHER SIM-ILAR DAMAGES ARISING FROM ANY BREACH OF THESE WARRANTIES EVEN IF THE WAITE GROUP, INC. OR ITS AGENT HAS BEEN ADVISED OF THE POSSIBILITY OF SUCH DAMAGES.

THE LIABILITY FOR DAMAGES OF THE WAITE GROUP, INC. AND THE AUTHORS OF THE PROGRAMS UNDER THIS AGREEMENT SHALL IN NO EVENT EXCEED THE PURCHASE PRICE PAID.

## COMPLETE AGREEMENT

This Agreement constitutes the complete agreement between The Waite Group, Inc. and the authors of the programs, and you, the purchaser.

Some states do not allow the exclusion or limitation of implied warranties or liability for incidental or consequential damages, so the above exclusions or limitations may not apply to you. This limited warranty gives you specific legal rights; you may have others, which vary from state to state.

# SATISFACTION REPORT CARD

Please fill out this card if you wish to know of future updates to
*Create Stereograms on Your PC* or to receive our catalog.

Company Name:

Division/Department:                              Mail Stop:

Last Name:                          First Name:                    Middle Initial:

Street Address:

City:                               State:                         Zip:

Daytime telephone:  (          )

Date product was acquired:  Month        Day        Year        Your Occupation:

---

**Overall, how would you rate *Create Stereograms on Your PC*?**
☐ Excellent      ☐ Very Good      ☐ Good
☐ Fair           ☐ Below Average  ☐ Poor

What did you like MOST about this book? _____
_____
_____

What did you like LEAST about this book? _____
_____

How do you use this book (education, diversion, relaxation...)?
_____
_____

How did you find the pace of this book?
_____

Please describe any problems you may have encountered with
installing or using the programs: _____
_____
_____

What is your level of computer expertise?
☐ New        ☐ Dabbler      ☐ Hacker
☐ Power User ☐ Programmer   ☐ Experienced Professional

Is there any program or subject you would like to see The Waite
Group cover in a similar approach?_____
_____
_____

**Please describe your computer hardware:**
Computer _____Hard disk _____
5.25" disk drives _____3.5" disk drives _____
Video card _____Monitor _____
Printer _____Peripherals _____

Where did you buy this book?
☐ Bookstore name:
☐ Discount store name:
☐ Computer store name:
☐ Catalog name:
☐ Direct from WGP        ☐ Other _____
What price did you pay for this book? _____

What influenced your purchase of this book?
☐ Recommendation          ☐ Advertisement
☐ Magazine review         ☐ Store display
☐ Mailing                 ☐ Book's format
☐ Reputation of The Waite Group  ☐ Topic

How many computer books do you buy each year? _____
How many other Waite Group books do you own? _____
What is your favorite Waite Group book?_____

Additional comments? _____
_____
_____

Send to:        Waite Group Press, Inc.
                Attn: *Create Stereograms on Your PC*
                200 Tamal Plaza
                Corte Madera, CA 94925

---

☐ Check here for a free Waite Group catalog           *Create Stereograms on Your PC*